BLINDSIDED

Blindsided

VICTORIA DENAULT

HeartEyes
Press

For Arlene 'Chickie' Cariola. The Hydras miss you.

MAGGIE

Pick up the phone for once, my brain hisses as I hook a left onto North Avenue and force myself to slow down. The last thing I need right now is a speeding ticket on top of everything else. Of course, since I'm headed to the police station I could just pay it when I get there, which would be convenient.

"You are seriously the only person I know who still actually calls people." My sister Daisy's voice fills my car suddenly. She doesn't even bother with hello. "Even Uncle Ben and Uncle Bobby just text. What is wrong with you? If you're trying to bring back phone calls, like high-waisted jeans or something, give it up."

"You know who doesn't text? Clyde," I say sharply.

"Because he's usually drunk," Daisy says about our grandfather. She's not being vicious, just factual. "And he dropped the only cell phone we ever gave him into a glass of whiskey."

"Well he couldn't text even if he wanted to right now because he's IN JAIL." I bark out those last two words as loudly as I can. My eyes dart down to my speedometer and I ease off the gas pedal.

"What?" Daisy replies, shocked. "Our grandfather is in jail?"

"According to my Tinder date, yes," I reply as the light in front of me turns red and I'm forced to stop, and curse.

1

"Your Tinder date told you Clyde is in jail?" Daisy repeats and I can picture her lying on the lounger on the balcony of our dilapidated rental, a textbook beside her, pretending she's studying when what she's really doing is soaking up some of the last rays of sun before the fall days turn chilly. "How is this getting more confusing?"

"My Tinder date turned out to be a cop named Matt and Matt was meeting me on his lunch break, in uniform, because—and I quote—chicks dig the uniform," I explain.

"Okay so we're not seeing him again," Daisy interjects flatly.

"No. We are not," I agree and continue. "Anyway, when I told him my last name he got this weird look on his face and asked if I knew an old man named Clyde Todd, because he just arrested him for getting into a fist fight at city hall."

"Who the hell was Clyde brawling with?" Daisy gasps. "Why was he at city hall? Are you sure it's not mistaken identity?"

"Clyde Todd, age seventy, owner of the Todd Farm out on Route 2A," I say and turn into the police station parking lot. I turn off my car and the call cuts out on my Bluetooth system so I grab my phone off the passenger seat next to my purse. "I'm at the police station now."

"Okay. Keep me posted."

"Will do."

I get out of the car and march across the small lot to the squat, one story red brick building. I burst through the front doors and beeline straight to the counter. "Hi there, I'm Maggie Todd," I say to the officer sitting there. His shirt says Martinez. Burlington isn't a big city, but I haven't had a lot of interaction with our police department, so I don't know him. "Officer Martinez, sir, I was told my grandfather is here. Clyde Todd."

"Ah yes. This morning's public disturbance. Don't know if we're charging him with disorderly conduct, battery or public intoxication. Maybe all three," he says easily, like this is no big deal. "Just have a seat over there with Mr. Adler. The arresting officer will see you both in a minute."

Mr. Adler? That could be a few different men, and none of them would be a welcome sight. I'd been so focused when I walked in I hadn't noticed anyone else in the lobby. I slowly turn from Officer Martinez to the pine bench against the far wall. Manspreading all over it like he owns it is my least favorite Adler. The one I have to spend every waking hour avoiding because we inhabit the same college campus. Tate Adler.

He's glaring at me so I glare right back, and then walk over and sit on the complete opposite end of the bench, pressing myself into the arm so I can be as far away from him as humanly possible.

I stare straight ahead so I don't have to see his shock of tousled dark hair and his wide shoulders or bulging biceps that poke out of his white T-shirt and always look like they're flexing even when they're not. But Tate is looking at me. I can feel his eyes still on me and I fight the urge to blush. I'm not embarrassed, but any time I get elevated emotions of almost any kind—from annoyed to sad to elated—my skin tends to pink. The joy of a very pale complexion. I blame the recessive redhead genes Daisy and I were both saddled with. I tap my foot as we wait because I'm so agitated the energy has to go somewhere.

"Can you *not* do that?" Tate's deep baritone fills the room and he drops his head into his hands, elbows on his widespread knees. "Just sit still."

"Don't tell me what to do," I reply coolly and tap my foot even harder, making sure the bottom of my sandal slaps the scuffed linoleum floor in the loudest way possible.

He groans to the point of almost growling.

"Am I exacerbating your little hangover? Maybe you shouldn't have gone on a bender last night."

"I'm not hungover. I'm just tired," he replies. "Unlike you, I don't go to every party on campus."

I raise an eyebrow at that. I *do* go out a lot. I'm a college student, enjoying my life. But he's a college sports star and last year, which was my freshman year as well as his, I saw him with a beer in his hand almost as often as a hockey stick. Not that I was looking for him, but Moo U and the city of Burlington are too small not to notice a guy you've known and disliked since birth. Especially when he's also a hometown hero, which is how a lot of locals see him. Small town boy with big time talent and all that crap. "Why are you paying attention to where I go and what I do? Stalker, much?"

"Hardly. You're hard to miss with the orange hair and ghost skin and that doppelgänger who follows you everywhere," he mutters, and my jaw falls open.

"First of all, doppelgängers are unrelated people who look identical," I correct him tersely. "And second of all, we're not twins. She's a year younger than me and I have freckles, but Daisy doesn't. I have hazel eyes, hers are brown. And she's taller by, like, two inches."

He looks up from the linoleum in front of him long enough to give me an apathetic smile as he shrugs. "If you say so. I've never looked at either of you long enough to find a difference. As soon as I see you coming I turn around and walk in the other direction."

"Really?" I shoot him a smile dipped in acid. "You usually have your head so far up your own ass I'm surprised you see anyone else at all."

"Are you two going to start brawling like your granddads?" Officer Martinez asks.

My head snaps back around to the dark oak desk where officer Martinez sits watching us with concern. "Clyde punched George Adler?"

"Why else do you think I'm sitting here?" Tate asks me.

"Not just punched," Officer Martinez says before I can answer Tate. "They were rolling around on the marble floor at city hall in front of the clerk. Kicking, punching, biting."

"Biting?" Tate and I say in unison and then glare at each other before turning back to Martinez who nods vigorously.

"Oh yeah. Well, there's no mark but George swears Clyde bit

4

him." Martinez chuckles but tries to cover it with a clearing of his throat. "I bet they'd have pulled each other's hair if either of them had enough of it."

He can't hide his chuckle now so he excuses himself and heads down the hall mumbling something about going to see what's taking the arresting officer so long. I turn back to Tate. "What did your grandfather do to get Clyde so upset?"

Tate rolls his eyes. "Oh please, everyone knows Clyde is an angry drunk."

I open my mouth to combat that claim only it's true. I could say something like "but it's noon, not cocktail hour," but for all I know Clyde had a couple before he left the house this morning. He usually carries a flask in his back pocket, so I don't really have a leg to stand on. "Well George isn't exactly known for his empathy and good cheer. At least not where we are concerned. He's attacked my family verbally as far back as I can remember, so I'm sure he's the one who escalated it to physical abuse."

"Your granddad once came to one of my hockey games to yell insults at me," Tate reminds me, those dark green eyes of his narrowed with disdain. "I was freaking twelve years old and he was in the stands chirping me like I was an NHL star on his most hated team."

I vaguely remember this story. I would have been twelve too and my uncle Bobby was the coach of the local team that Tate was on. "Yeah but didn't *your* grandfather used to show up to practices and scream obscenities at my uncle because he thought you weren't getting enough ice time?"

"Tate Adler. Maggie Todd," a voice booms from nearby and Tate and I both jump to our feet. Another police officer marches toward us. He's big, burly, and frowning. Beside him is Ethel, the town clerk. She's a tiny little silver-haired lady in a T-shirt with an airbrushed cat on the front. She's smiling at us, but it's awkward. The officer glances from Tate to me and back to Tate again. "You had a killer season last year, Tate. First time I can remember that a

Burlington defensemen has led the division in shorthanded goals."

Tate smiles, his shoulders go back and he nods. "Yeah, it was a great season. Although personally, I'd have liked to win the division."

"That's what this year is for, right?" The officer chuckles and I want to groan in disgust at this love fest but instead I bite my lip and read his name on his shirt.

"Officer Humphries, can you tell us what's going on with our grandfathers please?" I interrupt with a polite smile.

"We've got them back there in separate cells so they can calm down. So far neither one wants to press charges against the other," Officer Humphries explains. "I just finished taking Mrs. Morris's statement since the incident happened directly in front of her."

Tate smiles warmly at Ethel. "I'm so sorry you had to witness that. Is there anything I can do, Mrs. Morris?"

Ethel smiles at him like she's a schoolgirl looking at her crush. "You can call me Ethel, Tate you sweetheart. And you don't need to apologize. We all know George and Clyde don't get along, but I certainly never saw them come to blows. I guess it was bound to happen eventually, but I didn't expect it at the sign-up for the farmer's market of all places."

The fall farmer's market. Of course. I sigh heavily and lift my eyes to the popcorn ceiling of the police station lobby. I asked my dad if he would head to city hall today and sign us up for a booth. The market runs year-round but has seasonal sign-up sheets as a way to help rotate vendors. He has been complaining we aren't letting him do enough so I gave him this task. He probably wasn't up for it though and didn't want to admit it to me so he asked my grandfather, Clyde, to go.

My dad had a stroke in the spring – thankfully not severe, but it did affect his balance and his energy levels, which is a huge problem for a farmer. My uncles Bobby and Ben, who own a construction business, have begrudgingly jumped back into farm work part-time to help out, but it's not exactly working out. My uncle Bobby forgot to sign us up for summer and we missed out on valuable income from the busiest market season. And now this.

"What, exactly, happened?" Tate asks gently and folds his arms over his chest, which is ridiculously broad.

"Well today was fall sign-up and everything was going smoothly, but then we got down to the last spot." Ethel raises a hand to her chest like she's having palpitations. Dear God, leave it to Clyde to traumatize the sweetest woman in Vermont. "George and Clyde were the only ones left in line. George was technically before Clyde. Clyde said George flirted with Katherine Oleson, who let him slip in line behind her, in front of Clyde. George denied it and Clyde called him a lying sack of...doo-doo. But he didn't use the word doo-doo. And then George gave Clyde a rude gesture with his hands and Clyde yelled something I don't dare repeat. And then...they just started throwing punches. It happened so fast I don't even know who started it."

Now Ethel is fanning herself like she's about to faint. I step a little closer. "I'm so sorry, Ethel. Truly."

"It's not your fault either, honey." Ethel stops fanning herself and pats my shoulder. "But the fact remains. We have one booth and two farms."

"I suggested to George and Clyde that they should have to share it," Officer Humphries says and Tate and I both tense up like we've been simultaneously poked with a cattle prod. He notices. "Yeah they both had the same reaction. Why do your families hate each other so much?"

"There's not enough hours in the day to explain that to you, sir," Tate mutters.

"His family stole some of our acreage," I say confidently.

"Your family ran a tractor through our fence," Tate counters.

"The fence George built on *our* property?" I reply. "And the gas pedal stuck. Even the police said it wasn't our fault. You running over one of our goats on the other hand..."

"That wasn't me, it was my cousin Raquel, and it was the middle of a whiteout blizzard so she didn't see him. And *your* goat was in the middle of *our* driveway because you can't seem to keep them in your own damn field," Tate snaps.

I take a deep breath of the stale air in this stuffy room. "It was our first year goat farming. We didn't realize they were such escape artists. Maybe if Raquel could drive without texting she'd have seen—"

"Forget I asked," Officer Humphries interrupts. "The fact remains, though, if you guys can put these ancient grudges aside and share this booth, you both get to sell your products. Win-win."

"No," I say flatly.

Officer Humphries frowns. "Well then, unfortunately I have to tell you that my investigation shows there is no proof that George Adler cut the line. Ms. Oleson pleaded the fifth, and so it's Clyde's word against George's word. So then the booth would technically belong to Adler Apple Farm."

"What? Wait…"

"Okay then! Now that's settled, can I take my grandfather home, Officer Humphries? I don't mean to rush you but I have to get to practice this afternoon," Tate says, smiling like a Cheshire Cat. I have seen women all over my campus swoon over that smile, but I simply want to rip it off his lips.

"I'll release both Clyde and George, one at a time so they don't get into another tussle. If they brawl again—anywhere, for any reason—there will be charges. Do you both understand me?" Officer Humphries says firmly.

"Yes sir," Tate says with a smile. I nod curtly but can't bring myself to smile.

As Officer Humphries heads off to retrieve our grandfathers, Ethel gives us a wave and heads out the front door and I turn back to Tate.

"Maybe we should rethink this sharing idea. Snap decisions are never the best ones. We could just keep Clyde and George away from the booth to avoid problems," I say, backpedaling so hard I'm surprised I don't break into a sweat. "Daisy and I and that younger brother of yours—Jace—could mend the fences the older generations broke."

Tate laughs loud and hard and it makes my hands ball into fists. "I speak for both Jace and me when I say, no thank you. We're good with keeping the booth to ourselves and the fences unmended."

If we don't share that booth with these assholes, we aren't at the farmer's market, and that's a huge chunk of our fall income. And since we already lost our summer market income, it will be a big blow. Daisy is going to flip. My dad is going to melt down. My uncles are going to freak out. I am going to kill my grandfather.

"Do you even have enough apples to run a booth for three months?" I turn to face him, knowing my face is tomato red because I can literally feel the anger running through my veins like lava. "I know you've had some pretty dismal crops the last couple of years. Didn't you have a bunch of scab apple trees?"

If looks could kill, Officer Humphries would be calling the coroner to come collect my body right about now. "Guess what? Even if we run out of apples and apple baked goods, I will find something else to sell. Hell, I'll sell my body at that booth before I give it to you."

"You'd be better off selling the rotten apples," I shoot back, but he just smirks because he knows that's not true. Tate Adler is built like some kind of action movie star—six foot one, tanned a golden-brown from the summer farm work, and the parts of him that aren't muscled are chiseled. Ugh. Screw Tate Adler.

"You've only got your granny panties in a knot because it was my granddad who got there first," Tate replies coolly. "If it was your booth, you'd tell me tough shit too and you know it."

I turn to face him, arms folded across my chest. "You're one hundred percent right."

He isn't expecting that kind of candor and the frown he's been sporting disappears. Although I would never admit it out loud, even if I was tortured, his cupid's bow mouth has the potential to be all kinds of sexy…if it didn't spew the garbage his brain thinks up. "Is this some psychology-major mind game or something?"

"I'm a business major focusing on entrepreneurial studies, just like you. We have a lot of the same classes, like accounting," I say. Since the semester started two weeks ago, I've watched him look up every time he entered the classroom to see where I was sitting and immediately walk to the opposite side of the room, so I know he knows this. "Also, I don't wear granny panties. Anyway I'm agreeing that yes, I would have done the same thing, but you have the opportunity to be the bigger person here. Come on small town hockey hero, show the world you're a bigger person than me."

Was that too much taunting? I know hockey players love a challenge. Uncle Bobby, who was the last local player to get drafted to the NHL, has never turned down a challenge or a dare in his entire life. He swears it's because of the competitive nature he developed playing hockey. And for the quickest little second, I think Tate might take my challenge. But George Adler appears from the bowels of the station and comes marching up to us. He's a tall, burly man with a barrel chest and thinning gray hair that used to be dirty blond. His polo shirt and jeans are in good condition and show no signs of the scuffle he had with Clyde, but there's a slight red abrasion on his chubby right cheek.

George stops in front of Tate, turning his entire body so that I'm behind his back, out of view, and he says to his eldest grandchild. "I'm sorry they bothered you. I had them call Raquel but she didn't answer her phone, and they wouldn't let me leave without supervision. Like I'm a goddamn toddler."

Tate frowns. "If you don't want to be treated like a toddler, Gramps, then maybe don't get into infantile fights. Let's go. I'm late."

George and Tate leave without another word or even glance at me. Son of a…

The door to the back swings open again and Clyde appears in

all his hunched over, bloodshot-eyed glory. He has the audacity to walk right past me and grumble. "Hurry up. I want to get the hell out of here."

I follow behind, scowling at the back of his balding head. We're crossing the parking lot when Matt, my brief Tinder date, pulls into the lot in his police cruiser and lowers his window. "Hey gorgeous! So it was your gramps? That's wild!"

"Yeah. Wild," I say tersely. Clyde has kept on marching to my car. George Adler has climbed into the passenger side of Tate's beat-up pickup, which is only a parking stall away from where I'm standing. So of course Tate has chosen to stand beside his truck and eavesdrop over leaving. Great. Matt smiles up at me and I'm sure he's leering at me behind those mirrored shades. In the fifteen minutes our date lasted, his eyes kept sweeping from my chest to my ankles, which made me regret the short strappy sundress I'd chosen to wear.

"So...we should probably reschedule our date, huh?" Matt lowers the sunglasses long enough to wink at me. "We had one hell of a vibe going before you ran off, didn't we?"

I'm about to tell him the vibe he was getting from me was repulsion but I'm not in the mood for another confrontation or to have a cop in town on my bad side or to give Tate Adler more of a show. So instead I just make a weird sound in the back of my throat and mutter. "Call me."

"I ain't got all day, Magnolia!" Clyde barks, and I turn and leave Matt without so much as a goodbye wave. I keep my head tipped down, eyes on the pavement as I make my way past Tate. I do not want to see his reaction to any of this.

I wait a second, until Tate has pulled out of the parking lot, before pulling out myself. Clyde turns to me and opens his mouth but I slap a hand up between us. "I don't want to hear it. You can explain at the farm—to everyone—how you got arrested and cost us a spot at the farmer's market. Until then, not a word, Clyde."

"Mag—"

"Not. One. Word!"

TATE

My dad scrubs his face with his hand as he leans against the kitchen counter. "Can you say that again? My brain just isn't making sense of it."

"Because it makes no sense," I reply and glance at the clock above the sink. My hockey practice is starting soon. Too soon. I have to leave this instant if I'm going to make it close to on time. "Look, I have practice. Just ask grandpa why he got into a fist fight with Clyde Todd. He can probably explain it better than me."

I start toward the front hall but there are footsteps thumping on the stairs and then my younger brother, Jace, swings his body over the whitewashed pine stair railing and lands with a thud directly in front of me. "Grandpa got arrested?"

"I told you how I feel about eavesdropping," Grandma says sternly from where she's sitting at the kitchen table a few feet away.

Jace shrugs his hoodie clad shoulders innocently. "It's not my fault the heating ducts from the kitchen carry every word people say right into my room. You guys really need to stop having private discussions in here. Try the barn."

"What's left of the barn is currently occupied by Grandpa who is blowing off steam by working," I explain. "And yeah he was arrested. Not charged. Thanks to me."

"Please say that loser Clyde Todd is still rotting in a cell," Jace says.

"Nope. Unfortunately he was sprung by Maggie. I gotta go," I say and push past Jace. He almost looks hurt. I feel bad because I don't hang out with him much at all lately. Now that I'm back at school, and hockey practices have started even though the season doesn't start for another month I barely see him and I know he misses me. I miss him too. He is used to me not being around since I went to boarding school for high school, but I think he assumed I'd live at home when I got into Moo U. But my full ride included money for housing, so I spent my freshman year in the dorms and moved into the hockey house a few blocks off campus this year. "I'll be seeing you on Sundays now though, since we got a booth at the farmer's market."

"We got the booth? Over the Todds?" Dad says and I can hear the relief in his voice. "You should have led with that, son."

I glance back at him and he smiles at me. I smile back, but I'm not as convinced as they are that getting a booth is a good thing. I mean, our apple crop is pretty pitiful this year and part of the plan was to sell pies and strudels and muffins from our less-than-presentable apples, but that relies on my grandma, and the arthritis in her hands is worse than ever. Aunt Louise and my cousin Raquel are supposed to help her out with the baking, but they tend to do a half-ass job if they show up at all. They both work other jobs—part-time—so I almost can't blame them except that they always expect me to give up everything to help with the farm, and I have other obligations. But I do it, so they should too. Jace has tried to help with baking but he usually messes up an ingredient amount and whatever he's making ends up inedible. "We will have enough baked goods to supplement the apples, right?"

"We will have enough. I think," Grandma says not even trying to sound confident. She tucks a strand of salt and pepper hair back behind her ear. "I mean I sent Louise to the store this morning for more flour, but she isn't back yet."

I grind my teeth. If you looked up self-absorbed in the dictionary, you'd find a picture of my aunt Louise. I can't say that out loud because my grandparents adore her. Louise can do no wrong in their eyes. "Jace, can you head to town and track down Louise please?" I say calmly and then whisper so only he can hear. "Check the coffee shop and the shoe store. If she spent the money grandma gave her on herself…"

I don't finish the sentence because there's no point. If Louise did spend the cash she was given for pie ingredients on shoes or a lunch for herself, I can't do a damn thing about it except make more money to replace it. Louise knows it and I know it. Jace nods and walks to the front hall to grab the keys to the family SUV. Well, it's technically Grandpa's but since Dad's car died in July and we haven't had the money to get him a new one, it's a communal car now, as with Gram's relic of a hatchback. He swings open the screen door and steps onto the porch. I follow.

"I'll be back early Sunday morning to help bring everything down to the farmer's market," I call as I walk out of the house.

Grandpa is walking out of the barn. He's red-faced and sweaty. I wonder what he's been doing in there. I don't know if I should ask. He wouldn't speak to me the whole ride home. He told me he was sorry I had to come fetch him and that it wasn't his fault but that was it. George Adler isn't the strong silent type. He talks. In fact, it's usually hard to get him to shut up whether he's armchair quarterbacking the Patriots game on TV or giving instructions to the farmhands—when we could afford to have farmhands —or telling his lame jokes at the dinner table, he's always yapping. "Need to replace the brushes on the apple washer."

"What? Why?" I ask, my feet skidding to a halt on the dirt drive, dust rising around me. "I thought we just did that."

"We did. Brushes are too hard. Bruised the crap out of the

fruit," he tosses an apple at me. I catch it and examine it. He's right. It's all banged up. We can't sell that.

"Why did we buy brushes that are too hard?" I say, my voice tight with frustration. I run a hand through my hair. "There's no way you can break down the washer and get it back together by tomorrow is there?"

"I'll stay up all night if I have to. Your dad will help," Grandpa replies.

He doesn't sound confident, he sounds resigned. He'll get it done, but it won't be easy. I'm not anywhere near confident either. Last time he broke down the washer it took three days to put back together. "Why did we buy the wrong brushes?"

"They aren't wrong. They just aren't right," Grandpa mutters and that lame excuse of a defense means he's covering for someone.

"Louise bought the wrong brushes? Or was it Raquel?"

"It's my fault. I asked Raquel to order them online and I didn't make it clear which ones. I was trying to save a couple bucks because it's cheaper than the local stores," Grandpa says and waves a hand between us like he's trying to air out the tension I'm emanating.

"Grandpa, did you really get arrested? For clocking Clyde Todd?" Jace asks and I want to bark at him because he should be halfway to town by now tracking down Louise. Instead he's hanging his head out the SUV window while it idles, burning away the gas we can barely afford.

"Yeah well, he deserved it. Was trying to steal our farmer's market booth," Grandpa says and frowns.

"He says you flirted your way into the line in front of him," I say, and Jace laughs.

"Clyde is always calling you a womanizer," Jace laments. "You've been with Grams forever and he's the one with the runaway wife. How does that even make sense?"

Somehow, Jace's defense of him makes Gramps even more ornery. I'm more observant than Jace so I think I know why, but

I'm not about to voice that suspicion. "I was nice to Kathy Oleson and Clyde's blowing it out of proportion. He's a drunk jackass. He and that group of miscreants he calls a family can take their fancy hippie cheese and shove it up their patchouli covered—"

The screen door slams behind me and Grandpa stops speaking instantly. I glance over my shoulder and see Grandma standing there, arms crossed and a look on her face that seems like it's equal parts hurt and anger. "George Adler, you and that belligerent mouth of yours have some explaining to do. Walk with me."

It isn't a request, it's an order. My grandmother rarely delivers orders to her husband, so when she does, you know it's serious. George looks guilty as he marches by me and joins grandma as she starts toward the orchard. I walk over to the SUV, where Jace is chuckling. "Wow. Grandma is pissed."

I think it's because she heard me say Gramps was flirting with another woman more than because of his use of colorful language and brawl with Clyde. Because if the suspicions I've had since I was ten and Grandpa spent seven months sleeping on the couch in the living room are correct, he's done more than flirt in the past. But now is not the time to explain that to Jace because it would take time neither of us has. "I'm pissed too because you're still here and not tracking down Louise and getting her and the supplies grandma needs back to the house."

Jace rolls his eyes. "Relax. I'll find her. Can you believe Grandpa and old man Todd actually came to blows? Has that ever happened before?"

"I have no idea but I'd say it's likely," I tell Jace. "They've been enemies since the day we moved here, I think."

Jace cocks his head and the backward baseball cap covering his light brown hair almost falls off as the brim hits the headrest on the seat. He adjusts it, spinning it forward. "Huh. Why?"

"What do you mean why?" I question. "Because Clyde Todd is a drunken asshole, you know that."

"Yeah but there's got to be more to it. What happened to trigger a grudge that lasts decades?" Jace asks.

"Jesus, I don't know. Why are you always so full of useless questions?" I ask and grin at him. "Next thing you know you'll be asking me why Zebras have stripes."

"Modern day scientists feel that Zebras have stripes as a natural defense mechanism because the pattern wards off biting flies that can carry deadly disease," Jace tells me. I smile at that because of course he knows why zebras are striped. He's actually a giant brainiac. He would qualify for a scholarship in a heartbeat if he would just actually try to pass his classes, but he doesn't, not for the last couple of years anyway.

I pull my phone from my pocket and glance at the time and swear. "I gotta fly. Can you go find Louise? Make sure she bought the right ingredients for grandma and help Dad and Grandpa with the apple washer tonight, okay?"

"Will do."

I jump into my car and take off as fast as legally possible back to campus. Today is not going as planned but what else is new? Since I started college the only thing that has gone right in my life is hockey. In a way it's my own fault, I guess. If I'd checked in more from my prep school in Minnesota maybe someone would have mentioned to me that Grandpa wanted to remortgage the farm to tear out half our Golden Delicious trees and replace them with super expensive, already matured Honey Crisp trees. I would have done the Google search that Grandpa didn't do and figured out that, though they sell for more, Honey Crisp trees often produce significantly less sellable fruit due to birds, insect infestations, and because they bruise more easily. Maybe we wouldn't have lost over forty percent of that first crop. And last year if I wasn't enjoying college so much and skipping visits home to spend weekends partying, maybe I would have noticed the cider press was on the fritz and in need of serious maintenance before it caught fire and burned down half the barn.

Now here we are, I'm a sophomore hockey star with a solid chance at going in the first round of the draft this coming summer, but I can't enjoy any of it anymore. When I'm not running off to a job I'm not supposed to have, I'm running back here to solve some crisis, working my butt off at hockey practice, studying, or lying awake at night trying to decide what I'll do if I do get drafted. Stay in school or bail immediately for a hockey contract and much needed money?

And as if all that weren't enough, Grandpa is risking jail time just so he can continue his war with the farm next door. I huff out a frustrated breath as I pull into the campus parking lot closest to the rink and jog toward it. I hadn't a clue why George was in jail at first. He just called and asked me to "spring him from the hoosegow" and I rushed over there without even asking why. But then Maggie Todd stormed in like a tornado—all red hair and pink cheeks and long, toned arms and legs—and asked to see her grandfather and the pieces fell into place.

Admittedly, I'm a little hazy on the details of the long-standing feud between the Adlers and the Todds. But that girl—who turned into a hell of a beautiful woman, unfortunately—has gotten on my last nerve since I was a kid. We went to the same grade school, and she used to run recess like she owned the place. All the other girls loved her and flocked to her, playing whatever game she wanted to play, giggling over whatever she giggled over and all that crap. Adults liked her too. She was always the teacher's pet. She talked like an adult too, which was weird as a grade school kid. On the occasions I overheard her yammering in the schoolyard, she didn't sound timid and used words I hadn't learned yet. And she smiled at everyone all the time. Everyone but me. To me she only glared, even before I told all the guys in fifth grade to call her Maggot instead of Maggie…which I only did because she glared.

We did our best to ignore each other in middle school and then it was time for high school and my hockey skills brought me an offer to attend an elite boarding school in Minnesota with the best hockey program in the country, and Maggie and all the Todds blissfully became a distant memory. All but forgotten until I came face-to-face with her during freshman orientation here last year. In an unspoken pact we reverted back to middle school days and ignored each other—until today when I end up next to her at the police station listening to her slam her foot into the linoleum. And her glare—the one that gets under my skin worse than a sunburn —was back in full force so I made things worse by being a brat to her.

I make it into the locker room and my stomach sinks. Everyone is in their equipment with their skates laced, seconds from hitting the ice. Even our goalie, Josh, who is usually the last one dressed because he has so much damn equipment, is ready to go. I yank my shirt over my head and toe off my shoes while undoing my jeans. Lex, a freshman who has made a point of sitting beside me in the locker room at all our practices so far this year, stands up on his skates and starts handing me my equipment as I need it. "I thought maybe you were skipping."

"You can't skip practice, like unless you're legit dying and even then I'd still be here," I reply tersely and then feel bad. He seems like a good kid so I add a grateful smile as he hands me my pads.

"Let's do this!" Coach Keller calls sticking his head into the room and slapping the wall by the doorframe. His eyes land on me. "You forget how to dress for practice, Adler?"

"Something like that, sir," I say and give him a light smile that he doesn't appreciate in the least. "I'll be out there in a second, Coach. I'm sorry."

"Uh-huh," Coach says and turns his attention to Lex. "Let's go rookie. Let him tie his own laces."

I cringe inwardly as Lex shuffles off with the others. The guy is just being nice so I hope Coach doesn't take the piss out of him for helping me. Bart Keller is a tough but fair coach and most importantly he is good at his job. He keeps us focused and motivated and he has been instrumental in helping a lot of his former players make the NHL. And maybe he'll help me if I can get to practice on time. Fuck.

I get out there as quickly as possible but Coach doesn't let me off the hook. Even though I work as hard as I can in every drill and keep my mouth shut in between them, not daring to joke around with the guys, he still stops me when it's over.

"You were late getting here, you can be late leaving," he says calmly as he tosses five pucks on the ice. "Twenty minutes of individual stick handling drills, and then swing by my office before you leave."

I nod and make sure not to show him any kind of facial expression that might make him notice there's a groan of dismay trying to escape my lips. Coach has every right to penalize me for this. I suck it up and do the drills. After I've showered and changed back into my jeans and T-shirt, I head out of the locker room to his office at the end of the long hall across from the entrance. As I pass by assistant Coach Garfunkle's office he looks up from his desk. "Adler! Wait a second."

"Hey Coach Garfunkle," I say as he stands and starts to walk around his desk. I hope he isn't going to chastise me too.

"I told Coach K not to go too hard on you.," Coach Garfunkel says in a stage whisper as he comes to a stop beside me. "Told him I've been sensing your chi is off."

I blink. Magnus Garfunkle played college hockey right here in Vermont but was never drafted. On our team website it says he has a degree in sports management but what it doesn't say, but he will be sure to tell you, is he also has certificates in transcendental meditation, Buddhist theory and Reiki. As if that wasn't quirky enough, he's short and squat and mostly bald so he kind of actually looks like a Buddha.

"My what?" I mumble back, confused.

"Your chi. You know, life force. Energy. Spirit." Garfunkle waves his hands around in front of me like he's clearing smoke from the air. "It's been off ever since you got back from summer break. That can mess with everything from your ability to meet deadlines to your sleep patterns to your performance on the ice."

"And you told Coach K this?" I ask and he nods emphatically.

"He'll go easy on you. Meanwhile, here." Garfunkle pulls a leather rope out of his pocket and shoves it at me. There is a crystal hanging from it. "This is rainbow moonstone and it will clear the bad energy invading your chi. Wear it around your neck and hang it by your bed when you sleep."

"Uh…okay. Sure thing," I say because I don't want to continue this conversation. I loop the rope over my neck and tuck it in under my shirt so no one sees it.

Coach slaps me on my shoulder appreciatively. "Keep it close to your skin, good idea."

"Thanks for this. See you later Coach," I say not because I believe in any of this new age crap, but I just don't want to keep Coach Keller waiting any longer.

When I rap on his open door, Coach Keller is sitting behind his desk and I can tell by the expression on his face he heard the whole exchange with his new age assistant.

"Sit down. Shut the door," Keller commands and I do exactly that.

When I look back up at him he's frowning. "I'm going to say this just once. I don't want you starting the season the way you're starting the season. Late, lagging a little on drills, not quite as focused as you should be."

"I don't want to start the season like this either, Coach," I say and try not to let the frustration in me bubble up to my face where he will see it. "I'm going to try harder."

"Good." He nods and looks me in the eye again, his face stone. "Now that Garfunkle is taking care of your chi is there anything else I can do? I think my wife has a quartz paperweight I can lend you."

He isn't smiling in the least as he says that and for a terrifying second I think he's serious but then he grins. The appearance of Coach Keller's sense of humor is as rare a sighting as Big Foot, so

I'm thrown for a loop as he chuckles at his own joke. But I find myself smiling. "I don't need more crystals, sir, I need a winning lottery ticket."

"What?" Keller's smile evaporates and he's back to his resting-stern-face.

"Nothing. I'm kidding. I just…family stuff," I mutter and clear my throat. "But I swear I will not be late again. I'm dedicated to this team, sir. I swear."

"Working on your farm didn't prove to be a problem last year," Keller reminds me. "And it can't become a problem this year."

"It won't be. I promise."

He doesn't look all that assured but then again he never does. He barely cracked a smile when we made it to the semi-finals last year. I stand up as he turns his attention back to his practice notes. I head out into the hall and out of the arena. The day is bright and warm, not a cloud in the sky, which makes my dark mood even more obvious. Cooper is leaning up against the side of my truck as I approach. He's my partner on D almost every shift I'm on the ice and we're good friends off the ice too. "Hey sunshine."

He's being sarcastic so I give him a sarcastic smile in return. He pushes off the truck as I approach. "Need a lift somewhere?'

"Nah. Was actually making sure you knew about the party tonight," he says and pulls his sunglasses down off the top of his blond head to cover his eyes. "Big one at Delta Phi Epsilon. We're all going."

"Awesome," I reply and try to mean it.

"So you joining or bailing like you did last night?" Cooper wants to know and I frown.

"Technically I didn't bail last night. I never said I was going," I remind him.

Cooper rolls his eyes. He just wants to have fun. I wish I was him. "Anyway, you coming or what? It'll be fun. Do you know what fun is?"

"I remember fun…vaguely." My phone starts ringing from my back pocket and I pull it out.

"Be there, Adler," Coop says and gives me a friendly shove as he turns and walks away, but I barely acknowledge him as I stare at the number on the screen. It's Vickie. Ugh.

I know Vickie too well to send her to voicemail, even though I really want to. Another guy who works for her told me he sent her to voicemail one too many times and she wouldn't send him out on jobs for three months. So I sigh and hit answer. "Hey Vickie."

"Hey, honey," she says. She has a southern accent but it's fake. She's working on it with a dialogue coach. Normally she has a fairly thick Boston accent. Vickie, like all of us, has dreams. She doesn't want to run a maid service with half-naked male cleaners for the rest of her life. She wants to be a voiceover actor. "How'd last night go?"

I think back to the job I did last night. Two middle-aged women who shared a small house in Plattsburgh, New York. They were typical. They kept giggling and insisting they'd never done this before. But then one of them said how cute the costume idea was and asked when that started, meaning they knew not all the Manly Maids wore costumes to disguise themselves. Still, they were harmless. "Good. Fine."

"Awesome. Now, sugar, I need you to get me out of a little pickle this afternoon," Vickie says and I want to groan but I don't. Plattsburgh was over an hour away and the job last night had taken two and a half hours. I hadn't gotten home until way late. I don't take local gigs because I don't want people to find out about this little side hustle, and I didn't feel like another long drive to clean toilets in my undies. But I also can't afford to say no to work. "Before you say no, I'm willing to pay you twenty-two an hour for this one."

"What? Why?" I ask, confused. "And also, I'll take it."

Vickie already paid us well. Twenty bucks an hour, and she included commuting time. "Because I'm desperate, Tate. This client booked last week and Vinnie was all set to handle it but he ate bad mussels or something last night and he swears he can't leave his bathroom now. Everyone else is booked except you."

"Okay…" I've helped Vickie out of scheduling jams before and there's never been a pay bump so there's more to the story. "When and where?"

"Five o'clock tonight. 10 Greene Street," Vickie says and pauses dramatically before adding. "Burlington."

And that's why she wants to pay me so much. "I can't ever do Burlington, Vickie. I told you."

"I know. I know. But I'm desperate," Vickie whines. "And it's only one gig, Tate. One time. And you wear a costume. There's no way anyone will recognize you. And even if they become repeat customers, I swear I won't ask you to work there again. Even if they ask for you specifically. I promise."

"Vickie I want to help and I need the money it's just that I can't. If anyone recognizes me I'm screwed in ways I can't even begin to explain," I reply. I told her my parents were religious zealots and would disown me. Vickie doesn't know I'm a hockey player and I want to keep it that way. And she has no clue I'm on a full scholarship and that the rules for the scholarship indicate that we are only allowed to work part-time at an on-campus job. I figured the less people who know my secret the better.

"I'll pay you twenty-four an hour," Vickie replies. "And I'll give you my new client in St. Johnsbury. Twice a month. Vince covered it once already and says she tips like forty bucks every time. She's yours exclusively if you take this, just this once."

I shouldn't. It's risky but damn…the money is too good to pass up. "Just this once, Vickie."

"Thank you, stud," Vickie says and repeats the address before hanging up.

I hang up and close my eyes, rubbing my forehead. I really hope I don't live to regret this.

3

MAGGIE

"Who left all the pots in the sink covered in…" I stop mid-yell and stare at the crusty orange-ish gunk covering one of the three pots in the sink. "I don't know what this is."

"Jasmyn was playing around with a homemade marmalade recipe," Daisy replies as she walks into our tiny kitchen carrying a square Tupperware she's eating cereal out of because there're probably no clean bowls.

"We are heathens," I announce and sigh as I drop the pot back into the sink, which is filled to the brim with dirty dishes. "When is Caroline hiring that cleaning service?"

"She left it in my hands," Daisy replies as she shovels another spoonful of Cap'n Crunch into her mouth and sits in one of the chairs at the tiny bistro table in the corner, which is currently covered in junk mail and books. "I've hired someone. They're coming this evening."

"Aren't people supposed to tidy up before their maid comes?" I ask but Daisy shakes her head, her copper hair shimmying around her shoulders.

"That's for people who have shame. We do not," Daisy says with a grin.

I actually am embarrassed that we've let our rental get so out of control. Just not embarrassed enough to clean it. When we all first moved in together in July, I tried. Daisy, our mom and I were doing everything at the farm all summer because Dad was still recovering from his stroke and my uncles were too busy with their own business. I was exhausted every single day but I would still get home from ten hours at the farm and scrub the toilets, mop the floors and do the dishes. When I got completely fed-up with that, I made a schedule for everyone else to help but no one is following it and I refuse to do it all alone again, so here we are with stains on our countertops and rings around our toilet bowls and dust bunnies in our hallways. But then our roommate Caroline's dad dropped in for a spontaneous visit last week and was horrified. He said he would give her a monthly stipend specifically for a cleaning person. Thank God for a rich roommate who is also a really great, albeit messy, friend.

"When does the maid get here?" I ask as I give up on the idea of cooking something and walk over to the cupboard and pull out a bag of tortilla chips. Daisy smiles. I stop midway to the fridge to retrieve the jar of salsa. "What?"

"Nothing. The cleaner will be here at five. You're home right?" Daisy says and she's still smiling in that way she smiled when we were six and she put a grasshopper in my bed.

"Yeah...why?"

"I just want us all here...to supervise." Daisy shrugs and finishes her cereal. She leaves the Tupperware on a pile of mail and walks out of the kitchen.

"Weirdo," I mutter and grab the salsa from the fridge. I take it and the chips to my room. I hate eating in my room but at this point, it's the cleanest place in the house. Although I refuse to clean up after Caroline, Jasmyn and Daisy, I do clean up after myself.

I walk down the long hall, wide wood floorboards creaking as I go, to my room at the front of the apartment. We picked cards for rooms. I scored the highest card so I scored the biggest room. It's like winning the lottery in this quirky third story apartment in a building built in the eighteen hundreds. It has a teeny but private bathroom attached and a door to the large balcony that fronts the apartment. The other bedrooms are at the back and side, so if my roomies want balcony access they have to go through the door off the living room, which is next to my room.

I open the door and immediately relax. I love my room in all its quirky but clean glory. I open the door to the balcony and admire my flowers and plants for a second. I covered our balcony with flower pots and boxes of them hanging on the railing. Jasmyn attached a bunch of tiny pots to the wall with herbs. We bought some brightly colored plastic bucket chairs that are cheap but comfy. It is an oasis. I would love to sit out there right now and relax, but instead I walk over to my desk and crack open the salsa and dip a chip in as I flip open my laptop. I should be reading an assignment for my Sustainable Business Strategies class, but I am still stewing about not getting a booth at the farmer's market and want to brainstorm other moneymaking ideas.

When I told Daisy the whole story about Clyde she was equal parts amused and miffed.

"I was flirting with Hank. He works at Biscuit in the Basket now because the Adlers let him go. Not enough money for staff and he says a big chunk of their crop tanked again this year. They'll forfeit that booth before the end of the fall season and we can snag it up," she had said. Hank was five years older than me and had been a farmhand with the Adlers since he was in high school. He had a thing for Daisy and probably wouldn't lie to her. But still, I couldn't rely on their perpetual bad luck.

"Tate said he'd use the booth to sell his body before he lets us take it over," I had replied.

"Gosh I hope Clyde got a good left hook in. I hate the Adlers," Daisy had grumbled.

"George had a bruise on his face but Clyde's gonna have a black eye," I told her. "And he had the nerve to blame it on me. He said if I really wanted to prove I should take over the farm, I should make it a priority and I should have been the one to go down to city hall and reserve the spot."

"He's gonna sell it," Daisy predicted sadly. "He is just looking for any excuse he can because he cares more about money than family."

Daisy was probably right, which was why figuring out a backup plan took precedence over my schoolwork. Clyde had been threatening to sell the farm for a while now, which had Daisy and me both terrified and angry. My mom and dad raised us there, they dedicated their lives to it, as our two uncles had as well, and Daisy and I were actually planning to do the same. The last couple of years, we've all spent more time and energy than we should trying to convince Clyde to let us take it over. So now that we don't have the fall market, I have to figure out how to off-load our honey and cheeses. The stores we are currently selling to don't need larger supplies at the moment so I start contacting new ones via their websites.

I finished the entire jar of salsa and am in the middle of applying for a booth for a weekend fair in Upstate New York when the buzzer for the front door squeals through the apartment.

"The maid is here! I'll buzz him up!" Daisy hollers, way too excitedly. I chuckle as I crumple up the now empty chip bag. Suddenly there is a knock on my open door and I turn and see Daisy, Caroline and Jasmyn staring at me with grins so big they're almost scary.

"What?"

"Go get the door!" Daisy demands.

"I thought you let her in?"

"I buzzed them up but someone still has to let them into the apartment," Daisy explains and bounces a little. "We want you to do it."

"Why don't you get it?" I ask and the hair on the back of my neck starts to rise. Something is up. I don't know what, but I don't like it.

"Just come on! Before the…maid…thinks we're not home and leaves!" Caroline giggles and suddenly darts into my room and grabs my arm, yanking me off the chair.

"What the hell, Caroline!" I say as someone knocks on the front door. Daisy and Jasmyn are running along behind us as Caroline drags me around the corner and down the hall to the front door. I'm trying to dig my heels in to stop the forward motion, but I'm in socks on hardwood so it's futile.

"She's coming!" Daisy calls out as Caroline finally lets go of my arm when we reach the front door. I stare at it and then turn and face my roommates with my arms crossed.

"I'm not answering that," I say flatly.

"Why not?" Jasmyn asks, her big brown eyes wide with excitement, over what I have no clue, and that's exactly why I will not answer the door. Because something is up and everyone knows it but me.

"I hate surprises," I remind my sister, who should know this by now.

"It's just the maid. I swear," Daisy says, and the smile drops off her wide mouth…which has a pretty pink gloss on it. And her brown eyes are sporting eyeliner and mascara.

I glance as Jasmyn and Caroline who are also both wearing makeup suddenly. Daisy was clean faced and in sweats earlier. Caroline was still in pajamas. Jasmyn wasn't even home. There's another knock as I say, "What the hell is up?"

Daisy huffs in annoyance. "God, you're such a scaredy-cat."

She pushes past me and grabs the door handle, but she slides to the right with it as she swings it open leaving me face-to-face with…a man. He's in a very tight white tank top, ripped jeans slung oh so low on his narrow hips, a cowboy hat, a red bandana over the bottom half of his face and sunglasses over his eyes.

"Who the hell are you?"

He doesn't say anything, but I think he tenses up. Or flexes? Something makes all his muscles—and there are a lot of them—tighten. Jasmyn giggles beside me and Caroline makes a low almost-growl sound of appreciation as her eyes sweep over him. Daisy peeks around the door she opened that she's basically hiding behind. "He's our cleaner. We hired Manly Maids."

"Manly Maids?" I repeat, confused and look at him again. "What the hell is Manly Maids?"

"A cleaning service that only sends hot, buff, beautiful men to scrub you clean," Jasmyn explains. "Well, your house."

"Come in!" Caroline urges the guy and starts motioning with her hands.

He reaches for something and hesitantly crosses the threshold with a mop and bucket in his hand now and I notice a feather duster sticking out of his back pocket. And then, as Daisy swings the door closed behind him, and he is less than a foot in front of me, he puts down his cleaning stuff, takes off his cowboy hat, hooking it on the mop handle, and reaches up behind his back and grabs the thin tank top and starts pulling it up over his head.

My eyes can't help but follow the hem of the tank as it rises up his torso revealing ripple after ripple of well-defined muscle. I feel like the Count on *Sesame Street* as my brain shouts *one ab, two ab, three ab, four ab, five ab, six ab…ah, ah, ah!*

And of course, as the shirt rises higher and higher so does the heat in my cheeks. By the time he's shirtless I know I'm the color of a first degree sunburn. Daisy lets out a laugh followed by a snort. "You should see your face!"

"Why is he getting naked?" I croak and stare at his face, which is barely visible yet somehow—in the recesses of my mortified mind—I feel like I should know him. "They clean in their under-wear," Jasmyn says and Caroline giggles maniacally beside her.

"What? Why?" I squeak as his hands goes to the button on his loose jeans and my eyes follow. "Oh my God."

I cover my face as the sunburn color deepens to second degree. My roommates are all laughing so loud at my reaction I consider moving out. "Jerks!"

I can't stop myself from peeking through my fingers though. He is totally just in his underwear now. A pair of snug, black

Calvin Klein boxer briefs. *Sweet Mother Mary and Joseph.* The man is *fine.* Daisy moves beside me and slings an arm over my shoulder. "Hey cowboy, you can start in the kitchen. We bought the full meal deal, for the record."

My hands drop and I glare at her. "What does that even mean?"

Before she can answer I turn to our masked, mostly naked guest and say. "You don't have to do anything you aren't comfortable with. I mean, we're not like…this is so…we won't touch you or anything. This is a safe space. I'm so sorry."

I'm rambling on like a complete insane person at this point, drowning in embarrassment. Jasmyn is laughing so hard tears are streaming down her cheeks and Caroline is doubled over, leaning on the wall for support. Daisy stares at me like I have lost my mind. "Full meal deal means he'll do the dirty dishes and clean the toilets as well as mop and dust. Get your mind out of the gutter, sis."

I look at her and back at him. He holds up a feather duster. And tucks the handle into the side of his very tight, very complimentary boxer briefs. My embarrassment sunburn shade kicks up to third degree. "I'm going to go hide in my room."

I start down the hall but Daisy grabs me. "Oh no, honey, we didn't hire him to do this without an audience. Show him where the kitchen is and supervise his work."

"This is ridiculously sexist," I blurt out but she's dragging me down the hall and I'm letting her because, if nothing else, I can protect him from my suddenly lecherous roomies.

"They have topless maid services, you know. Hell, they even have a topless coffee shop in Maine," Daisy argues calmly. "Those have been in existence for years, so this service is just balancing the scales. We're actually being feminists by using it. Keeping things fair and equal."

"I think you need to enroll in law school because that's the best argument I've ever heard, even if I don't believe a word of it," I reply.

He's right behind us as we enter the kitchen but he stops abruptly when the sink comes into view. It's as gross as it was earlier and now I'm aware of the smell I must have blocked out before. The room has a faint odor of rotten vegetables and musty water. We're lucky he's got seventy-five percent of this face covered so we don't have to witness his look of disgust. Even though it's saving me from further embarrassment I question it. "Do you have to wear the costume? Can you even see in here with sunglasses on?"

He turns his head toward me but doesn't speak. He just gives me a curt nod and walks over to the sink. There is something about the way he moves—his walk, the shape of his broad muscular shoulders and the round curve of his bubble butt…this guy doesn't just work out to get that body. He plays a sport. Or he did. He moves like an athlete.

"We're busy, hardworking women, cowboy, so we just don't have time for dishes," Jasmyn says leaning on the door frame and full-on ogling this poor dude. He glances over his shoulder at her but doesn't seem to mind. I guess if this is his job, he's used to it.

"Thank God a big, strong man like you is here to clean our plates," Caroline says and it sounds so bloody cheesy even he groans. And it's not only sexy but also familiar. I've heard that groan before…recently.

How have I heard that groan before?

"So are you from around here?" I ask as Daisy sits at the kitchen table, chin in her hands and stares blatantly at his ass.

He isn't even attempting to answer me as he scrubs a pot. Caroline doesn't like that. "You're dressed as a cowboy, not a mute. Is talking extra or something?"

He glances over his shoulder and looks in my general direction and shakes his head.

"Okay so you're not from here. But you must live nearby?"

"Maggie this is a cleaning service not a dating app," Daisy says sternly. "Save your questions for your next Tinder date.

Maybe next time you'll swipe right on a cowboy instead of a cop who tells you he arrested your grandpa."

I start to turn red again which seems to delight my sister. Caroline and Jasmyn are finally paying attention to something other than the naked hottie. "What? Your grandfather was arrested?"

"And you're dating a cop?"

"Yes and no. I'll explain later," I reply and my eyes go back to the Cowboy.

"Explain now," Jasmyn begs.

"Our asshole neighbor, George Adler, has always gone out of his way to push Clyde's buttons and, long story short, they got into a fist fight at city hall," I mutter. "And I found out when I went on a date with a cop."

"I don't even know what to say about that," Jasmyn shakes her head. "Was the cop at least hot?"

"Yes," I say absently, still focused on our maid. Why is my Spidey-sense going off like a smoke alarm? "Hey Mr. Manly Maid. You must do more than just go to the gym, right? I mean to be this...fit. Do you play a sport? Soccer?"

He shrugs those amazing shoulders and seems to scrub the dishes more aggressively suddenly. My eyes slide down over that well sculpted butt and then to his thighs. His thick, muscular, strong thighs. "Hockey? Do you play hockey?"

"That is definitely a hockey ass," Jasmyn whispers.

"Just stop talking and enjoy the view. It's what you paid for," he snaps and while my roommates and sister gasp in horror at his rudeness, I gasp in shock because I *know* that deep voice overflowing with snarky attitude.

I walk over as he starts to turn to face us and I reach out and tip his hat off his head. In an attempt to catch it, he leans forward as it tumbles to the ground. Knowing he's off guard, I quickly grab the edge of his bandana and give it a swift tug. He jumps back and his sunglasses tumble to the floor next to his hat.

And then there he is—Tate Adler half-naked in *my* kitchen. For once, I'm not the one turning red.

4

TATE

I knew I shouldn't have taken a job in Burlington. And now I am totally and utterly screwed. There were warning signs all damn day that I ignored. The address was the first. A ton of students live in this area of town because it's affordable and has a lot of rental properties. The name of the client was Caroline S. To protect privacy Vickie never gives out last names for our clients like she doesn't give out our names at all. But I know Caroline Schneider. She had a brief but intense fling with a guy on my dorm floor last year. And she drives a custom painted matte teal Fiat, which was parked across the street as I parked next to the apartment building. I noted it, which is why I decided to keep my sunglasses on which isn't normally part of my costume. In case she lived nearby and saw me.

As soon as I heard the giggling behind the door, I knew I was fucked. I knew they were college girls, which meant they were Moo U girls. And I was about to leave when the door flew open and Maggie Todd was standing in front of me. The very pretty, ultra-annoying bane of my existence. I should have turned and run down the stairs and out the door as fast as my legs would take me but I didn't. I told myself I could get through this—but I couldn't. And I didn't.

And now she's basically holding my proverbial balls in her hands and she knows it. Maggie Todd is a lot of things but stupid isn't one of them.

"Holy shit!" Caroline gasps as my identity is revealed.

"You go to our school!" The girl who had been laughing like a Tickle Me Elmo doll says. I don't recognize her at all, but they've called her Jasmyn a few times.

"Adler?" Daisy whispers in shock.

"Tate Adler," Maggie grins and crosses her arms and tips out a hip. She couldn't look more smug if she tried. "You've got some explaining to do."

"Actually what I've got is a really disgusting apartment to clean," I reply sharply because if I'm going down, I might as well do it swinging. "You girls live like animals and that says a lot coming from a guy who lives with a bunch of other perpetually sweaty jocks."

I go back to washing what's left in the sink, ignoring the parts of my costumes that fell to the ground because there's no point hiding now. I hear them all approach and know they're hovering right behind me full of judgment and questions. I'm so furious with myself for getting into this situation and my brain is running at a million miles an hour trying to figure out a way out of it.

"This was only fun because he was a stranger who didn't judge us," Jasmyn announces and walks out of the room.

Caroline frowns at me. "You know we are all really busy. I've got an internship this semester and a full course load. Daisy and Maggie work part-time on their farm and Jasmyn goes to college for business and takes cooking classes almost every night so…"

"You don't owe me an explanation," I interrupt because I don't care, honestly, that they live like pigs. "I'm not going to tell anyone. I'll keep my mouth shut and clean this entire house if you all keep your mouths shut too."

"I want a ten percent discount," Caroline demands, surprising me but I nod without hesitation. "Lips sealed."

She turns on her heel and also leaves the kitchen. Great, now it's just me and Satan's redheaded minions. I put the last dirty dish on the drying rack, which is stuffed to the brim, and walk over to my mop and bucket and lift the bucket to the sink.

"I'm not so big on the keeping my mouth shut part," Daisy says.

"Of course you're not," I say and turn to her. "Because you're mean and selfish like your grandpa."

"No. Because this is hysterical and you're a dick," Daisy replies and then, before I realize what's happening, she's pulled a phone out of her back pocket and I hear the distinct snapping sound.

I charge toward her and reach for her phone. "No pictures! It's in the damn rules."

Daisy is fast and out of the kitchen before I can grab her phone. I chase her down the hall, Maggie is running behind me yelling my name but I ignore her. I don't know their apartment or where the hell she's going but she turns and heads back toward the front door then takes a left into what must be a bedroom and slams the door a millisecond before I can cross the threshold. I bang on it with my palm. "Seriously! No pictures! It's in the online consent form. I'm going to sue your ass if you don't delete that!"

My heart is racing and I turn to Maggie and I know I look like I'm having a panic attack because, well, I might be. I have no idea what those feel like. Maggie's face morphs from amused to concerned immediately. "Okay, okay, calm down."

"That's a breach of terms of service. A total violation," I snap.

Maggie looks like she's fighting an eye roll. "Dramatic much? We took your picture we didn't grope you or anything."

"I'd rather you did," I bark back and instantly regret it but hey, I'm suddenly an expert in doubling down on stupidity so when her eyes grow wide I lift both my arms and take a step toward her. "Seriously, you can touch whatever you want. Get a good feel. Pinch my ass. Try to figure out what jock size I wear. I don't care if it means you'll delete that damn picture and keep your big mouths shut about this job."

Maggie's big hazel eyes are blinking so rapidly in disbelief that they're fluttering. And that pale complexion of hers is rapidly gaining color again. "You're so worried about the picture you'd let me molest you?"

"I could list a lot of your faults Maggie but your IQ wouldn't be one of them," I reply and she looks rightfully offended. "You're here on a full ride just like me and so I know you know the rules about scholarships. So go ahead and molest the hell out of me— you can all take turns—as long as the picture disappears."

"First of all, gross," she says and shudders. "Touching you would be a punishment not a reward."

"Please. You may hate me but let's be honest, physically I've got more to appreciate than that cop you're dating," I say flatly and with confidence which I know sounds egotistical but I'm great in bed, and hockey and farm chores have given me a body I know women appreciate because they tell me. Not just on every job but at school parties too.

"I'm not dating the cop. It was one date. And let's get back to the scholarship and the rule about how if you're in need of a part-time job you must consult with Financial Aid and they will match you with an on-campus job," Maggie says and that smug smile is back playing on her lips. "Because students on a full scholarship are only allowed to work on-campus jobs on a part-time basis only as to not interfere with schoolwork."

She recites the regulation almost verbatim. I'd be impressed if it wasn't so upsetting. "Yeah. So it shouldn't shock you that I'm willing to do anything or let you do anything to keep this between us. I need this scholarship."

"Excuse me? Are you going to finish cleaning this apartment," Caroline calls out and Maggie and I both snap our heads around to see she's popped her head out of her bedroom door down the hall by the kitchen. "If not, I'll still pay if that touching option is still on the table."

"I'll clean it," I reply and turn back to Maggie. "After Daisy deletes that picture. For all I know she's already posted it to Instagram or some garbage."

Caroline disappears back into her room with a disappointed huff. Maggie sighs and brushes past me to knock on her sister's door. "Daisy open up and give me the phone."

There's a pregnant pause but the door opens a crack and a pale arm extends with the phone in hand. I step forward as Maggie takes it but she puts a hand out and her palm bumps my bare chest. "Not so fast there, cowboy. You've got a job to do, remember?"

"Cleaning this pig sty? Yeah. I'll do it. Now delete it," I reply tersely.

"Clean," Maggie replies just as tersely.

I want to hurl every insult I've ever heard at her, but I grit my teeth and force myself to head back into their dirty kitchen where I grab my mop and bucket and get back to work.

An hour later, the kitchen and bathroom are clean and I'm both disgusted and exhausted. This place is messier than the hockey house, and we're not exactly clean freaks. "Vickie described the job as kitchen and bathrooms, plural, so where's the next bathroom?"

"This way," Maggie—who has been following me around, watching me like a hawk the entire time—says. She walks down the hall and I follow, dragging my supplies with me. Daisy, who has been sitting at the kitchen table reading a magazine and smirking at me while I work, doesn't follow. Caroline and Jasmyn have only occasionally popped their heads out of their rooms to sneak a peek, but I haven't seen either of them in fifteen minutes. At the end of the hall, near the living room, Maggie swings open a door on the left. I walk in bracing myself for another pig sty but don't find one.

The room is simple—a double bed with a vintage quilt, an old wooden desk, some floating shelves with neatly stacked books, and a ridiculously oversized bean bag chair near the bay window and the door to the balcony. Even the throw rug beside the bed looks like it was recently vacuumed. "Whose room is this?"

"Mine. Bathroom is over there." Maggie points to a closed door next to an open closet. I walk over and pull it open. It's truly the smallest bathroom I have ever seen. It's barely bigger than a phone booth.

"I don't even think I can fit in here to clean it," I mutter and try. I am basically touching everything the second I step in there. My calf is touching the toilet bowl, my hip the sink and my shoulder the shower curtain for the teeny stand-up shower. I turn awkwardly to face the door and she's standing in it, so she's basically right on top of me. I try to take a step back, but there's nowhere to go and I hit the sink with my butt and stumble to the side and basically trip into the shower, almost ripping down the shower curtain.

"Careful clumsy!" Maggie scolds.

She moves into the space with me which is impossible, only she does it anyway, and now I'm not just touching every surface in the bathroom, I'm touching her too. More importantly, she is touching me. Her chest, covered in what I now know feels like a very soft, very thin T-shirt, is brushing against my bare chest. Her left arm grazes my hip and as she bends down and reaches for something under the sink, her long silky hair ghosts across my belly and her shoulder skims the front of my boxer-briefs and my dick. Maggie Todd just touched my dick.

"Okay this is insane," I blurt out jumping back and stumbling out of the small space. I almost fall onto her bed in the process and manage to readjust the suddenly expanding bulge in my briefs as I right myself.

My dick is still tingling from the brief brush of her shoulder. I *cannot* get hard over *this* girl. Not her. Anyone but *her*.

She's giggling behind me. "I'm amazed you play hockey as well as you do, because you seem about as coordinated as a baby deer on a frozen pond."

"Why the hell would you try to get into that postage stamp of a room with me?" I ask her as I slowly turn around making sure my body parts are all behaving before I face her. "How do you even function in that space?"

"I manage." She tosses something at me and I catch it a second before it's about to smack me in the head. "There are those lightning fast reflexes the local paper raved about last year."

"You read about me a lot, do you?" I mutter and smirk at her before looking at the thing she tried to assault me with. It's a box of Lysol bleach wipes.

"I clean the bathroom with these. It's easier than trying to cram a mop in there and there's only like a foot of tile anyway," Maggie explains as she steps back out of the bathroom and makes a grand gesture for me to enter again. "And unfortunately I had no choice but to read about you and hear about you last year. Your rookie season was all anyone talked about. Local kid leads the entire division in shorthanded goals. NHL scouts itching for him to enter the draft, blah, blah, blah."

I feel my chest inflate just the slightest despite her "blah, blah, blah" part. "Yeah well, I worked my ass off. And all that hard work will be blown out of the water if you post that picture anywhere."

It only takes three wipes and a minute and a half to clean her bathroom, not just because of the size of the space but also because it wasn't very dirty to begin with. I wipe the floor last which is basically six large porcelain tiles and scoot my way out as I do it. When I turn to face her she's the color of marinara sauce again. I cock my head to the side. "What's got your face all tomatoey again?"

"Nothing. It's just actually kind of stuffy in here." She barges past me to the three windows that make up her bay window and tugs open the middle one. I have the brief, startling revelation that she might be on fire this time because she liked the view—of me. But I don't have time to use that egotistical thought to tease her again because I have real problems to solve.

"Will you delete the damn picture now? From the Cloud too?"

I ask. I want to get that photo deleted and get the hell out of here and go back to pretending she and her pesky little sister don't exist.

"You're getting paid for the cleaning. You want the photo gone forever, you gotta pay for that," Maggie replies coolly as she sits on her bed, leaning back all casual, like she isn't fucking with my entire life.

"You want your money back? Fine. But I can only pay you what Vickie pays me. She takes a cut, you know. I don't get to keep it all and I'm broke, so I can't give you anything more than I get," I explain and grit my teeth because the idea of not being paid for this humiliation pisses me off.

I walk over and stand in front of her which I instantly realize isn't a great idea. She's now eye level with my junk. Her hazel eyes seem to grow two sizes and that alabaster complexion is changing color again. And she tries to stand up, but I'm too close and she ricochets off my chest and lands on her back on the bed. I can't help but laugh, which clearly annoys her, so I swallow down the last bit of my chuckle and take a step back. Pissing her off isn't going to help me.

"You want the picture, you're going to have to give us half your booth at the farmer's market," she announces as she stands up again, this time without calamity.

"I'm sorry, what?" I wasn't expecting that but as soon as she announces it, I realize I should have been. "When? This Sunday?"

"Yep." She nods firmly and puts her hands on her hips. "And every other Sunday of the season."

My jaw drops. "You're fucking kidding."

"I don't kid about business, Adler," she replies, cool as a cucumber again. I angrily grab my feather duster off the floor and point it at her, about to tell her off, but then she pulls the phone from the back pocket of her jeans and snaps another picture. I lunge for it but she's much more graceful and catlike than she was a minute ago and she manages to leap onto the bed and off the other side. Her fingers are busy punching things on the screen as I dart across the room to try and grab it again.

Maggie quickly drops it down the front of her shirt, probably tucking it into her bra. I freeze and she smiles. "If you go for it I will punch you square in that pretty face of yours. And also, it won't do a lick of good. I just emailed it to myself."

Argh! I hate this woman.

"The entire season? That's bullshit," I argue even though I know there's no point. I have to give her what she wants. "My family needs the money from this more than yours. That's a fact and you know it."

"We lost this market because my dad's recovery isn't as quick as we'd hoped and he couldn't go to the sign up and sent ornery and apathetic grandpa Clyde. And this summer, my darling but unreliable uncles forgot to sign up," Maggie confesses. "So we need it more than you think."

"Town gossip is that your family's done an excellent job of moving to goat milk from the dwindling cow milk industry, despite what happened to your dad. And that you sell your specialty honey to a chain of organic stores based out of Boston," I tell her, folding my arms across my chest. "Not that I was paying close attention but other farmers talk—a lot. That's also why I know you must know the situation my family is in with the lost crops and the cider press causing a fire in the barn." I sigh and run an exasperated hand through my hair.

She shifts from one foot to the other. "Can you get dressed?"

"Sorry. I guess you're not used to seeing men's bodies," I mutter and start toward the door to her room because my pants and tank top are still on the floor in her front hall. "At least not really good ones."

"Wow. Conceited much?" she demands as she follows behind me. "And what the hell is that supposed to mean anyway?"

"I saw your little police officer boy toy this morning," I reply and start to pull on my pants. I turn to face her as I do them up.

"And he's definitely been to the donut shop a few too many times."

"It is so not your business but as I said before, he is not my boyfriend," she says and crosses her arms. "But regardless, your comments make you just as much of a vain jerk as I thought you were."

I smirk. "Tell yourself whatever you want, Firecracker, but I noticed you didn't take your eyes off me the whole time I was cleaning."

"I wanted to make sure you did a good job and didn't steal anything," Maggie shoots back.

"Uh-huh," I say but what I'm really saying is "bullshit" and she knows it.

The door to Daisy's bedroom cracks open and her head pokes out. I lied when I said to Maggie at the police station that I can't tell them apart. I was just trying to annoy her because I remembered when she was little she hated how everyone confused them. It likely didn't help that Daisy skipped second grade and was in the same year as Maggie. But despite the obvious resemblances as soon as I came back from school in Minnesota and saw them at the Biscuit in the Basket I could totally tell them apart. Daisy is pretty but Maggie is stunning. The type of girl I would totally pursue if it wasn't for her personality.

Now Daisy raises an auburn eyebrow and gives me a snarky glare. "You're hot. Big deal. You're ugly on the inside where it counts for girls like us. Now can we get back to the business? Do we release the photo or are we partners at the booth?"

"Eavesdrop much?" I snap at her because that inside remark stings.

"She has ears like a bat," Maggie explains. "She can hear you whisper through a closed door on the other side of the house. It's her super power."

"What's yours? Blackmail?" I scowl but then I relent because I have no other choice. "Fine. But if our grandfathers end up killing each other I'm going to make sure that the police know it was your fault. And if my gramps disowns me, that's on you too."

"Tell your grandfather the police changed their mind and mandated that we share the booth to keep them from being charged," Maggie tells me. "That's what I intend to tell Clyde."

"Wow. You've planned this whole thing out," I remark. I'd be impressed if I wasn't so outraged.

"I had to think of something to take my mind off you being naked in my house." Maggie shivers like she's traumatized and despite the fact that I give less than zero fucks about what she thinks, it still kind of stings.

I'll be damned if I will let her see it though, so I just roll my eyes. "Whatever. Delete the photos. Now."

Maggie holds out the phone and I watch her delete the images. "But they're staying in my email until the farmer's market season is over, and then I will let you delete them yourself. I promise."

"Your promise holds little value to me," I reply because it's the truth. "The Todd family is about as trustworthy as a snake in a tree in the Garden of Eden."

"Yeah because the Adlers are a bunch of saints." Daisy snorts and rolls her big brown eyes.

I pick up my mop and bucket. "I guess I have no choice but to say I'll see you Sunday."

"See you then!" Maggie grins and waves as I step out into the hall outside their apartment.

"Toodles!" Daisy calls out, a smile as equally fake and saccharine as her sister's on her face.

"You two are my own personal version of *The Shining* twins, you know that?" I say. Their response is to slam the front door in my face.

What did I ever do to deserve this? It's going to be the longest and worst semester of my life.

5

MAGGIE

Almost a week later and I'm still feeling great. It helps that the summer weather has wrapped its arms around September and refuses to let go. Midway through the month and we're still in the midseventies with the sun down. I take a slow deep breath, filling my lungs with the smell of pine and grass that swirls in the night air, and smile.

"I didn't think you'd come tonight, to be honest," Jasmyn says as she links her arm with me and we climb the steps of the Alpha Zeta fraternity house. Her boyfriend, Rhys, is a member and they're having a games night, which usually ends up with people dancing on the pool and ping-pong tables rather than playing on them.

"I need to celebrate my first hostile business takeover," I say and wink. Daisy giggles as she and Caroline climb the stairs behind us.

"The first of many," Daisy adds. "Only the next time we take something from the Adlers it won't require half-naked blackmail pictures."

Jasmyn reaches for the door handle. You can already hear the music pumping inside. "What are you going to take next?"

"Hopefully their farm when the bank forecloses," Daisy replies and the door swings open and we step inside.

It's a big, old, brown-brick two story. The rooms off the front hall are large and packed with people and games tables. Two ping-pong tables in the living room, an air hockey table in the dining room as well as beer pong set up on the table in the kitchen just beyond. The whole house smells like beer and sweat. It was midseventies outside but it's mideighties inside thanks to all the bodies.

"I can't believe you two are going to take over another farm," Jasmyn says in awe. "I feel like I'll be lucky to get a job at McDonald's when I graduate."

Daisy reaches over and wraps an arm around Jasmyn's shoulders as we push our way toward the kitchen. There's a loud cheer as a girl beats a guy on the ping-pong table to our left. "You can come and work for us when you graduate. If we can snag their farm, we're turning it into an events venue."

Jasmyn's whole face lights up at the idea, which makes me smile. I love the idea too.

"They've got really beautiful land with a lake and yeah their barn is falling apart, but their farmhouse is huge and in good shape. It's going to be a bed and breakfast and my uncles are going to make tiny container home-style suites and we'll pepper them down by the lake and then add a gazebo for weddings and a barn we can turn into a hall for conferences and wedding receptions."

"We'll need more than one talented chef versed in farm-to-table food for the B and B," I say, smiling, and Jasmyn smiles back.

"Don't get my hopes up, but if you do take it over, I'm your girl," Jasmyn replies as we enter the kitchen.

Caroline sighs and pouts as she leans on my shoulder. "My life is going to be so boring after college. You girls will all be working together and I'll be in dental school staring at molars."

I pat her head. "You can visit anytime."

We're about to turn left as we enter the kitchen but Caroline, who is leading the way, stops dead and we all bump into each other like dominos. She lifts a hand and points, but my eyes already see what she sees, what stopped her in her tracks. The two sets of French doors that lead out to the expansive, covered back porch are wide open and Tate Adler is playing ping-pong on the table out there—shirtless.

"That six pack looks familiar," Jasmyn whispers in my ear. "I hate to say this, but he really is gorgeous."

"He's okay," I mutter and wiggle past Daisy and Caroline to the kegs, which are on the other side of the kitchen island. I grab a red plastic cup off the island and start to pour a beer. A group watching the ping-pong match on the porch erupts in cheers and I can't help but look.

Tate has both arms raised in victory and the biggest, brightest victorious grin on his face. The abundant muscles in his bare chest and abdomen are taut and rippled and gleaming with a slight shimmer of perspiration. His dark hair is ruffled perfectly, and I notice for the first time the matching chestnut hued hair that dwindles its way down from his belly button to the top of his faded jeans.. And those damn V-cut muscles on either side that I was all hot and bothered by—against my will—when he was cleaning our apartment are on display again tonight. Ugh. I look up from his treasure trail, lock eyes with him and immediately look away, which is good because my cup was about to overflow.

Caroline grabs it from my hand and as she raises it to her lips she says, "You look parched. You should do something about that."

She caught me checking him out but I refuse to admit it, so I feign innocence by blinking my eyes rapidly like I'm confused and then grab another cup to pour another beer. It's almost full when another hand takes it from me. This time the hand is wider and bigger than Caroline's and as the fingers brush mine there's a roughness to them. A shiver runs down my spine without my permission. "Thanks, Firecracker."

"That's the second time you've called me that nickname and I like it even less than the first time," I reply more calmly than I feel. Why am I suddenly rattled by him? I level him with an indifferent stare and he just smirks.

"It could be worse," he says and pauses to take a sip of beer while I reach for yet another cup to fill. "I could call you Maggot like I used to in grade school. But that will make the time I'm about to have to spend with you even harder."

"Why are you shirtless?" I ask and wrinkle my nose so I look disgusted.

"All your freckles turn into one big blob when you do that," Tate replies and points to my face. Jerk. "And I've been playing ping-pong for an hour straight. Can't seem to lose a match. Anyway, I got hot."

"Yes you did." Caroline nods and I glare at her.

Rhys, Jasmyn's boyfriend, has walked up and is standing right behind Tate.

"Speaking of ping-pong, champ. I'll take a rematch," Rhys says but Tate just hands him his paddle.

"I don't need to kick your ass twice," he says and Rhys shrugs and takes the racket, leading Jasmyn toward the table with him. Tate is still staring at me and I'm fighting the urge to blush.

"Well, enjoy your night," I say nonchalantly and turn, grab my sister by the hand and walk out of the kitchen, Caroline doesn't follow. She stays with Tate, which annoys me but whatever. It's her life.

For the next half hour, Daisy and I chat with friends in the living room and I almost forget Tate's even here. But then I go to get a second beer and he's still standing by the keg and still shirtless. And now he's holding a bottle of Malibu coconut rum, pouring it into shot glasses lined up on the island. Caroline is still right there beside him. I reluctantly walk over and she laughs like she's drunk, and she probably is. "Tate is pouring shots!"

"I see that," I reply coolly.

Caroline blinks. "Oh...right. We're not supposed to like him."

Tate chuckles smugly at that. I glare at him for a second and turn back to Caroline. "You can like him. There's no accounting for taste. But I'm vetoing him."

"Vetoing me?" Tate says, evidently confused. "What does that mean, exactly?"

"House rules," I explain and lean on the counter waiting for him to stop pouring his shots so I can get to the keg without accidentally brushing up against him. "When we all moved in together we put a veto rule into effect. We can hook up with whoever we want but if the other roommates don't like a guy, then he's not allowed in the apartment. Hookup must happen at their place."

"We're not like that," Caroline tells me, her tipsy expression growing serious. "God, you're dramatic tonight."

"Caroline's right. We're not," Tate agrees. "But if we were, that would be a stupid rule. I've already been in your apartment."

He hands Caroline a shot and then one to a buddy of his, some blond guy from the hockey team, and then he hands me one. I shake my head.

"Can't handle the strong stuff, huh? Clearly you don't have Clyde's genes."

Ouch. Low blow. "I can handle my booze just fine. But unlike you, I have to work tomorrow. People will actually want to buy our products, unlike your subpar apples."

"More drinking. Less bickering," Caroline demands.

"I agree. This is way too much drama for me," the blond guy says.

"Cooper wait!" Tate calls but Cooper keeps walking.

Caroline leans forward to clink her shot glass with Tate before she puts it to her lips and tips it back. He does the same but doesn't do a little shimmy afterward from the harsh taste of it like Caroline does. Tate smiles at her reaction and I grab the remaining shot glass.

"I'm going to need this if you two are going to flirt," I mutter and down the shot in one big swallow. I force myself not to react as it burns its way down to my stomach and slam the shot glass on the counter.

"I'm not flirting," Caroline replies.

"Neither am I," Tate says and turns to me, leaning on his side of the island to bring our faces closer together. "Trust me, you'd know if I was."

"Gross," I reply and grab the bottle of rum, pouring new shots into their now empty glasses and filling a new one for me.

"Guess there is a little Clyde in you after all," he remarks and my hand not holding the bottle balls into a fist.

"The only way I'm like Clyde is that I also think you, like your grandpa, need a punch to the face," I shoot back.

He grabs the first full shot glass. "So you admit Clyde hit George first."

Caroline grabs me by the shoulders and pulls me away. "I'm over this drama. Let's go Maggie. If I don't get you out of here you two are either going to fight or fuck, and I don't want to see either."

My jaw drops. The last thing I see as she hauls me out of the kitchen onto the back porch is Tate looking equally as startled by the comment. Once out of earshot on the porch she lets me go. "How drunk do you have to be to suggest I would have sex with that reprobate?"

She laughs and flips her blonde head back dramatically. "Oh come on. You two are seriously throwing out the strongest hate vibes I've ever witnessed."

"Yeah," I agree as she jumps up to sit on the railing of the porch and reaches for the bottle of rum I'm still holding. "Hate vibes. Not sex vibes."

"There is a fine line between love and hate and an even finer one between hate and lust," Caroline explains. "Trust me on this. Best sex I've ever had was with that jerk Matt this summer."

"Matt? You slept with Matt? The guy from your high school who told your boyfriend to break up with you right before prom your senior year?" I say because I know this sordid story all too well. Caroline will never get over going to prom alone, heartbroken.

"The one and only. I still hate him by the way, but the sex…" She started to fan herself and then takes a swig directly from the bottle of rum. I gently put a hand on it and pull it from her lips.

"Easy there slugger. We've just had the apartment cleaned. I don't want you puking all over it later."

"You two up for some beer pong?" Tate's voice calls out and I turn and see him setting it up on the ping-pong table with cups, his eyes on Caroline and me. "I'm undefeated in this too, so you'll lose but it'll give you something to do other than huddle in the corner talking about me."

"You're an egomaniac," I reply but find myself nodding. "I'll play if for no other reason than to wipe that stupid smirk off your face."

I snatch the bottle from Caroline as she's about to drink from it again and hand it to some random guy standing nearby. "I need you to be able to see the cups, sunshine."

Caroline pouts but lets me drag her to the table. Tate tosses me a ping-pong ball. "Good luck. You're going to need it."

We're about to start our third game when Caroline announces she needs a potty break. I groan and as she disappears into the crowd, Weston, Tate's teammate at beer pong and ice hockey apparently, announces, "Not here for the next game that's a forfeit."

"She'll be back!" I argue but he's already walking away. "She's just peeing! If she gets back and you aren't here we win!"

Weston either doesn't hear me or doesn't care because he disappears out of sight into the living room. Tate is grinning at me from across the table. "Weston is right. Caroline bailed first. That's a forfeit and we win."

We're tied one game each so this is a very serious matter. I shake my head. "No. I refuse to agree to that."

"I refuse to care what you agree to," Tate replies, still grinning.

A girl walks over and rests half a butt cheek on the corner of the table, staring up at Tate like a puppy looking at an owner who has a treat. "I'd love to play you next Tate."

Tate smiles at her. "I'd love to play with you too, but first Firecracker needs to admit defeat."

I roll my eyes and subtly grab the corner of the table because it makes me a little dizzy. I'm well past tipsy. "You're delusional. I didn't lose. We tied and even that is questionable because you cheated a little."

Tate's eyebrows both shoot up. "Excuse me? I never cheat."

"You're an Adler. It's in your DNA," I shoot back, and I realize instantly that drunken quip is actually a much bigger insult than I intended. George is apparently a womanizer after all. Rumor is years ago when Tate and I were kids, George cheated on his wife with a cashier from a hardware store in Montpelier. She showed up in town and caused a big scene or something. The details are sketchy for me, but I know that's why Clyde always says he's a womanizer and he's said it wasn't the first time. Now, even through the beer goggles I'm wearing, I can see the hurt that flickers across Tate's face.

"I'm going to go find Caroline," I announce and march off into the still overly crowded living room. Just like always with these type of nights, the games have stopped and people are dancing instead as music blares out of Bluetooth speakers. I find the downstairs bathroom and there's a line. Caroline isn't in it. I wait, and the girl who comes out of the bathroom isn't her either. It's getting really hot in here and I need some air, so I decide to weave my way to the back porch. Maybe air will help me sober up. Our first farmer's market is tomorrow, and I'll be struggling, I know it.

There's a bunch of people circling the ping-pong table out there where our beer pong set up used to be, but it's already been removed. I can't see exactly what they're doing instead, so I stumble closer. There's an empty wine bottle in the middle of the table and a tall guy leans over and gives it a spin and I watch and fight the urge to roll my eyes. Are they playing spin the bottle? Am I so drunk that I stumbled back into ninth grade?

I watch as the bottle slows and points to a blonde girl who smiles brightly at the guy who spun it as he walks around the table and kisses her. It's a crazy deep, full-on kiss, not the pecks I got in junior high when we played this in Jasmyn's basement at her thirteenth birthday party. Finally the couple break apart and she leans over the table to spin the bottle.

"You get off on watching, Maggie?" Tate's voice is way too close to my ear and I jump and turn around. He's right behind me.

"I've just never seen adults play such a stupid childhood game before," I tell him. "They must be really drunk."

"Or just really smart," Tate replies. "I mean what better time to play the game than after we actually learn how to kiss."

Of course he sees it that way. I ignore him and watch as the blonde girl walks over to a short-haired brunette girl because the bottle landed on her, and the two girls kiss. Again, there's little restraint. I'm about to go back inside to find Caroline when someone calls out. "Hey Tate! You and your girl wanna play?"

My eyes lock with Tate's and he looks as horrified as I feel at the mistake. "I'm not his girl!"

"I'll play," Tate says and pushes past me to join them. "Maggie isn't into anything remotely interesting, so she'll sit this out."

Some people snicker and I feel my blood starting to boil. "Actually, I'll play."

Did I really just say that?

Everyone is staring and smiling except Tate, who is staring with his mouth hanging open, so yeah, I guess I really did say that. So I walk over and wedge myself in between two guys. There's now eleven of us playing which is simply ridiculous to me. Eleven college kids who don't have anything better to do than play a childhood game. Each time the bottle spins I feel a flutter of confusion in my belly because half of me is terrified it will land on me and half of me is terrified it won't. All I need is a smaller bra size and some braces and it really is junior high again.

After the third spin it still hasn't landed on me but it has landed on Tate. It's a short girl with waist-length blonde hair. She's smiling shyly as she walks slowly around the table and puts a hand on Tate's shoulder as she rocks up on the tip toes to plant one on him. He circles her waist and leans down but his eyes are on me—liked locked with mine and it's absolutely awkward and yet…exhilarating. Their lips meet and his green eyes finally break their battle with mine because they slide closed and suddenly, I don't want to play this game anymore. I don't know why because I've watched all the other people kiss, but watching Tate feels wrong. Luckily it's over quick.

Tate smiles at the girl and as she skips back to her place he sips from a beer bottle in his hand and then leans across the table and spins the bottle so hard it blurs. I watch, kind of wishing it would spin right off the table and shatter so we can all stop playing this stupid game. But it doesn't. It stops. On me.

"Shit," I whisper.

Tate doesn't move. He stares at me from his position across the table.

"Are you gonna do this so we can keep going or what?" someone asks.

"Just keep playing," I say and wave my hand like I'm shooing away an annoying mosquito. "We can skip this round."

"So you're forfeiting?" Tate asks and laughs. "That's two forfeits in one night. Forget Firecracker. I'm gonna call you Little Miss Quitter from now on."

"I am not quitting," I say firmly and then shrug. "You landed on me so if you don't follow through, you're the quitter, not me."

Oh shit. He's walking toward me.

He wouldn't. I mean he hates me as much as I hate him. Probably more now that I'm blackmailing him. He's not going to actually kiss me.

He's standing right in front of me now.

He's probably waiting for me to panic. My face starts to flush so badly I think I might break into a sweat. He's gonna lean in and expect me to jump back and then he'll claim he's won again and…

He leans in and I don't move. He will not win. His lips are an inch from mine. I can feel his breath on my cheek as his head slowly tilts to the right. I feel a hand on my hip so I put one on his shoulder, not to be outdone. He hovers there. I try to read his expression but he's too close. He's a blur.

"You're not backing down," Tate murmurs, and I can't tell if he's disappointed or impressed.

"I don't back down," I whisper.

"Neither do I."

And then…Tate Adler's lips are on mine.

They're light and soft and warm and… I refuse to pull away first. He's not going to win. So I press my lips into his and open my mouth just the slightest.

He slides his arm around my lower back so I slide mine around his neck.

Is that…his tongue? Yep, his tongue most definitely just slid against my bottom lip. That rat bastard. If he thinks that's going to make me run, he's got another think coming. I am *not* going to let him win. I slide my tongue out too and then, our tongues touch. It's like I stuck it in a socket. Electricity shoots through me right down to my toes and up again to start a fire in my belly. Well, slightly lower than my belly. Oh shit.

He's going to stop this insanity now, right? But he doesn't break the kiss. He doesn't jump back. He doesn't quit first. He pushes back against my tongue and slides his into my mouth and…I am fully and completely making out with Tate Adler in front of half the damn school and the most horrible thing about it is that I'm liking it. A lot. Tate Adler is making my toes curl and my panties damp.

I jump back at the very same second Tate does. I don't wait to see his reaction or let him see mine I just turn and storm back into the house, ignoring whoever it is who yells out after me. "Hey! It's your turn to spin!"

Back in the kitchen I see Daisy standing by the beer pong. "Hey! Where were you?"

"I was just outside." *Getting completely turned on by my mortal enemy.* "Getting some air."

Daisy's eyes slide over my shoulder and narrow as a frown starts to curve her lips downward. "What are you doing here?"

I don't dare turn around. If I look at Tate I will turn crimson... and maybe kiss him again. No. I will definitely not. I think. I just can't turn around.

"Your sister owes me a tiebreaker game of beer pong," I hear him say.

Daisy shakes her head. "Nope. Not gonna happen. I'm calling it an official tie."

"No! No ties!" Tate barks. "She doesn't play, she forfeits and I win."

Daisy stares at him then me and shakes her head. "You two are going to be a mess tomorrow. Remember tomorrow? First farmer's market of the fall season?"

"Right. Shoot. Okay. Let's go!" I sound overly enthusiastic suddenly and I know it. I take a couple steps too quickly and end up grabbing the wall because it keeps the floor under my feet from tilting too much. I can't help but steal a glance at Tate who just smirks his smirkiest smirk of all smirking time. "If you don't wanna play another game of pong, we can go back out onto the porch and play more of the game out there. If you want to. I think you want to."

"Are you trying to make me puke?" I ask and my voice might be ice-cold but my face is red-hot.

"No more games for this Pong Princess." Daisy sighs heavily and she doesn't even know what game he's talking about, thankfully. She would blow her top if she did. "Let's go. Jasmyn already took Caroline home."

"You're forfeiting, Firecracker," Tate calls out.

"I'm better than you, the end," I call back as Daisy tugs me toward the front door. "If I wasn't you wouldn't be sharing your booth with me."

"Let's see if you can even make it there tomorrow," Tate calls back and somewhere in the back of my brain I wonder if this was his plan all along. To get me drunk so I'm too hungover to show up tomorrow.

"I'll be there with bells on, Tater Tot," I call out and someone we're passing snickers at the nickname I just invented.

Once we make it to the sidewalk out front and start down the street I turn to Daisy. "I don't care if you have to throw a bucket of ice water on me tomorrow morning, you make sure I get my ass up and get to the market. Got it?"

Daisy laughs. "Whatever you say."

The only good thing that might come from this drunken night is maybe I won't remember kissing Tate when I wake up in the morning. And I don't care if it feels like I've been smacked across the forehead with a two-by-four tomorrow, I will be at that farmer's market.

6

MAGGIE

It feels like I have been smacked in the forehead with a two-by-four. Or maybe ten of them. Ugh. I was so jealous when I hauled my hungover butt out of bed at seven this morning and Caroline and Jasmyn were still tucked snug in their beds, sleeping off their hangovers. So jealous.

And now, as if this pounding headache, foggy brain, and dry mouth aren't enough of a problem, I've got Clyde staring at me with his hard, mean, bloodshot eyes and for the millionth time I wonder what it's like to have a grandfather who isn't a bitter, hateful little man. The kind you see on TV shows and movies that wraps you in gentle hugs and pinches your cheek and has cute nicknames for you. I'll never know. My mom's dad died when I was one and all we've got is Clyde.

"I flat out refuse to work with that asshole," Clyde announces. He's standing there in his battered old overalls and green plaid shirt, which hangs off his emaciated frame. All he needs is a straw hat and it would look like we have a scarecrow on our porch to anyone driving by on the street. Clyde needs to consume something other than alcohol. I've never known him to be anything other than painfully skinny, but there is one picture on the mantle of him sitting in a camping chair down by the lake, a fishing pole in one hand and a smile on his face, and he's heavier. His body more like my dad's with a thicker waist and broad beefy shoulders. My dad is in the grass at his feet with his own tiny, plastic toy fishing rod and he's about two or three, which means the picture is from the year my grandmother ran out on them.

"That's okay, Clyde," Daisy responds for me. "We can do this without you, like we do everything else."

"I work hard young lady. You don't think I work hard? You two are off galivanting around your fancy campus so you don't know nothing," Clyde barks and our dad pats him on the shoulder as he emerges on the porch, the screen door to the house banging shut behind him. I wince at the noise which feels like a firework going off too close to my ears.

"Dad, they aren't galivanting. They're learning," our father clarifies, leaning heavily on the cane he now uses every day. "And we all know you work. Daisy, apologize."

Daisy sighs and rolls her eyes dramatically which makes Clyde turn a new shade of red. "Sorry, Grandpa. But with all due respect, it's better if you're not at the farmer's market. You *are* the reason we don't have our own booth anyway."

"It's that George Adler's fault. He butted in line. I was last, sure, but if he hadn't gotten all flirty with that Oleson woman in front of me then he'd have been standing behind me. That dirty, slimy, womanizing—"

"Relax!" Dad repeats, cutting Clyde off before the expletives start again. The man swears like a drunken sailor, especially about all things Adler. Uncle Bobby rounds the corner of the barn. He's got two of our Cashmere goats with him, Blair and Jo.

Clyde huffs. "I'm not going to the damn market. Not ever. And you know what I'm going to do with my free time?"

"Clean the goat pens? Milk the goats? Check on the beehives? Make the cheeses?" Bobby asks lightly, but it's a dig. Clyde won't officially give the farm over to any of us but he's stopped doing much of anything here, except drinking and bitching. Clyde gave the reins over to my dad a couple years ago but now that my dad is unable to handle full-time farm work, Clyde thinks selling it is a better option than holding onto it until Daisy and I graduate and can take over.

"I'm gonna go to that realtor in town to see if that client she had is still interested in buying," Clyde announces and storms back in the house.

He stomps off around the porch to the back of the house where the extension with his self-contained apartment is located. This summer a real estate agent came by and told Clyde she had a buyer looking for farmland in the area and was willing to pay a decent price. Clyde didn't say yes, but told her he would keep it in mind, and he's been threatening us with it ever since. Now, I turn to my dad with worried eyes. He shakes his head. "Ignore him Mags. He's just mad you're working with Georgie Boy."

"Yeah," Uncle Bobby agrees with an easy smile. "Besides, the realtor works at the same agency as Tanya Adler, so Clyde won't step foot in there and likely won't sell through them either. Especially since I told him Tanya would make money off the sale."

"He believed that? It's not Mrs. Adler's client or her agency, so she won't," I say, and Bobby's grin deepens.

"Let's not explain that to your grandpa, okay?"

Daisy laughs. I want to laugh too, but I'm scared it will make my head pound harder. Ugh. I am never drinking again. Despite their reassurances, I let my eyes sweep wistfully over the property.

I grew up in the large, white, clapboard farmhouse. My chubby toddler hand prints are pressed into the concrete steps that lead up to the porch on Clyde's side. Daisy got her first set of stitches after wiping out on her bike in the driveway when she was eight. I helped build the cheese barn that sits across the drive on the only hill on our land when we shifted to goats. I spent hours as a pre-teen in the towering sugar maple down by the road when I wanted to escape my family, reading or daydreaming. I may not own this land, but I *am* this land. I do not want to lose it.

"I keep forgetting how this feud works," Bobby jokes with his standard, lazy lopsided smirk on his face. "Are we the Capulets or the Monahans?"

"It's Montagues," I correct with a smile. "And who knows?"

"I was never the scholarly one in school, that was your uncle Ben," Bobby replies about his twin brother. "Anyway, I for one am proud of you two putting aside the differences for the benefit of the business."

"Thank you," I say and he winks at me. As much as my grandfather is a disappointment, my uncles are quintessentially perfect. They're twins, a year younger than my dad, and are disarmingly charming, hardworking, fun-loving guys. They've been nothing but supportive of Daisy and me since birth. Even though they don't want to continue farming and have a successful construction business, they fully supported our idea two years ago to shift the farm's main income from dairy to goats and bees. We had to present it to Clyde like it was their idea, and my dad's since everyone knew he wouldn't take the idea of two high school girls seriously.

"But I have to say, I'm shocked the Adlers agreed to this," Dad says as Bobby disappears around to the other side of the house. He's taking Blair and Jo to the pasture where the other cashmere goats are, like Tutti and Natalie. We name all our goats after old TV and movie characters. Everyone gets to name some, and those were named by my mom. "Old George hates Clyde with the same amount of venom."

"Like I said, the police said either we shared or they took the booth away from both of us," I lie easily.

The screen door on the porch swings open again and Mom comes out with a picnic basket in her hand. Her dark hair is swept up in a messy top knot. she's wearing zero makeup, as usual, and just like always my dad's face lights up when he sees her. I will never grow tired of seeing how Billy Todd looks at Violet Hill Todd.

"Packed you all a lunch," she says with a smile as she hands

Daisy the basket. "I'm hoping you'll be so busy selling you won't have time to find your own."

"Thanks Mom. Let's hope you're right," I say and she smiles and then the smile grows softer as her eyes shift to my dad. "Put a thermos of coffee in there too. I saw you yawning earlier."

"You're a dream, Vi. Thanks!" Dad kisses her cheek before walking off toward the cheese barn. I try not to stare as he goes. It hurts my heart to see him move so slowly and so uneasily.

Mom pauses in front of me and tucks a lock of my hair behind my ear and gently cups my face. "Have a good day, lovebug. Don't let your dad over do it. And don't let the Adlers annoy you, or him. I know they'll try."

"I won't Mom," I say.

"I think we're ready to fly!" My uncle Ben calls out coming out of our regular barn tugging a squeaky dolly which has two tabletop cooler display cases on it.

"Shh! No yelling today. Please," I beg and press my fingertips to my temples.

"Are you…hungover?" Mom asks, and I know the answer will make her upset. She's always been worried we'll turn into drunks like Clyde. We've been getting speeches about how alcoholism is hereditary since we were ten.

"Yeah, she already let an Adler get to her," Daisy adds, unhelpfully. She means the beer pong but I think of the kiss. "Tate challenged her to beer pong last night."

"Beer what?" Mom is horrified. Great.

"It's fine. I'm fine," I promise. "And I won't be doing that again."

"I hope not because you're underage young lady and the police may look the other way on a tussle between two old grumpy men, but they'll have no problem charging you with underage drinking," Ben reminds me.

"He's right Maggie. And I don't want you two drinking at all, whether you're legal or not," Mom says. "I know that's not a real-istic dream but I have it anyway."

I hug her. "I'm sorry."

"I nursed one tiny beer the entire night," Daisy says proudly. "And like I said, if it wasn't for Tate, Maggie would have done the same."

"If he offers you booze at the market…" Mom starts but I raise a hand and stop her.

"He won't. He's not a complete idiot," I reply. "See you tonight."

I bounce with as much energy as I can muster to the truck Ben just finished loading. "Daisy will go with you and I'll take Dad."

Ben nods and he and Daisy get into his truck. Dad shoves his cane into the back seat and pulls himself up into the passenger seat of the beat up Kia Soul I share with Daisy. I start down the drive and turn onto Route 2A toward town. The Adler Farm whizzes by, and Dad cranes his neck to look up their drive. "Wonder if they've already left."

"Who cares?" I reply. "Maybe if we're lucky Tate is more hungover than me and he slept in."

"You're partying with the Adler boy?" Dad raises one bushy blond eyebrow.

"Not *with* him. I went to a party and he happened to also be there. And he insisted on annoying me the entire time and…" *Kissing me like his life depended on it*, my brain reminds me but of course I don't say that out loud. I suddenly feel hot and put down the window. "Let's just say I understand Clyde's impulse to punch Adlers now."

Dad chuckles. "So you hate the Adlers now too?"

"Don't we all hate the Adlers, always?" I ask as the truck hums along. Dad lowers his window too. It's a cool fall morning but the sun is already warming it up.

"Yeah. I guess we do," Dad replies.

"Why is that?" I ask as the sun starts to gleam off the road and I pull my sunglasses off my head to shield my eyes.

"It's a long and sordid history, Maggie. I don't even know where to begin," Dad says.

"Okay. I'll begin," I say. "One of my first memories was Clyde screaming obscenities at George because he thought that George had built the fence between our properties too far onto our side. George responded by throwing rotting apples at him and Mom had to call the police."

Dad huffs out a breath and I don't dare take my eyes off the road to see if it's out of frustration or amusement. "Before that we didn't have an official fence. Just some rope tied to posts in the ground only about hip high. George put in that six foot chain link monstrosity two feet past where the original one had been so he did steal some of our land. We have always wanted to take it to court but don't have the money for that. We did get the police to make him take down the barbed wire he had originally placed on top of it."

"So all this is over two feet of land?"

"Nope. Honestly Mags, I don't know exactly when it started. George and Clyde have been fighting my entire life," Dad explains and puts sunglasses on over his blue eyes. "Tate's dad Vince and I used to go at it too. We got into at least four fistfights in high school. Both of us got suspended for it the fourth time, which is the only reason I think we stopped. And one time I made Vince and Tanya storm out of the grocery store. Left a cart full of stuff in the middle of the aisle, because when I saw them there, I stood in the produce aisle and started to loudly talk about how bad the quality of their apples was."

I smile. "Tate's mom, Tanya, threatened to shove a cupcake up Mom's ass at the fourth-grade school bake sale."

Dad laughs deeply. "I remember that. First time I think a parent has ever been hauled into the principal's office."

"Did Grandma used to fight with George Adler's wife, Faith, too? The way Clyde and George go at it and Mom and Tanya did?"

I steal a glance at his face this time because this topic can be touchy depending on his mood. No one in the family likes to talk about his mother, Elizabeth Todd. Dad is in a Zen mood today though because he doesn't tense or frown he just shrugs. "Don't remember. I was only three when she left, remember?"

No, I don't remember because I wasn't alive. As usual I only have Todd family folklore to go off of. "And Ben and Bobby were barely two."

"Yup."

"And...we don't know where she went?"

"Maggie not this again, please," Dad says, and by the hard edge to his tone I know I've finally annoyed him. "We don't know where she went and we don't care either. Now can we stop talking about my deadbeat mother?"

"Fine. Fine." I sigh and bite my tongue. The fact is I don't actually ask about my grandmother all that much. I learned at a young age, when I was doing a family tree project in sixth grade and Clyde saw the poster board and tore it up when he saw her name next to his, that Elizabeth Todd was a taboo subject. But the older I get, the more interested I am in our family history. And lately Daisy is positively obsessed with finding out more about her, and our roots in general, so I hear it a lot since we live together. We've never even seen one picture of her.

"My mother decided she didn't want Clyde and I don't blame her. But she also decided she didn't want her children, which is the unforgivable part," Dad says as I slow the car and turn onto Pine Place that will take us to Pine Street, where the farmer's market is held. "I mean hell, Vince and Tanya Adler divorced what, like ten years ago, but she still sees her kids. She is still a parent. My mother never reached out. Not a Christmas present or birthday card or even a letter. She didn't care what happened to us, so we aren't going to care what happened to her."

I carefully tuck into a spot in the grass lot where all the vendors park and Dad opens the door and gets out before I turn off the engine. I try to ignore how he struggles to find his balance for a second. He doesn't like when we fuss over him.

I hop out after him and give him a smile, walking around to

the back of the car and popping the trunk. "I'm sorry. I shouldn't have brought it up."

He grabs his cane and joins me, pulling me into a hug. "Clyde is a jerk a lot of the time but he didn't abandon us. He raised three little boys on his own. He always found the money to give us school trips and hockey equipment and whatever reasonable request we had."

I hug him back, pressing my cheek to his chest. My dad gives the best hugs. He almost makes me forget I'm hungover. "Now we just have to convince him to not sell the farm."

"He's bluffing on that, I think," Dad assures me as he lets me go and grins down at me. "Just don't tell him you're partying with an Adler."

I laugh but it quickly catches in my throat and disappears when I glance across the parking area and see Tate. He and his little brother are hauling bushels of apples out of his truck. It looks like it's their last load, not their first, which means he got here extra early. And he looks well-rested and perky and I hate him even more.

Seven minutes later we find the booth in the long row of booths and I frown. "Are you kidding me, Adler?"

From the other side of the booth Tate looks at me innocently. "What?"

I point up at the tent awning above the booth. "Adler's Apple Farm?"

He rolls his eyes like I'm some overdramatic girlfriend and that starts to make my blood boil. "What? You want a coverless booth? So we can get rained on or sunburned? Your smelly cheese will melt if it isn't in the shade."

"Our cheese is not smelly. Except the garlic one but it's supposed to be. Well, and the blue goat cheese but…" I huff and now I'm equally as frustrated that my cheeks are starting to pink. "Listen, the booth can't just say Adler's Apples because it's not just Adler's Apples."

He shrugs and his little brother Jace, who is arranging apples in baskets on one side of the table is smirking like a little shit. Because he's a little shit. "Maggie, we don't have a co-branded tent. Too bad."

"You could just take your stinky hippie cheese crap and go home." The voice comes from behind me and I turn and see George Adler walking up with a heaping basket of baked goods I assume all have apples in them.

"Hi, Mr. Adler. You gonna hit one of us like you did Clyde?" Daisy asks, smiling sweetly as she walks past him to the empty side of the booth and drops a cooler of cheese down with a thud. She spins and faces Tate and his brother, copper hair whipping around from her ponytail and almost slashing George across his throat. I smile. "So here's what's gonna happen boys. My uncle is going to throw our tent topper over your tent topper on the one side. Okay? Great."

"Good idea, Daisy," Dad says and Daisy puts a stool down behind him as Uncle Ben is wheeling over the display coolers on a dolly, the wheels squeaking angrily. The sound makes it feel like a cat is actually sharpening its nails on my brain. Ugh. I can't help but wince and Tate notices and grins. I hope he gets incurable jock itch.

We set up our side of the booth, Dad sitting on his stool arranging stuff as we haul it over from the parking lot. We ignore the Adler clan but talk amongst ourselves about what cheese to display where, how to stack the honey jars, whether the goat's milk soap will melt in this heat. "Why are you all so chatty? So much noise," George grumbles.

"Gramps..." Tate mutters in a warning, which surprises me a little.

"Those girls are so chatty. Yak, yak, yak," George growls. He turns to my dad, who is standing at the back of our side of the booth. "You should teach your girls to be seen and not heard."

"Sorry, we don't live in the Stone Age old man," my dad says calmly. "I'm pretty sure my girls have more intelligent things to say than you do."

"Are you gonna stand in my booth and insult my intelligence?" George growls and takes a step toward our side but Tate and Jace both jump in front of him.

"If you're going to stand in *my* booth and insult my daughters then you bet your ignorant ass I am," Dad declares in a calm, firm voice.

"You piece of—"

"Walk it off Gramps." Tate's loud voice overtakes anything George was going to say.

"Did you hear what that punk said?"

"Yeah and I heard you tell him his daughters shouldn't speak," Tate replies coolly. "I'm not taking sides here but you never say that to Raquel. Or Louise. They both talk more than I'd like."

Louise is his aunt and Raquel is her daughter, Tate's cousin. I went to school with Raquel and I was not a fan to say the least. Louise isn't my cup of tea either, but for Tate to challenge his grandfather like that in front of us, and more importantly because of us, shocks me. George mutters something under his breath that I can't hear, rips an apple fritter off the stack Jace was making on the table and storms off.

"Great. Now I have even more work to do since Gramps won't be helping," Jace complains and turns and glares at Daisy and me. "Thanks a lot."

"Yes because your grandfather's anger management issues are my fault," Daisy mutters.

"Let's all just stop talking and keep working," I say and wish I could have found the Advil this morning, but I couldn't and my head is still pounding.

An hour later, we're fifteen minutes from opening and everything is perfect. Dad got our topper folded and clipped on top of one side of the booth. Now you can see the Adler logo and ours. The table looks really good, on both sides if I'm honest. The Adlers have their apple products displayed nicely, Tate even polished each apple before he wandered off somewhere while Jace artistically stacked the jars of apple jelly and caramel apples. Our side has all the different goat cheeses on display in the cooler, the soaps stacked nicely on one side and the jars of honey from our beehives on the other. On top of the mini cooler is what always sells out the quickest, our goat's milk caramels. And now, instead of taking a moment to snack on the food Mom gave us or drink the coffee she sent, like Daisy, Ben and Dad are doing, I decide I need to hunt down some headache medicine and a Gatorade or this hangover will most definitely kill me before the end of the day.

I tell my family I'll be right back and head out of the market down the road toward the gas station because they usually carry those travel-size packets of Advil. Of course they're out—just sold the last pack to someone not ten minutes ago, the attendant told me. I buy a bottle of Gatorade and am on the sidewalk debating whether it's worth walking another block to the drugstore when I notice Tate coming out of the bagel shop across the street. He doesn't look as perky and fresh as he did earlier. In fact, his shoulders are slumped and he's wiping his brow with the hem of his shirt like he's sweaty. Alcohol sweats? He's got his own Gatorade tucked under his arm and a big paper bag in his other hand. I watch as he takes something out of his pocket and tosses it into his mouth. He looks up and I notice his skin is paler than normal. I start walking crossing the street but he tries to pretend he doesn't see me and starts marching off, back toward the market.

"Not so fast!" I call and lunge forward, grabbing his forearm. He's way too easy to restrain for a big burly hockey player. "You *are* hungover!"

"Whatever." He yanks his arm free and the effort makes him look like he might barf and that brings me such joy.

"Ha! I'm not the only one!"

"Quiet already. God you're so damn loud!" Tate groans, his eyes snapping shut.

"Do you have headache medication?" I ask. "Did you buy the last pack from the gas station? I saw you take something."

"See you back at the booth," he says, ignoring my question completely as he starts walking again.

"Oh no. You're not getting away," I say and grab his arm again.

"I've got bagels for my family," he says angrily and shakes the bag in my face as he breaks free of my grip again. "Some of us don't have a mommy to make us lunch, okay?"

"You have a mom," I argue back. "She lives a couple blocks from here. Stop being dramatic and give me an Advil already."

He sighs and then, when I think he's going to tell me off again, he starts to grin and I get a sinking feeling in my belly. "Okay. You want it? Admit I kicked your freckled butt at beer pong last night."

"You didn't kick my butt. We didn't get to break the tie," I reply calmly. "That is not my fault."

"Caroline disappeared and didn't come back. That's a forfeit."

"You threw like three shots with your elbow over the table," I reply. "I called you on it and you ignored me. Those shots should have been forfeited."

"Enjoy your headache." Tate turns and starts to walk away.

"Argh!" I let out a disgruntled cry of pure annoyance. "Fine. Okay. You won the beer pong. Aren't you a big hero. Such an important skill to have in life. Congrats!"

He turns back to me grinning that annoyingly adorable smirk he has. "I beat you. Say it. Say Tate Adler kicked Maggie Todd's freckled ass at beer pong last night."

My only response is a snort.

"It's either that or admit you enjoyed the hell out of that kiss," Tate says. My jaw drops. He grins. "Say I kissed Tate Adler and it was the best kiss I've ever had."

"I didn't kiss you. You kissed me," I reply. My face feels like it's on fire. "I would have walked out if I'd spun that bottle and it landed on you but you seemed damn eager to get your lips on me."

"I'm about to become a professional athlete. I have a competitive streak that doesn't stop because the challenge is...undesirable," Tate replies and shrugs.

Well, that's such a good burn I almost want to congratulate him.

He holds up the small travel pack of headache meds and gives it a shake. "So which is it, Firecracker? Are you going to say I kicked your freckled ass or I gave you the hots? Or are you going to suffer through the rest of the day unmedicated?"

I sigh irritably. We stare at each other and I swear his smile keeps getting more smug. I ball my fists. "Tater Tot Adler kicked Magnolia Todd's ass—which is not at all freckled but you'll have to take my word for it because you will never ever get anywhere near it—at beer pong. Good?"

Tate stares at me wordlessly and I feel that stupid flush happening. Then he bursts out laughing. "It'll do, I guess."

He pulls out the small packet from his pocket and hands it to me. He was the one who bought the last pack from the gas station. I shake two pills out of the packet and pop them in my mouth, swallowing them down with a swig of Gatorade. "Thanks. Bye."

I start off back toward the market. He's walking behind me the whole way, but I refuse to walk with him and he clearly doesn't mind. Good. We are not friends. But I decide I need to stop him and say something before we get to the booth so I grab him again just before we turn into the market.

"You really just can't keep your hands off me, can you?"

I roll my eyes. "Reality check time. That kiss was part of a stupid game and no one ever needs to know about it."

"You think I'm going to brag about it or something?" Tate questions and laughs. "In case you haven't noticed, my family hates you and if they ever found out I even played beer pong let alone touched you in any way they'd probably disown me."

"Good," I say flatly. "Because you mention that gross kiss again and I will plaster that picture of you in your undies holding a feather duster on a billboard in town."

"We don't have billboards in this town," Tate replies.

"I'll build one," I call back as I walk away.

The market is officially opened now, so I pick up the pace and scurry behind the booth. Tate comes up behind me a second later pushing his way past us to get to his side. My dad, Uncle Ben and George Adler have all disappeared so it's just Jace, Tate, Daisy and me.

"Where did you disappear to with *him*?" Daisy demands, her hands on her hips and her eyes narrowed like she's Mom catching me out after curfew.

"I went to seek out headache meds and he was doing the same," I explain. "Trust me we are not friends."

"You better not be," Daisy replies.

"We are in a hostile alliance. Nothing more. Now go chop up some of our caramels and offer them as samples," I say shooing her. "We need to get people to buy those over the stupid caramel apples the Adlers are peddling."

The day passes much faster that I thought it would given my physical condition. But we're busy and every customer is in a great mood. A lot of people are thrilled to see us back after missing the summer season. Jace and Tate try to lure our customers away as we're talking to them by interrupting and suggesting apple products and it even works a couple of times. Two customers put down our honey and our goat's milk caramels to buy some apple butter and caramel apples. Daisy gets even by telling me loudly, when there's a group of about six people crowded around the Adler side of the booth, that she thought she read that there was an *E. coli* outbreak linked to apples.

By the time the market closes at two we are almost sold out of everything. The Adlers did well too, but I think we did better judging by the scowl on their faces as we pack up. "See you boys next Sunday!" I call merrily as we leave, which only deepens the sour looks on their faces.

"It's going to be a long fall," I hear Tate grumble as I climb in my car and I smile.

7

MAGGIE

"Umm...hello? Did you even hear what I said?"

I blink and tear my eyes away from the ice and shift on the hard cement bleacher to look at my sister. "You dragged me to this game against my will and now you're complaining because I'm paying attention?"

"Who, exactly, has your undivided attention, Magnolia Todd?" Caroline asks in a sing-song voice that annoys me to no end because she's caught me. Only I won't admit it. Ever.

"The team I'm rooting for, the girls' team," I reply coolly and shoot laser beams out of my eyes at her before turning back to Daisy. "Now, what did I miss?"

Our women's hockey team is playing our men's hockey team in an exhibition game. I had no intention of going but everyone else was, and Daisy insisted I join. So now I'm sitting here on the cold concrete bleachers, breathing the cold, dry arena air, getting all warm inside when I look at number seventy-six.

Daisy huffs her annoyance at me. "I was telling Jasmyn and Caroline how much it bugs me that we don't know anything about our grandmother."

"Our grandmother was born and bred in New Hampshire. She still lives there today in the house our mother grew up in, on a lake just outside of Concord New Hampshire," I say and can't seem to stop my eyes from darting down to the action on the ice. It's only an exhibition game but it's really good. Currently the women are winning by one goal and there're only six minutes left in the game.

"Not Mom's mom. I was talking about Dad's mom," Daisy says, exasperated.

"Dad didn't have a mom," I reply. "That's what he keeps telling us, and I think we should finally respect that."

"I don't know," Caroline says as I watch Tate steal the puck from one of the forwards on the women's team and make a break for it down the ice. People cheer and I have to sit on my hands to keep from joining them. "Maybe there were circumstances involved no one knows about. Don't you two have a right to find out for yourselves?"

"One day. Maybe. But if we keep bringing it up right now it will only get everyone mad. And we don't need Clyde angrier than he already is," I reply but I don't know if anyone hears it because Tate Adler just took a hard slap shot on goal and it sailed over the female goalie's shoulder and into the net. The stadium erupts and gets on their feet. I do too. I can't help it. It was a really sweet goal.

Daisy reaches up and yanks me back down. She aggressively waves her pink foam finger with the words Moo U and the female symbol on it in my face.

"Oops. Right," I say sheepishly. Caroline smiles knowingly over Daisy's shoulder but I pretend she doesn't exist. "So about Dad's mom… Why are you so obsessed with this suddenly?"

"It isn't sudden. It's been bugging me since ninth grade biology when we learned about hereditary diseases. Dad's stroke just made it all too real. The doctor said there could have been hereditary factors," Daisy says. "We know nothing about this woman's side of the family. What if there's something else we need to know? What if there's breast cancer? Or ovarian? I'm finally old enough to investigate this without permission and I'm going to and I want your support."

I don't think Daisy is wrong. I've always been curious about where Elizabeth Todd disappeared to and why, but I don't want to go behind my family's back. "How are you going to do that without Dad or one of our uncles or, God forbid, Clyde finding out?"

I turn back to the game. Tate is on the bench now. He is squirting water into his mouth from a water bottle and he's talking with a teammate and smiling. His skin is rosy from exercise and his eyes are sparkling with a fire of competition. He's actually *really* hot right now…like he was when he was just about to kiss me. I tell myself it's not a crush. It's just an indisputable fact of life. Tate is hot. His bone structure is pronounced without being angular. And even with the war wounds from sticks and pucks —the faded nicks and stitch scars that are visible up close, when he's about to make out with you—somehow make him more attractive, not less. But his personality ruins it, I remind myself, and that's something I can never ever let myself forget. Because I need a crush on Tate Adler like I need a bee in my bathing suit.

"I told Daisy about all the DNA, genealogy and ancestry websites out there," Jasmyn says sucking my focus off Tate and back to our current conversation. "You can go on one and fill out all the info and send in a swab from your cheek, and if others who match your profile and fit in your family tree are also open to find potential relatives, they'll alert you."

Daisy perks up beside me. "I knew about the sites but I didn't know they matched you with other people from your family. So I'm going to join a couple and see what happens."

"It's a way to possibly find out more without pissing Dad off," I agree. "But I doubt she'd register for something like that. If she wanted to be found by us, all she would have to do is come back. Our family has been on that land, in that exact farmhouse, since Clyde's grandfather."

"True," Daisy says and bites her bottom lip for a second. "But screw it. I'm going to try anyway. If nothing else, maybe I'll find some other cool relatives too. Like maybe we're related to a celebrity or historical figure or something."

"My great, great, great grandfather wrote the music for 'O Canada' and then moved to Boston," Caroline says.

"Very cool," Daisy says but as they continue to talk about Caroline's relatives, I refocus on the game...otherwise known as secretly admiring Tate Adler. He is really good at hockey. I knew that because he got into that fancy boarding school and everything, but I never really paid much attention to him when he actually played. By the time the game is over, I'm convinced that Tate Adler will actually be drafted into the NHL. That's awesome for him but potentially awful for us. If Tate is drafted and signs a big contract, he'll have the money to save his family's farm, which means my family won't be able to buy it and grow our business the way Daisy and I had hoped and planned.

I voice this concern to her, while we wait for Jasmyn and Caroline to use the restroom so we can head over to the Biscuit in the Basket for some food. Daisy looks as concerned as I feel. "Maybe he won't want to save the farm. I mean, maybe he'll get drafted somewhere far away, settle down with a local puck bunny and use his millions to move his whole family to wherever he is."

That little fantasy Daisy just invented makes me feel queasy instead of hopeful. I don't know why. Maybe my blood sugar is low. I barely ate lunch after all. I shrug. "I don't know. If he's playing like this all season and enters the draft this summer, he'll make it for sure and then he'll have enough money to not only save the farm but hire a ton of people to run it for him."

"According to Clyde, George Adler moved here from New Hampshire with his wife when she was pregnant with Vince because he cheated on her in New Hampshire and they were looking for a new start together. He had been in construction before that, so farming isn't a family tradition or anything for them."

"Yeah and then George set about ruining the town with his seedy-ass existence, not to mention ruining perfectly good farmland Clyde had wanted to buy and add to our land mass," I say because Clyde has told the story many times through the years.

"Yeah, so maybe they'll just give it up anyway," Daisy says and crosses her fingers.

"I'm worried," I mutter and stuff my hands into my jacket pockets. "I wish he wasn't so damn good."

"I could go all Tonya Harding on him and take a pipe to his knee caps next Sunday," Daisy offers and grins like a psychopath. I laugh and she laughs too.

"What's so hysterical?" Jasmyn wants to know as she and Caroline exit the ladies' room.

"Long story but you know what's not funny? How hungry I am. Let's get to the Biscuit. There's a burger with my name on it," I say, and we start out of the arena.

The Biscuit is packed, as is always the case after a home game, even an exhibition one. The hockey players and fans love this place. We get a high top table directly next to the long high top with a placard on it marked 'Reserved'. I know instantly who it's reserved for. The hockey players always congregate at the same table at the Biscuit.

"Maybe we can find a table on the other side of the place," I say hopefully, but looking around, I know it's impossible. "Or we could go to Tito's instead."

"I don't want to hang out at my work on my one day off this week, Maggie," Jasmyn says with a sad look on her face, so I give in and sit.

A smiling server with the name tag Gail walks over and hands us our menus. "Can I grab you all some drinks while you look that over?"

We all order drinks and she smiles and nods as she walks off.

Gail hands us our drinks, but Jasmyn can't decide on food, so she gives us a few more minutes. Ugh. I want to order, eat as fast as possible, and get out of here before the team shows up. Maybe

Tate won't join them tonight, I think hopefully. But then, suddenly, they wander in—a line of well-built, happy-go-lucky hockey jocks in Moo U T-shirts, hats and sweatshirts. And Tate Adler *is* with them because the universe loves torturing me.

Gail walks back over, smiling. I hand her the menu back immediately because I never needed it. "Veggie burger with goat cheese and bacon."

"We don't have veggie bacon," Gail warns and I nod.

"The real stuff is what I'm going for," I explain. "I'm not a vegetarian, just like the burger."

Gail nods and jots down the order. "Cool, just double-checking."

Daisy orders her usual inferno hot wings, Jasmyn gets a cheeseburger, and Caroline gets a barbecue chicken burger. We also order nachos for the table.

"Veggie burger with real bacon makes no sense," I hear as soon as Gail walks away.

I look up and see Tate staring at me from his seat as he lifts a pint of beer to his mouth. A Moo U T-shirt is painted over his muscular chest and a backward baseball cap, probably with the hockey logo on it, covers his thick dark hair. The table is over-flowing with his teammates, all dressed about the same, and girls are peppered around them, some even sit on their laps. Tate's lap is empty though.

"I like the taste of the veggie burger and the taste of bacon," I reply coolly. "Why do you care?"

"I don't care but I find it amusing that you can't even order food that isn't irritating," he quips and his buddy beside him—that hot blond guy Cooper—snorts.

"You know what's even more annoying?" I reply. "The fact that you can't seem to mind your own damn business."

Caroline leans over to look at the hockey table. "Great game tonight guys. Sorry about the loss."

"We weren't giving it our all," Cooper says with a shrug. "Exhibition and all."

"Oh right. Sure," Daisy rolls her eyes. "Because a bunch of women couldn't have beaten you if you were really trying, right?"

Cooper is about to nod but Tate cuts him off. "Actually this group of women could. They won the championship last year in case you weren't paying attention. Honestly, I'm just pleased they didn't smoke us in a shutout."

Daisy doesn't know what to do with that honest, non-misogynistic response and quite frankly neither do I. Tate notices he's stunned us into silence and winks at me, turning back to his teammates.

I pretend to ignore him for about an hour after that as we eat but for some dumb reason, I am hyper-aware that he is there. Tate and I have been in the same space lots of times. Last year, we were in this very restaurant at the same time a lot. We were in the school cafeteria together more than once because we both lived in dorms last year. We even lived in the same dorm on different floors. We had two classes together, but he was somehow easier to ignore then than he is now.

I think it's because we broke the seal of silence, thanks to Clyde and George's brawl, and I'm sure the fact that I know what it feels like to have his tongue in my mouth doesn't help. Ugh. Once the Burlington Farmer's Market is over, I can get back to forgetting he exists.

As Gail clears our empty plates, Tate's server brings him something he must have ordered. As he picks up his burger I smile and he catches me. "This is real meat, with real bacon not some giant contradiction on a bun, FYI."

"It's the four cheese bacon burger, right?" I say an he nods. "You know why that tastes so good?"

"The garlicky cream cheese stuff they put on the bun," he replies. "It's magical."

"It's not cream cheese. It's our goat cheese," Daisy interjects and as my grin grows, Tate's wilts.

"What?"

"We sell our garlic and herb goat cheese to the Biscuit and they use it on that burger," I explain. "It was actually Daisy's idea and she made a version of it and had the chef try it, which is probably what sold him on it."

"Huh," Tate says and looks at the burger and back at me. He's impressed and he's fighting with his face inwardly because he doesn't want to show it. "We sold our apple cider to Whole Foods across the tri-state area."

"Past tense," I remark. "Because your cider machine imploded and took half your barn with it. So what have you done to mitigate *that* loss?"

He scowls at me. "I go to school for business lectures, I don't need them here."

"Touchy, touchy," I mutter and bite back my condescending smile because I actually want him to open up to me, not shut down. I tuck a piece of hair behind my ear and take a sip of my iced tea while I watch him take his first bite of burger and try not to reveal how much he enjoys it.

I glance at Daisy and she picks up on what I'm trying to do, like a good sister. "Sorry, Tate. Maggie gets overzealous about the business side of the farm. It's been her dream since she was like six, like yours must be playing hockey—professionally."

Tate chews slowly, savoring it and then swallows and before he can answer, one of his teammates—one of the twins on the team, but I don't know which one because I can't tell them apart —does. "Tate's got a real shot at going first round in the draft this summer."

"So you're entering the draft?" I ask casually.

Tate smirks. "Why do you care? Gonna miss me?"

"Not in the slightest," I reply swiftly and the twin laughs. Tate glares at him, so he gets out of his seat and wanders down to the other side of the table.

"What are you going to do with the farm if you're playing across the country or something?" Daisy asks and I glare at her. I don't want to be so blunt with Tate.

"Why do you want to know?" Tate asks.

"Well I know you're having…financial issues," Daisy says and I kick her under the table. "Ouch!"

"She means that we Todds hold out hope every day that you might sell it so we can get some neighbors we actually respect," I say and Jasmyn winces and Caroline stares at me.

"Harsh much, Mags. Geeze," Caroline whispers.

Tate's dark green eyes narrow and his jaw tenses. "Sorry to burst your bubble but we have no intention of selling the farm. And yeah, losing the cider press like you mentioned earlier hurt us a little. We sold out of almost everything we brought to the market yesterday except the caramel apples because you kept poaching our customers with your goat chews."

"Goat's milk caramels," I correct with a hiss. "And they're better than your caramel apples. Sorry not sorry."

"You guys should have a friendly competition," Caroline suggests and I kick her under the table too. "Ouch! God. Why so violent? All I'm saying is whoever makes the most money next farmer's market, the other one has to stop selling their caramel product. It's either that or you two arm wrestle for it and no offense Mags, but you'll lose."

Tate swallows down another bite of his burger and shakes his head. "I'm not going to stop selling anything. It's our booth, technically."

"You know you'll lose. We sold way more than you and we'll do it again next week," I reply smugly. "We're a better farm on every level. Sorry if the truth hurts."

Tate frowns. "Fine. I'll make a bet. But I want bigger stakes. Whoever makes the most money next market has to skip the following Sunday."

"That's a little crazy," Daisy replies.

"Scared, huh?" Tate smirks.

"Hardly," I say as Caroline and Jasmyn stand up and drop money on the bill Gail brought us earlier. I dig out my wallet and add my money to the pile.

"So it's a bet then?" Tate says and wipes his hand on his

napkin before extending it toward Daisy who tosses her money on the table and walks away without taking his hand.

I take it though and give it a short shake before pulling back like touching him was painful. The problem is that it wasn't. At all.

"We'll win and we'll be doing you a favor. Give your family an extra day to fix the side of your barn, which still has a giant hole in it thanks to your cider making skills," I say, making exaggerated air quotes as I say the word skills. Then I turn on my heel and stomp off, shoulders back and head up high.

"The machine malfunctioned! We're just waiting on the insurance money!" he calls out defensively but I ignore him completely.

As we walk home Daisy looks at me, her dark eyes serious. "If he makes the NHL, it sounds like he'll keep the farm."

"Maybe," I say. "I'm not convinced. Yet."

"That land is perfect for our business expansion," Daisy reminds me, like it wasn't my idea in the first place.

"I know. I know," I say and sigh. "We'll just have to spend our Sundays convincing Tate he really doesn't want to keep the farm."

"Or maybe you could actually try to build an actual truce with them," Jasmyn suggests and her wide mouth parts in a smile, which I'd like to think is sarcastic but I think she actually means what she says. "You guys could forge a friendship and then tell him you want to buy it. I bet they'd consider selling it to you if this insane feud was over."

Daisy and I stop walking and stare at her, then each other, then back at Jasmyn. "Yeah, no," Daisy and I say in perfect unison.

"You two are doing this the hard way," Jasmyn warns and Caroline is nodding her blonde head beside her.

"It's not possible to fix it. Trust me this is our only way," I say.

Neither of them say anything as we turn onto our street but Daisy nods in agreement, and that helps quell the doubt that has sprouted in my gut.

8

TATE

The hardest part of this entire plan has been keeping a straight face all week when I saw Maggie on campus. And for some reason I've seen her more than normal. Well, I've noticed her more anyway. I blame the damn spin the bottle game. If I had kept my lips off her, maybe I wouldn't be so hyper-aware of her existence. It was dumb. I knew it when I was doing it—and I really didn't want to do it. But I'm competitive to a fault so I couldn't just walk away after that damn bottle landed on her. She'd take that as a win. She can never win. Not against me. So I kissed her, fully expecting it to be as disgusting as if I was kissing my cousin or something but…it really wasn't. It was good. Great. Hot as fuck.

Maybe that's what has given me the inspiration I need. Maybe I should be thanking her, I think with a wry smile as I wait impatiently in the parking lot for Lex, Jonah, Cooper, Patrick and Paxton, who all volunteered to help me. Well, I kind of strong armed a couple of them into it, but hey, it was a perk of not being a rookie anymore. I lift my butt off the tailgate of my truck as I see my teammates making their way across the parking lot to me. "On time and everything. Thanks guys!"

"Wouldn't miss it," Patrick says with a smile. Paxton just nods beside him. He's not as up for trouble like his brother usually is. And this is most definitely trouble.

A truck I recognize as Bobby Todd's and Maggie and Daisy's familiar mini-SUV come down the road and park a few cars up from us. The girls get out first and Maggie makes sure to glare at me as she walks to the back to open the trunk and takes out whatever goat products she's packed in there. Daisy opens the back passenger door and pulls out a long, rolled up thing and kicks the door shut with the heel of her Ugg-covered foot as she struggles with it.

She starts to march toward us as their uncle Bobby and their menace of a grandfather Clyde are fussing with whatever's in the back of their truck, and arguing just loud enough that I can hear the venom in their tone but not make out the words. Maggie stops what she's doing and hisses in their direction. "Clyde, best behavior, you promised."

"You're not the boss of me, Magnolia Todd," Clyde snaps. "You need me today because your dad got too tired last market. Just another reason why I should sell the damn place."

His vile mood makes my grin deepen. "Perfect. They're already ornery, and Clyde is likely to explode when he realizes what I've done. If I'm lucky he'll make a scene and get them all banned from the market forever."

Patrick shakes his head and grins as he says, "I don't get it. She's hot. Make love not war, Adler."

"Hey I didn't start this feud. I'm just going to end it, once and for all," I say with an easy shrug, like I don't have a care in the world. But I do. On top of wanting this to go so well for Adler Apples that Maggie gives up, takes her goat cheese, and goes away, I also need this to make us some good cash for another reason. Jace was frantic when he called me Tuesday about the amount of apples that were damaged in that mini freak storm we had around four in the morning. The winds were insane and a ton of apples dropped and were banged up to the point where selling them at the market would be embarrassing. The solution I came up with was borrowing a dunk tank from Jace's best friend's dad, Otis—who owns an events business—setting it up just across from the booth in the field near the parking lot and having my teammates volunteer to get dunked by customers paying to throw our banged-up apples at us. It had to work because it was all I had to beat her in sales today.

A second later, Maggie is carrying two coolers past as I motion for the guys to each grab a barrel of apples, and I grab one too. We start walking a few steps behind her. She twists her head to glare at me over her shoulder. Her long hair is pulled into a low ponytail and a few pieces have already escaped and are curling around her face. I think of what Patrick said. She is hot, even with that sour look on her face, there's no denying it. If Maggie Todd wasn't Maggie Todd I would probably try to make that spin the bottle kiss a hell of a lot more. But she *is* Maggie Todd—the enemy. The mortal kind, not the kind you...

"What the ever loving sweet baby Jesus is *that*?" she says.

Paxton, Patrick and the rest of the guys stop dead and I slow my gait but continue making my way directly to the dunk tank Jace is filling with water. Lex is on a step ladder hanging the banner across the top that says "Dunk A Hockey Hunk."

It was ridiculous and shameless and not at all what I asked Jace to put on the banner. But he was busy all day yesterday working on rebuilding the wall of the barn and then he apparently got stung by a bee, which he blames the Todds for because they have beehives. So Jace sent Raquel to go see Mikey—our banner guy who Jace goes to school with and who works out of his parents' basement—and Raquel came home with this.

"This is an extension of Adler's Apples booth today," I say casually like it's no big deal. I walk over and drop my barrel of apples beside it.

"You're..." Maggie looks around and realizes she's surrounded by hockey players. "You're...cheating. This is cheating."

"This, Firecracker, is winning," I reply with a grin.

Daisy is now walking up, carrying a bunch of crap in her arms and her steps slow to a halt. Her dark eyes dart around furiously from me, to Maggie, to the dunk tank, to the rookies, to Paxton and Patrick. A roll of tape tumbles from her pile of stuff and Patrick bends and picks it up.

"No," Daisy says in a dark, deep rumble.

Patrick smiles. "No? I haven't even hit on you yet and you're already saying no?"

Daisy glances at him, wrinkles her nose and then walks toward me. "You can't run this stupid thing and the booth. That's...that's che—"

"Cheating. Boy you and your sister share more than just some flaming hair and attitude, you share a brain too, huh?" I joke. "Well I hate to break it to you both, but there was never a word uttered about how we made the money this Sunday. The bet is just whoever makes the most money."

Daisy and Maggie glare at me and then each other. Bobby Todd, their uncle who used to be my hockey coach when I was little and was the last local guy to be drafted into the NHL, surveys the situation and shakes his head begrudgingly. "Shit, Adler, you got more brains than I thought."

He continues on toward the booth. Daisy makes a sound in the back of her throat, like a cat cornered in an alley, and she storms off after her uncle. Maggie keeps glaring at me. "You... I... All of you...argh!"

She flips me her middle finger and stomps off after the rest of her family.

"Umm...what did you get us into?" Jonah asks nervously.

"Relax. She'll only take it out on me." I clap him on the shoulder reassuringly. "Now take off that shirt of yours and climb into the tank. You're up first."

"I am? Why me?" Jonah asks, but when I don't answer he just sighs and tugs his T-shirt over his head.

It takes almost an hour after the market opens before we get our first customer, which almost sends me into a full-blown anxiety meltdown. It was bordering on pitiful watching Jace and Paxton calling out to people from the card table we're using as a ticket stand, trying to lure people over to play. Finally two high school girls drinking kombucha buy three apples each. When neither of them manages to dunk Jonah, I throw them a free apple and the blonde one nails the target. When Jonah drops like a sack of potatoes and bounces up soaking wet, they squeal with delight. Jonah turns red but it draws a couple more customers.

Two hours after that, I am finally able to take a deep breath. We've got a line of people excited to dunk my teammates with our rejected apples. It's working. "When you taking a turn, brother?"

I glance at Jace and shrug. "Eventually. Right now I'm just basking in my success."

"The banner helped. I know marketing," Raquel says with a confident smile as she flips her bleached blonde hair.

"I don't know if it helps but it doesn't seem to be hurting," I say because I still think the banner is a bit much. When Paxton saw the cheesy slogan his face scrunched up like he'd smelled something foul.

"It's a bit…over-the-top," Jace says.

Raquel huffs, hurt. I would feel bad but my cousin has spent her life being hurt by everything. She's always been a drama queen because it works for her. Aunt Louise, and even Grandpa and Grandma have always coddled her. "I need a coffee break," she announces and gets up from the booth, stomping away before I can say anything.

Patrick walks toward us holding a towel as he dries off. "An eighty-one-year-old woman just nailed the target and sent me swimming on the very first try."

I laugh. "The Sox should sign her."

"Seriously." Patrick nods chuckling as he rubs the towel over his wet hair. "Also, I said I would help and I helped. Now I'm going home to dry off. Your turn to get your butt wet, Adler."

"Yeah, yeah." I know I should do it.

"I'll pay double for the apples if I get to dunk you," someone says and I look over and see a girl I vaguely recognize from campus standing two back in the line with a friend. The friend starts nodding profusely. "Me too."

"If you're paying double you get VIP access," Jace says motioning them forward. "Front of the line for you two."

They giggle and walk over to him. I am about to talk them out of it, tell them they don't have to pay more, but a flicker of red in the corner of my eye catches my attention. Maggie is watching— intently—from the corner of the booth. So instead I grin, wink at the girls and walk toward the tank.

"Hold up, Lex!" Lex freezes on the ladder. He was about to go for his second turn. "I'm gonna take this one."

He just shrugs and climbs back down the ladder. I make a big stupid scene about taking off my T-shirt. At least it feels that way because I'm purposely removing it slowly. I know the girls buying the apples are staring, but the show I'm putting on isn't for them. It's for Maggie. And hers are the only eyes I can feel on me. I finally get it over my head and I drop my T-shirt on my shoes, which I've toed-off. I sneak a glimpse in her direction as I tug off my socks and realize that the reason I feel her gaze is because she looks like she's trying to melt me into a puddle of flaming goo with just her eyeballs. There's nothing hot about that, sexually-speaking, and for a second I find myself disappointed.

I stupidly forgot to bring my swim trunks like the other guys did so I walk over with just my faded jeans on and begin climbing the ladder. The sun is warm but the wind that blows softly has a bit of a bite, and I realize I owe my teammates more than ever for helping me with this. As I drop my butt into the center of the wooden platform, I lock eyes with Maggie and give her a small wave to let her know I know she's staring. I can see her cheeks pink from all the way over here and it makes my grin widen.

"Here we go," one of the girls holding one of our bruised

apples says excitedly, and I turn to face her. She lobs one and it hits the ground almost a foot left of the target. "Oops!"

She giggles. Her friend tells her to go harder next time and she does, but she still misses the target. I swing my legs, my toes skimming the water. I'm thinking they may be the only part of me that gets wet today.

"Line up the target with the apple before tossing," I hear Maggie call out. "You can do it!"

The girl tosses her last apple and misses again. "Boo!" she calls out, disappointed.

Maggie is marching toward her and she grabs her hand, pulls her toward the pay table and drops three dollars in front of Jace. "Give her three more."

"Umm…"

"My money not good enough for you?" Maggie challenges, her shoulders back and fists balled. Jace cowers, takes the money and hands the girl three more apples without a word.

"Did you fail Intro to Business last year?" I call out to Maggie as they walk back toward the toss line with the fruit. "Because giving money to me when we're competing to see who earns the most today is not good business."

"Shut up or you'll get water in your mouth," Maggie shoots back and turns to the girl to give her more throwing advice.

The girl listens intently and nods a lot and then tosses it and comes close to the target but not close enough. I smile. "Sorry sweetheart. I think you need a better coach."

Maggie glares at me. The girl just smiles because I called her sweetheart. Maggie takes the remaining two apples from the girl who stops smiling and hands them to her friend. "Maybe your bestie has a better arm."

The friend is up for the challenge and for a second I think she'll hit it as the apple sails with some good force toward the target, but she, too, misses.

"Damn it!" Maggie bellows.

My grin is beyond cocky now. I know it, and I make no effort to control it.

"What are your names, ladies?" I ask.

"Courtney and Sandi."

"You know what, Courtney and Sandi?" I say. "For the last one, you can take a step closer because I feel bad you have to deal with this crazy goat-farming lady."

They both glance at Maggie who is still standing beside them smoldering like a match sliding across sandpaper, about to erupt into flames. Courtney looks back at me. "We don't even know her."

"Consider yourself lucky. She's obsessed with me," I reply and then it happens so fast I don't even realize what's going on until I'm submerged under water.

What happened was Maggie spun toward Courtney, snatched the apple out of her hand and spun back toward me, hurling that bruised fruit like a major leaguer. I barely even heard the ding of the metal target compressing before I was under water.

I pop back up and try not to sputter and cough but the dunk was so unexpected I inhaled half the tank. I push my hands through my hair trying to get the wet mop out of my eyes and give my head a shake. Wiping my eyes, I see Maggie jumping up and down in victory, a triumphant smile plastered from ear-to-ear and Courtney and Sandi are clapping and staring at me like I'm... well like I'm cleaning their kitchen in my underwear.

And then I realize, when I start climbing the ladder and something catches my leg, that I am actually *in* my underwear. My very wet, very white, very see-thru boxer briefs. The weight of the water drenching my jeans had tugged them halfway down my thighs.

"Oh my God!" Maggie gasps and covers her eyes.

I drop back into the water and duck down to grab my jeans and yank them back up. Jace is laughing so hard he's doubled over and Patrick and Paxton are using each other for support or else they'd be rolling on the ground. Jonah is embarrassed for me,

I can tell, because he's covering his open mouth with his hand and trying not to look me in the eye. Lex is running toward me with a towel as I make my way up the ladder and my jeans start to slip again. He's my new favorite teammate.

Getting out of the tank while keeping my pants on is not a graceful display but thankfully I manage it and as soon as my feet hit the grass, I grab the towel from Lex with a slightly humiliated smile. Courtney and Sandi come rushing over to me.

"Sorry she stole your last apple," I say to the girls. "If you want to press charges there's usually a police officer at the Community booth."

Maggie snorts from laughter.

This did not go as planned at all.

9
MAGGIE

I can't believe I hit that target on the first try. That says a lot about how angry I am because normally I wouldn't be able to hit the side of a barn. His pants falling down was just an added bonus I hadn't planned on and luckily he was too embarrassed to notice how my face went scarlet when I saw his almost completely see-through boxer briefs. I would never admit this to anyone, but I got a *good* look. Even though my brain was screaming for them to focus anywhere else, my eyes refused to move from his groin and I ended up having to cover them with my hands to stop staring.

Tate Adler has a nice package.

The two girls from our school also enjoyed the show and unlike me aren't ashamed to admit it. They make their way over to Tate now and fawn all over him. Argh. That isn't what I wanted to have happen. I want him to wallow in his embarrassment. "Way to go Maggie, looks like you got him two dates to go along with his win over us."

I turn and see Daisy standing a few feet away. I walk over to her. "He's not going to win. We still have a chance. People loved the free flowers we're handing out with purchases."

"*Were* handing out," Daisy corrects. "We're out."

"The apartment and the farm?" I ask and when Daisy nods my

heart breaks a little. I decided after seeing Tate's dunk tank we needed something more, so I had Clyde and Bobby go and cut my beloved flowers. They pillaged the tiny flower garden on the farm I've had since I was ten and the pots and flower boxes on our apartment balcony too. I had gladiolas, dahlias, roses, sweet peas and marigolds. I'm not looking forward to going home tonight and seeing nothing but dirt. If we've lost—and I think we have—I gave up my flowers for nothing.

"Bobby is working his magic on every woman who walks by the stand though," Daisy says trying to bring my spirits up. "Two moms bought like four jars of honey from him. And one lady bought six different flavors of goat cheese because he winked at her."

Yes, we were totally and without shame pimping out our handsome, single uncle. Desperate times, desperate measures. Daisy suddenly frowns as the wind whips her hair into her face and she pushes it back, annoyed. "But now Clyde is back at the booth, and we all know he's the worst salesman ever."

"Go send him on an errand," I say giving her a shove. "Tell him we need batteries and send him off to the store."

"Batteries?" Daisy looks confused.

"Batteries. Water. Coffee. Whatever! Just find a way to keep him away from the booth. We've only got an hour left," I say. Daisy nods but she doesn't look confident as she heads back to the booth.

I'm about to join her when I overhear a conversation that makes me freeze.

"No. I swear I know him!" a woman is saying. I turn and follow the voice. It belongs to someone I've never seen before. She's tall, curvy, middle aged and smiling excitedly as she stands at the ticket table talking to Jace and Tate's teammate, Lex.

"Do you follow the local college sports?" Lex asks her. "Because we're all players for the college team. Maybe you recognize him from that."

"No, I live in New Hampshire. I'm just here for the weekend

visiting a friend," she says and her eyes are locked on Tate who is now taking pictures with Courtney and Sandi. "I've never been here before and I don't follow hockey, but...he looks so familiar..."

It hits me like a ton of bricks how she might know him. She might have hired him. I start to walk over at the same time Lex stands up and turns to call Tate over. "Adler! This lady thinks she knows you."

Tate's green eyes lift from Courtney and Sandi and land on the woman. The color drains from his face in the blink of an eye and I know my suspicion is right. I start walking faster directly toward the lady. His expression seems to flick the switch on the lightbulb in this lady's head and her eyes flare and she claps her hands.

"I know! I know it!" She exclaims loudly and then points at Tate. "You are the guy who—"

"Sold you apples," I finish for her in a voice abnormally loud but I need to drown out the revelation she's about to express. "He probably sold you apples. Anyway, I hate to interrupt but your friend is at our booth and she wants your opinion on which cheese to buy."

"Anne Marie is here? Where? I thought she was working this morning," the lady says, confused.

I take her arm and lead her away, toward my booth. "I'm sure it's your friend. Come with me. Do you like goat cheese?"

"Maggie..." Tate says my name kind of under his breath but I hear it.

I look over at him his face is still void of color and he looks positively terrified. I remain cool and give him an icy smile. "Just shut up and look pretty while I take this woman to sample cheese."

"She's stealing a customer Tate! That's not fair. We should win by default," Jace announces and Tate walks over to his brother, but his eyes stay glued to mine and his expression softens as he realizes what I'm doing—saving his ass.

The lady is completely and totally perplexed as she gets to our stand and realizes her friend, Anne Marie, is nowhere in sight. I act bewildered. "I swear I thought she was here. I mean there was a lady looking for her friend and I assumed it must be you. I'm so sorry. Look, do you eat goat cheese? I can give you a free tub of our creamy and delicious roasted garlic goat cheese spread. You'll love it."

I grab a tub from the mini-fridge and hand it to her. She looks at it and at me, more baffled than ever. "Please. It's the least I could do. Also if you like honey our lavender honey is the best in the state and completely organic. It's magical. You should try it. It's on sale."

Daisy is watching our interaction with one eyebrow cocked. Luckily, Uncle Bobby and Clyde are nowhere to be found and Raquel is on the Adler side of the booth, trying to get a good selfie with her iced coffee, ignoring us.

"I do like honey," she says with a nod but she turns to look over at where the dunk tank is. "That guy works for this maid service. I swear he cleaned my house this summer."

I shake my head. "Nah. Not him. You must have him confused with someone else."

She cranes her neck to look at Tate again and then turns back to me and shakes her head. "No, I'm sure of it. See, it's this service my girlfriends got me for my birthday as a joke. And let's just say it's not his face I..."

I step closer to her and lower my voice. "Are you saying you recognized my fiancé's...body?"

"Your fiancé?"

I try to look like I'm on the verge of tears. "Are you saying you've seen him without his shirt before? When? If that man has already cheated on me, before the wedding, I swear I will—"

"No. No. I think I have it all wrong," the woman says, her voice suddenly soft and soothing. She reaches out and pats my arm. "I think he just looks like someone I know. I'm sorry. Thank you for the goat cheese and you know what, I will take a jar of that honey."

"Great!" Daisy pipes in and hands her a jar. "That'll be four bucks."

She hands Daisy a five and tells her to keep the change before almost running away. I watch her go, happy she isn't trying to return to the dunk tank. When she's completely out of sight, I turn back to the booth and am confronted with Daisy's judgmental stare. She crosses her arms over her chest, over the Todd Organic Farm logo on her shirt, and says. "What on God's green earth just happened?"

I sigh and tug her across the path, away from the booth before I whisper. "That woman was about to announce Tate's little part-time job, so I intervened."

"Why?"

My brain short circuits for a second. Why did I do it? I did it because Tate was about to be hurt and I didn't want that to happen. But there is no way I can confess that to my sister so I scramble to find a different reason. "Daisy, if his teammates and family find out about the maid thing, then we lose our leverage."

There. That makes sense. Phew.

Daisy mulls that over, chewing on her full bottom lip. "Smart. He'd definitely kick us out of the booth if we didn't have that secret to hold over his head."

We head back to the booth. An hour later, the last of the customers wanders away and the market is officially closed. But there are at least half a dozen people still in line at that stupid dunk tank. I tell Daisy and Bobby to count the money and march over. "Market is closed. Any sales after this moment can't be counted toward today's total."

Jace gives me a cool smirk. "No worries. We are out of apples to toss anyway."

"Oh," I frown. They had a lot of apples. We're screwed.

"Nothing left to do but count the cash," Jace says confidently. "It should take a while, so have a seat."

I huff like a disappointed toddler and stomp my way back to the booth. I know Tate is watching me go. I can feel his eyes on me, but I refuse to look at him. If he's smiling as smugly as his brother, I will have to kick him in the shins or something.

Back at the booth, I go about packing up with Clyde while Uncle Bobby and Daisy count the money. Raquel and Louise are also counting their profits. I watch Raquel out of the corner of my eye while she skims a couple twenties and tucks them into her bra. I will tell Tate about that at the end of the season but for now, her petty theft works to my advantage.

I pack a round of stuff into the SUV and when I get back to the booth Daisy motions me over.

"Four hundred and forty-four dollars and fifty cents," Daisy whispers in my ear as she tucks the money into our metal lock box and hands it to Uncle Bobby.

"Hope it's enough, Mags because we don't want to lose a day here." Bobby tucks the box under his arm as he starts to pull our loaded dolly back to his truck. "See you girls at home."

"Here he comes." Daisy tips her head toward the dunk tank.

I turn and walk toward him, meeting him in the middle of the path that runs the course of the booths. I do not feel the least bit confident but I am determined to fake it. I place a hand on my hip and wait. "So…what's your number?"

"What's yours?" he counters.

"I asked you first."

"Okay, but this isn't kindergarten, so just tell me your number so I can get this over with and go home," Tate barks. "Being admired by the entire female population of Burlington is exhausting."

"Your ego needs its own zip code," I reply.

"Before we begin, we should set up a margin where we will call it a tie," Tate says. "I mean do you really want to win by like one penny? I'm proposing if we're within fifty bucks of each other, it's a draw. Sound good?"

"Why on earth would you do that?" I ask before I can stop myself. Honestly it's to my benefit because I'm almost one hundred percent sure we lost this. If we come in under fifty we will be able to attend the next Sunday, so I should just shut up.

"Tell me I have bad business sense, I don't care. I'm just trying to be fair." Tate shrugs. "I bet we beat you by more than that anyway. Now just tell me your sales."

"Okay, I agree to the fifty buck rule," I mutter and take a deep breath and close my eyes and spit it out. "Four hundred and forty-four dollars and fifty cents."

I keep my eyes shut and wait for the laughter, the judgement, the hoots of victory. But there's nothing but the rustle of the fall wind through the nearby pussy willows. I open my left eye.

Tate is staring at me with his mouth hanging open. "Say that again?"

I give him the total again. He shakes his head. "Damn it…is it too late to reconsider that fifty dollar thing?"

"Yes. Why? What's your total?"

"Four hundred and sixty-six dollars."

A twenty-two dollar difference.

Tate shrugs. "Okay, well, see you next Sunday then. I have to take a load of stuff back to the farm while Jace takes the dunk tank back to his buddy."

He turns and walks over to his truck, which Louise has loaded with stuff. She gets in the passenger seat and he hops behind the wheel and I'm still staring as they drive away, the tall grass scratching at my jeans in the cool wind. What the hell just happened? I should be relieved. I should be thrilled, but something isn't sitting right.

He lost his mind over a beer pong tie but he's giving us a fifty buck buffer?

I walk back to the booth to grab the last box of stuff. Raquel is still there and she sighs in typical Raquel fashion—loudly and dramatically. "Where is my cousin? I have to give him the sales figures."

"He left," I mutter and then her words hit me. "You have to give him what?"

Raquel looks annoyed. "The sales figures. The jerk left? Why am I even here? He said he needed me to run the stupid booth and count up the sales as fast as possible as soon as it closes and the brat didn't even wait for them? I swear he is so annoying."

"Tate didn't have the sales figures?" I find myself saying—out loud—in shock.

Raquel turns and glares at me. She's been doing it since she was born, so I'm used to it. "Not all of them. I counted the cash but I forgot to count the sales we made through cards. And mind your own business."

This *is* my business, I think but I don't say it to her. I just turn and march over to my car with a new fire building inside me. That asshole had to have known he didn't have all the sales. That means he beat me and purposely let me think we tied. Why? There must be a nefarious reason for this because Tate Adler is not about to let a Todd—any Todd, but especially me—get a free pass on something.

Daisy is standing at the trunk of our car pushing it closed because it's packed full already. "That'll have to go in Uncle Bobby's truck."

I nod and hand it to her. "You'll have to go with him too. I need the car for an errand."

She looks confused but doesn't argue which is great because I want to figure out what he's doing before I let her in on it. Despite the nickname Tate uses exclusively for me, Daisy is actually much more of a firecracker than I am. She tends to shoot first and ask questions later. She'll just flip out on him and make the situation worse. I want to know what he's up to so I can plan the appropriate revenge successfully. I jump in our car and am out of the parking lot before I even click my seatbelt. The drive to his farm is the same as the drive to mine so, despite wanting to get there as soon as possible, I take a small detour around the town center so Bobby's truck doesn't follow me the whole way there. If Daisy figures out I'm on my way to the Adler farm, she'll show up there too.

When I turn onto our road, the sun is low in the sky and the road is empty. It looks really beautiful this time of year when the trees are starting to show little patches of color here and there and light is so golden it almost makes the road glitter. I love this time of year most of all in Vermont but I don't let myself enjoy it right now because there's a growing knot twisting in my belly with Tate Adler's name on it.

I drive right past our open farm gates and hook a left onto the Adler's property. There're two ways in. The main one that everyone uses and this little, blink-and-you-will-miss-it dirt lane that hooks around the back of their barn. It used to be fenced off, but last year a tree crushed the old, rickety wooden gate when it fell in a windstorm. They never fixed it and despite the tall, unmown grass at the foot of the lane, I turn onto it. I want to avoid alerting every Adler in the place I'm on their land. I park my car halfway up the lane and walk the rest of the way toward the barn. As I crest the small hill, the lake gleams ahead, all serene and sparkling. The farmhouse is to my left and beyond that, the orchards. My right has the barn. Well, what's left of it, which is three walls. I don't have much of a plan in place except to sneak around the Adler Farm like a member of the Scooby gang until I find my villain, Tate.

I don't have to go far as he's on the main drive on the opposite side of the barn, unloading market stuff from the back of his truck. There are about six other cars peppering the drive and I can hear the murmur of voices and I realize their farm is open for apple picking today. That means his father and George are in the orchard handling the customers. I steal around the side of the barn and as he turns to haul something into it, I block his way. He jumps like a scream queen in a horror movie and drops the box he's holding. I would laugh if I wasn't hyper focused on exposing his lies.

"Why did you let us win?"

Tate blinks repeatedly and regains his composure. "What are you doing here?"

"Raquel was looking for you because you forgot to count the receipts from people who paid electronically," I say flatly. "Which means you won. We didn't. You lied and said we did."

I stare at him with laser focus waiting—hoping—to see some look of shock which should be quickly replaced by excitement that he beat us. He won. He gets the booth to himself next week. But instead he just blinks those eyes the color of wet moss, all dark and lush, and shrugs. "Raquel doesn't know what she's talking about. And honestly, neither do you. You didn't win. We tied. Big difference."

He bends to pick up the box he dropped and walks around me toward a small, aluminum storage shed beside the barn. I follow so close behind I almost clip his heels with the toes of my Converse.

"Go home Maggie."

"No," I reply. "I want to know why you're lying."

"We tied. Let it go," Tate barks. "You know if my grandfather sees you here, he'll call the cops or get out his shotgun. Or both."

"You didn't count all the money," I repeat and he opens the shed door aggressively and drops the box inside. "What are you up to? I'm not an idiot. I know you aren't letting us win out of the goodness of your heart. You'd kick a puppy if you thought it was mine. So I don't get it. And whatever your reason I'm here to tell you that I don't want your charity."

"For the love of all things hockey, woman, stop talking," he huffs and his eyes dart over my shoulder, and then he's suddenly hooking my arm and hauling me into the dilapidated barn. I open my mouth but as a startled squeak starts to escape, his big hand clamps down over it.

The forced silence allows me to hear the rumble of a car coming up the drive.

My back is pressed up against the side of the barn just left of the door, and Tate's very large body is pressed against me. He changed after his dunking into a pair of school logo sweats and a T-shirt with the hockey logo on it. The fabric of both are supple and thin so I feel every part of him. Every hard curve, bump and twist of his athletic body. I stop breathing but I don't know if it's out of shock or fear or something else. The swirl of emotion in my belly is definitely…something else.

A car door opens and closes and then I hear Jace's voice. "Tate! Where you at?" Tate doesn't answer. He doesn't move. I think he's staring at me, but there're too many shadows to know for sure. Jace calls his name one more time and then I hear the distinct slam of their porch door. Tate's hand over my mouth instantly loosens, but he doesn't move it away from my lips. Instead he leans closer to me and whispers. "You really need to learn not to make mountains out of molehills, Magnolia."

I bite his palm.

Not exactly gently but not enough to draw blood or anything. So when he jumps back wincing and cursing in a stage whisper I roll my eyes at his dramatics and put my hands on my hips.

"Tell me what the hell you think you're doing lying about the bet results, and I'll decide if it's a mountain or a molehill," I reply.

"You are the biggest pain my ass has ever experienced, you know that? And I once took a slap shot to the ass, so that's saying something," He runs a hand through his hair and curses under his breath again before turning back to me. "Yeah. I lied about the cash we made and technically, I guess my farm won the bet. But you did something nice for me so I was just returning the favor. I didn't want to owe you. The end. Now go home."

"I have never done anything nice for you!" I declare like he just accused me of some kind of act of treason. In a way, he kind of did.

"You stopped that client from revealing my job in front of everyone," Tate replies. "I saw the whole damn thing, so don't pretend it didn't happen."

"That? That wasn't about you. That was me being selfish," I say casually and shrug.. "I don't want your charity."

"And I don't want *your* charity," Tate barks back. "I could have run my own interference and gotten her off the subject myself. I never asked for your help."

"You were too busy trying to keep your pants on to help your-self," I scoff. "You won the bet and we won't be at the market next week."

I start toward the barn door, and he grabs my arm again. I spin and shove him. "Do not manhandle me!"

There are supplies—timber planks piled up and a couple tool boxes—on the floor behind him and my shove makes him take a step back, which causes him to trip on the pile of stuff and he starts to fall backward. I lunge forward and grab him. He didn't need my help and was already righting himself so my yanking causes him to lurch forward, and the next thing I know we're chest-to-chest again. And that warm, electric feeling I would love if it was caused by anyone else in the world is swirling in my belly again. I try to take a step back but his hand is suddenly around my waist holding me in place.

"You just can't stop saving me, can you?" he asks but his voice is low and gruff and filled with a husky tone I haven't heard before.

"If you impale yourself on a plank I can't...my leverage..."

God, he's strong. Solid. Warm.

"Did you forget how to form a sentence?"

His hand slips lower. Oh God. *I like it.*

"I'm not taking your charity. The end," I say, acting like I don't feel the hand that is firmly palming my ass now. I want to applaud myself for sounding so unaffected. My pulse is racing, my blood is heated, my girl parts are dancing—and my hands are slipping down his chest, fingertips riding over every ripple of toned flesh under his T-shirt.

"Fine. You lost today." He tilts his head just the slightest bit to the left and inches a millimeter closer. He has a good neck. I've never said that about a guy before but I'm staring at his, and it's long and thick and perfectly tan.

I find myself leaning into him, moving closer to his neck. It's pure and utter insanity. He's done it. Tate Adler has caused me to lose my mind. He tilts his head further the closer I get and then I feel his breath ghost my own neck and then his lips skim the shell of my ear. "You and your family better not be anywhere near the booth next Sunday. You lost. I won."

"Exactly," I whisper. "So stop being nice to me."

"Fine…if you tell me the truth." His lips skim along my jaw, the graze of his stubble creating ripples of heat on my skin. The desire igniting in me could probably light this barn on fire. Again. "Why did you really do it? Stop that woman from exposing my job today?"

"Because you had this look on your face of pure panic and impending doom. The look of someone who could see their world crumbling. Your face looked like Daisy's did when we woke up and found our dad collapsed on the kitchen floor after his stroke," I confess. "No one should feel the way that look says they feel. Even you."

His lips stop moving. Now they're just pressed to my cheek ever so lightly and I want to press my skin against them but I don't. Then he speaks, his lips still against my skin so its muffled but I not only hear but feel every word. "Thank you. And I'm sorry about your dad. That you went through that."

"We hate each other," I remind myself as much as him, but the whisper is so breathless and weak I don't think my brain, or his, really hears it.

"Uh-huh."

And then his lips slide across my cheek to brush mine and I swear to God I see stars. My hands slip around his neck and into his hair and I open my mouth just a little. Mostly out of shock at my own behavior. When he squeezes my ass—hard—my mouth opens wider and Tate's tongue barges in.

He's pushing me now, hands still firmly planted on my ass so my body stays glued to his, and he walks me backward until I'm pressed up against that barn wall he had me up against earlier. Then his hand slips from my ass to the crook of my knee and as he tugs my bottom lip between his teeth, he pulls my leg up by my knee and grinds into me and I feel him, long, thick and so hard it makes a heated flush explode across my face, and even in the dusky barn he sees it and smirks.

"Fuck you," I pant at the smirk as he pushes into me again, grinding his length across my core in the most perfect way.

"Is that want you want?" His voice is rough and hard and it's the most sensuous thing I've ever heard. "Me to fuck you?"

"Yes," I answer before I can even think to stop myself. I grab the back of his neck and kiss him again because if he smirks at how much redder my face just got, I'll die before he can give me what I want.

Our hands move in a frantic dance to remove each other's clothes. He gets my pants down to my ankles and I kick one leg free as I tug his shirt over his head and throw it behind him. He reaches up and tugs on my ponytail, tipping my head back and then he puts his mouth on my neck, just above my collarbone, and attacks it with just the right amount of bite and suck so that I feel it between my legs. My hands reach and shove his sweat pants down. Thank God they don't require work because my brain is short circuiting and my hands are shaky and uncoordinated with need.

He's not wearing underwear. My eyes fall and land on his erection—thick, long and eager as it points toward me like a weather vane in a storm. I bite my bottom lip and make a noise in the back of my throat that I've never made before in my life. Tate smiles and bends down and for a panicked second, I think he's going to pull his sweats up.

"What are you doing?"

He pulls something out of the pocket of the sweats and holds it up between us as he stands. "Protection."

"Of course you carry them everywhere you go." I roll my eyes.

He laughs and leans his whole body against mine again. "Only you would somehow make safe sex a character flaw."

He kisses me hard holding my chin for a moment and the

pulls back. "Besides," he looks down and I hear the distinct rip of a wrapper. "Borrowed these sweats from Patrick. He carries condoms everywhere."

He slides the condom on and then moves to kiss me again, his hand sliding down my side and around my hip as he pulls back just enough to speak. "Take your shirt off."

I want to tell him I don't take orders from him except that I want to take my shirt off. So I do and before it even hits the ground he's yanking the strap on my bralette down and moving those gifted lips to my left nipple and I groan so loud he has to clamp a hand over my mouth again.

"Shh!" He commands, his words a gush of hot air against my breast. "They can't find us."

I nod and snake my hands into his hair again, pushing him closer to my nipple which he gladly circles with his tongue over and over before moving to the other one. "Now do you promise to shut up so I can put this hand to better use?"

I can't answer because my mouth is covered so I bite his palm again. He yanks it away and unfortunately pulls his mouth from me too. "Don't bite."

I smile. "Don't talk."

I start to push his head down to my breasts again but now his other hand is in my underwear and without a lick of hesitation he slides two finger across my entrance and now it's Tate who is making the strange noises. "You're ready, Firecracker."

"So don't keep me waiting," I reply shamelessly wrapping a leg around his hip, opening myself up against his fingers, which slowly slide inside. "Oh God…"

"If this is only happening once, I'm going to enjoy it. And so are you," Tate whispers against my mouth before his tongue pushes its way inside again.

Definitely only once, I agree in my head as his thumb makes slow circles against my clit. I dig my fingernails into his shoulders. And he breaks our kiss and our eyes connect. His gaze is heavy and heated but there's a flicker of hesitation to it too, like he's waiting for me to come to my senses. His fingers slip from me and, knowing with every fiber of my now-on-fire being that I am never going to stop this, I push him back a bit and then push my underwear down my legs and pull my left foot free.

He's watching me with a look of awe and lust.

"Now or never. What's it going to be?"

Tate steps into me again, his wide hands cup my ass and he lifts me up off the ground. "Now. Then never," he replies. "Hold on."

He pulls me off the wall and takes a couple steps to the left, where there's an empty pen with a door with metal rails. Probably where they used to keep their cow when they had one. He presses me against the rails now, kissing me hard and deep, and I can feel his sheathed cock bump against my entrance. I grab the rail on either side of my head and wrap my legs loosely around his waist. I watch with baited breath as he grabs himself and rubs his tip against my slit. We both inhale loudly at the same time.

His eyes dart up to me and then back down as he places one hand on mine on the railing and he guides himself into me with his other hand. Just the tip, then a little more, then a little less, then a little more… I hook my ankles behind him and as he starts to slide a little bit deeper again, I use my legs to keep the momentum and pull him closer and closer until he's all the way in. He buries his face in my neck biting down on my shoulder as he grunts and my head tips back and I bite my bottom lip to keep my own moan from escaping.

Tate's hips start to move immediately, and because this day isn't insane enough, my body is overwhelmed with the urge to topple into orgasm. How is that even possible? I whimper and tilt my pelvis into the thrusts, trying to fight my orgasm and chase it at the same time. His hand grips my ass and his other one moves to cup my chin, tilting my face to his. "You feel…this feels…"

"No talking. Just fucking," I beg. "Hard."

His hips drive harder and he grabs my chin again to guide my mouth to his. I feel Tate everywhere—inside and outside—and it's too much and not enough. Everything feels like it's happening too fast but in slow motion. My limbs are all numb because every nerve ending in my body has shut off except for one: the one Tate's bumping and grinding against at a deliciously relentless pace.

I gasp into our endless kiss as my body tightens and shudders and my climax rips through me with abandon. As my body goes limp Tate's gets more rigid and he pushes harder and faster for a few more strong, hard thrusts and then a groan rumbles up and out of him and I slap a hand over his mouth this time as he finds his own release.

For a few disorienting moments we stay there, body-to-body, hearts hammering against each other, breathless. His lips are the only thing moving, still gliding over my neck, my jaw, my ear and then my mouth. He's gentle now. Slow and soft and it feels divine. I drop one arm across his back and slip my fingers through the hair at the nape of his neck. It's soft and damp from exertion, and he must like me playing with it because he nuzzles my neck. But then he whispers. "I have to pull out."

And he does, stepping back so I let my legs drop to the floor. I feel like a newborn baby goat taking its first steps—wobbly and uncertain. So much for marching out of here like nothing happened.

I, as quickly and gracefully as possible, get dressed. Tate does too and before he can say anything, I'm leaving. He's right behind me as I make my way out of the barn. "This was a mistake."

"No it wasn't," Tate replies. "It was either this or we kill each other. At least now neither of us will end up in jail like Clyde and George."

I stop. Turn and look at him. His skin is pink and he's still breathing unevenly like he still hasn't caught his breath. Good to know I have company in that department. "But it's one and done."

"Couldn't agree more. One and done," Tate repeats with a nod, but then our eyes lock and a smile starts to tug the corners of the lips that feel so good on my skin, and I feel a blush start to crawl up my cheeks and I can't help but smile too, and suddenly we're grinning like total lunatics...until the screen door slams.

"What is *she* doing on *my* property?" George Adler's voice booms like a cannon going off.

Shit.

"Finishing up some market business," I respond trying to sound calm and professional and not like someone who just let his grandson pound her into blissful oblivion in his barn. "Relax. I'm leaving."

I can hear George stomping down the porch steps but I don't bother to turn around. I keep walking but George keeps following. "You and you wretched family aren't allowed to set foot on my property for any reason."

"Gramps, stop!" Tate barks. "You're being rude."

"I'm being rude? Her family has a history of making our life hell," George replies, yelling at the top of his lungs. "They killed our cow."

"What? Gramps, Milkshake was an escape artist with a death wish," Tate replies. "She used to get off the property at least twice a week. And she wasn't hit by one of the Todds."

"No, but it was the fence that borders their property that she got through the day she died. The one Clyde keeps trying to tear down," George says. "And why are you defending them?"

"I'm definitely not defending them," Tate says, but he sounds...guilty.

"What the heck is everyone screaming about?" Comes a new, annoyed voice.

"Nothing, Dad. Don't worry about it," Tate says.

"Why is Maggie Todd here? What's going on?"

Finally I turn to face them. Vince Adler is standing on the porch with his arms crossed and an annoyed scowl on his face. George is walking toward me pointing at me with a stubby fat finger. Tate is following along behind him.

"Do not touch me, old man," I warn when George gets close enough that his hand is a foot from my face.

"I have a right to stand my ground and protect my property," George announces. "You're trespassing, so consider yourself lucky I don't get out my shotgun."

"Gramps, we don't have a stand your ground law in Vermont, and if you pull out your shotgun, I'm calling the cops on you," Tate barks.

"Stop defending her," George demands.

"I'm leaving!" I holler, loudly. Everyone stares at me. I make a point of looking each of them in the eye defiantly but calmly. Until my eyes land on Tate and I feel my girl parts shimmy as my brain fills with images from moments ago in the barn. Before I can blush, I force myself to look away from him and push the memories out of my head. "I just had to settle something with your grandson. It's settled. I promise it will never happen again."

"Never ever again," Tate repeats and George turns and levels him with a stare, his old wrinkled face twisted in bewilderment.

"Bye!" I say and march away as fast as I can without actually running.

By the time I get to my car and haul myself inside, my skin is crimson, but it's not because I was berated and chased off by George. It's because I just saw Tate naked. And he saw me naked. And our parts merged...

I had sex with Tate Adler and I liked it. A lot. More than I have ever liked sex before.

Oh my God, this is a nightmare.

TATE

"What the heck are you doing?" Lex asks me as he stumbles down the back stairs and into the kitchen, in workout gear, sleep likely still blurring his eyes. "It's like, the crack of dawn."

"I've got to do some work at the farm before class," I lie. In truth I took an early morning cleaning session Vickie offered me. The gig is an hour away, so I have to get up early. "And my room is so damn stuffy with this summer weather that won't end. I couldn't sleep much."

He looks almost guilty at that. He's the rookie and you would think that means he has to take the smallest room in the hockey house, but we decided to play a shootout game after the first practice to decide who gets stuck in the third floor room with sloped ceilings, one tiny window, and that was barely big enough for a double mattress and a desk. I lost.

He glances at the mop, bucket, feather duster and other cleaning supplies at my feet while I finish the last of my coffee. "You don't have cleaning supplies at the farm?"

"We're out so I picked these up last night," I say. "To bring by today."

"Oh. Okay." Lex shrugs. "I'm off for a run."

"Don't overdo it, rookie. We have practice tonight and if you're lagging, Coach will notice," I warn him.

He nods. "Same goes for you. I heard you walking around the house half the night. These creaky floorboards hide nothing.."

"A lot on my mind." I shrug and put my empty coffee mug in the sink.

"You won that weird bet against those sisters. Shouldn't you be worry-free?" Lex questions.

I just had mind-melting sex with one of those sisters, also known as my blackmailer, so the idea of being worry-free is hysterical. I start laughing. Great. Now he's looking at me like I'm looney tunes.

"It's complicated," I say when I regain my composure. I pick up my cleaning supplies and head out the door. "See ya at practice."

I toss everything in the back of the truck and start on my way. I really do not want to work today—especially this job—but I can't afford to turn down work. After what happened at Maggie's I wanted to quit, but the fact is we are now officially two months behind on the mortgage payments on the farm. The dunk tank stunt helped though. I make a mental note to remind Jace to drive that cash down to the bank today. I don't have time between working, classes, and practice.

I think of Maggie the entire drive to the gig, just like I thought about her nonstop since our post-market sex two days ago, which is why I haven't been sleeping much. I lay awake at night and think of her. The way she felt, the way she sounded, the way she looked when she came—because I made her come. *Hard.* And she returned the favor. And now the mental juxtaposition of how great it all felt and how wrong it actually was has my head spinning. It doesn't help that I can't say a damn word to anyone about it. I just can't. My teammates won't get it. My brother will lose his mind and possibly tell the family and the only other person I would normally confide in I don't talk to anymore.

Hank Knight had been a long-time employee of our farm. He

was about five years older than me and started working for us when he was fourteen. I thought he was the coolest kid ever and looked up to him like an older brother. He dropped out of high school in his senior year and started full-time with us. And when I went away to boarding school for hockey, I actually kept in touch more with him than anyone else at the farm. But then a few months ago, after the fire in the barn, we didn't have enough money to keep paying him, no matter what I did with accounting. We let him go. I have been avoiding him ever since. I heard he works at the Biscuit now, so I avoided it all summer. He wasn't there after the exhibition game earlier this week, but since we go there after all the other home games during the season, I know I'm bound to run into him. Still, it's obvious I've been avoiding him, so I can't exactly call him up and ask his advice.

But damn, I know Hank would be able to give me some solid advice. Maybe he'd know the exact words I need to hear to make me stop thinking about her and the sex. Because the more I think about it, the more I find myself searching for a way to let it happen again. And it can't happen again.

I pull off the highway and focus on listening to the soothing voice on Google Maps as it directs me to the house I'm cleaning. I get there five minutes early and sigh as I'm grabbing my stuff. I upgraded my costume to a Zorro-type mask from the bandana I used to use because of how easily Maggie yanked it off my face. Can't have that happen again. I always cover my face because my mug is on the university website more than a few times on the athletics page, and it makes the paper sometimes. Last year the university had a billboard with the team on it. I can't risk being recognized.

I make my way to the door and ring the bell, bracing myself for whatever comes next. I've been lucky—really lucky—with my assignments because the women have been flirty and fun and sometimes even embarrassed but never aggressive or inappropriate. Mike Danvers, my former teammate who told me about Manly Maids, said he had a few who stuck their hands in his underwear. He let a few of them too. I was not going to turn this into something like that. It wasn't that some of these women weren't hot—they were. But cleaning half-naked for money and sex for money were two different things. I wanted to keep it legit. Mike was a senior on the team last year and wasn't on a scholarship so he did the Manly Maid gigs to pay his way through school. He'd done it all four years of school and graduated last year debt-free.

The door opens, and I almost fall over. The woman who is standing there is probably about seventy. Her long, white hair is pulled back in a bun. She's in a pair of pink polyester slacks and a white blouse with pink peonies all over it and a pink cardigan. She is also wearing pink slippers. "Uh. Hi ma'am I'm... I..."

She smiles brightly. "Oh good! I was hoping you'd be a brunette. When do you take off your shirt?"

"You...ordered a maid?" I ask because I thought for sure I had the wrong address.

"Not just any maid, a *manly* maid," she says still smiling like she is the gentle old gran in a cookie ad or something. "And boy, did they deliver."

Her blue eyed gaze slowly rolls up and down my body. "Won't you come in. You'll remove some of those clothes though, right?"

"Yes ma'am," I say. She moves to the side and I step in. I put down my supplies to pull my shirt over my head. She sighs and then claps when I drop my pants too. Oh God, this is going to be an interesting one, I think, and then I hear another set of footsteps.

"Nana! Who is at the door?"

A pretty woman, who looks like a thirty-year-old version of the flirty, dirty grandma, walks into the front hall and screams like I'm a cat burglar. Granny turns around. "Calm down, Patty. Has it been that long since you've seen a half-naked man that you're scared of him?"

"Who are you and why are you naked with my nana?" Patty says as she steps forward, grabs Nana by the shoulders and moves Nana behind her.

"I was hired to clean. I'm a Manly Maid," I explain.

"I hired him," Nana announces proudly. "You haven't been on a date since the divorce. You won't even join one of those app thingies to talk to men. You just sit here and take care of me. I need you to have a life while you're young."

Patty still looks horrified. She turns her nana by the shoulders to face her. "So you hired me a man?"

"Just to clean," Nana explains. "It's legit I swear. My friend Barb told me about it at canasta last week because her grand-daughter hired one. They keep their skivvies on, and you aren't supposed to touch them. But I figured this way you don't have to clean today and maybe seeing some hot young thing will get your motor started again."

"Oh my God." Patty looks at me and covers her face with her hands. "My motor is fine, Nana. Sir, you don't have to do this. I am so sorry."

I am amused by this whole situation so I just grin and shrug. "I've been paid up front so let me just clean. If you don't want to watch, you don't have to. Go out for coffee or read a book. But at least let me save you scrubbing toilets."

"That would be nice," Patty replies and the pink color of her cheeks reminds me of Maggie.

"Well I'm gonna stay and watch," Nana announces and I chuckle.

"That's fine too," I reply and pick up my mop and bucket. "Let me know where you want me to start," I ask and Nana claps and Patty covers her face again.

Two and a half hours later I'm parking in front of the hockey house again. It turned into one of the funnest and easiest gigs I've had in a long time. Unlike Maggie and her roommates, Patty and Nana kept an immaculate house, so the work part was easy. Nana followed me from room to room fanning herself and making small talk. She was a hoot. Patty hid in the kitchen drinking pot after pot of tea and trying not to die of embarrassment. They were great but traffic was heavier than I anticipated coming back, and I missed my first class of the day. I'm kicking myself as I walk to campus now.

It was Intermediate Accounting for Small Business, and I barely made it through Intro to Accounting last year. Math is not my thing. I can't be skipping classes. And also...Maggie is in this class. I can't decide if not seeing her is worse or better than seeing her. I mean, it's probably for the best because running into her for the first time in a crowded classroom might make it even more awkward. Or maybe it would have made it less? I don't know.

I decide to hit up the Green Bean for a coffee and something to eat before heading to my next class. I pull open the door and almost trip over my own feet. Maggie is in line. She's staring at her phone and doesn't see me. Her hair is down and kind of wavy today. Just like it was when I yanked the elastic out in the barn and buried my fingers in it while I was sliding into her...

I panic. I don't know why, but I suddenly think seeing her here like this in public is a really bad idea. I turn and almost crash into a dude leaving holding two coffees. My shoe makes a terrible squeaking sound as I come to an abrupt stop.

"Watch it!" The guy barks at me, and it's loud. Too damn loud. Out of the corner of my eye I see her turn toward him.

And, like her gaze is a magnet pulling me toward it, I turn to look at her as she looks at me. Our eyes lock. She looks really pretty today in a really loose, white cotton dress and dark high top sneakers. The dress is short and her long, pale legs—the ones that wrapped so perfectly around my waist—are on full display.

"Dude, are you coming or going?" the guy says, irritated.

"He's probably going," I hear Maggie say. "He's already come."

I stare at her trying not to let my jaw hit the floor. She's smiling —smugly—and then she turns around, eyes on her phone again like she didn't just hurl the mother of all double entrendres right at me. I step out of the way and even hold the door for Mr. Bitchy Pants before walking over to stand directly beside her.

"There's a line," she mutters, her eyes still glued to her phone.

"Yeah, but I'm buying you a coffee," I say and glance at her screen, which she quickly angles away from me so I can't see what she's looking at. "Checking out my hockey profile on the Athletics page?"

"Ha. No," she says humorlessly. Her eyes shift up and join mine for just the slightest second. They're a really cool kaleidoscope of hues. Starbursts of amber and light brown with a mossy greenish-gray ring around the outer edge. I've never really studied them until now. "Stop staring. Also I don't need your free drinks."

I blink. Did I just analyze her eye color? Why did I do that? I can't even remember the eye color of the last girl I slept with before Maggie and I *liked* her. What the hell am I doing? "Well, it's not charity. I know you're allergic to that. It's a bribe, so you should be fine with it."

She looks up at me again, frowning a little this time. "A bribe to keep my mouth shut? Don't worry. I don't want to remember what we did in that barn let alone share it with anyone."

Ouch.

Okay so the weird tingle I am still feeling, like residual lust or attraction or something, is definitely one-sided. Got it. I clear my throat. "I need to borrow your notes from class this morning. Accounting. I missed it."

"I noticed," Maggie mutters as the server calls out for the next customer, which is us.

I step up but she doesn't, so I have to reach back and grab her wrist and tug her forward. She glances around like she's horrified someone might see me touch her and gently pulls her wrist back. "I'll have a non-fat iced vanilla latte and an everything bagel with cream cheese. And she will have…"

"Coffee. Black," Maggie spits out at me.

"Coffee. Black," I repeat to the server. "Like her heart."

The server starts to laugh but when he realizes Maggie isn't joining in, he quickly stifles it, rings in the order, and I pay him.

We move to the side to wait. "So can I borrow your notes. Please?"

"Yeah. I guess," Maggie mutters and crosses her arms. She's rocking ever so slightly at her hips, like she's antsy or nervous or something. "I'll print them off and give them to you tomorrow."

"Thanks," I say. "But can you maybe just email them to me?"

She shakes her head, no, without even thinking about it. "You want my notes, you can have them, but printed out only. When I find the time to do it. It's called punishment for not getting your lazy ass out of bed like the rest of us."

"I was up at the crack of dawn to go to work," I say. "And it ran late, so that's why I missed it."

"You worked the farm this morning?" Maggie says, shocked.

"No. The other job," I lower my voice an octave and watch as she makes a face like she just gargled lemon juice with a mouth full of paper cuts. "That's a pretty judgy face for a woman who was once a client."

"Daisy hired you, not me."

"No you just ogled my ass while I worked," I remind her and I can literally see her struggle to keep a blush from hitting her face. She turns away as someone calls out our order and I walk over to collect it.

"So," I say as I hand her coffee. "Any chance we could run over to the student center and print those notes now? I'm going to need them before class tomorrow."

"Yeah, you are. We have a quiz tomorrow," Maggie replies and opens the door, not bothering to hold it open for me and leaves. I have to wedge my foot in it to keep it from slamming closed in my face.

"Magnolia, seriously. Please," I say, and I'm getting annoyed— not just with how she won't give me her damn notes but also because the windchill she's blowing my way is brutal. "Or maybe I should just ask someone else."

I start to break off from her and veer left as she veers right but then suddenly, she reaches out and grabs my hand. I turn to face her and she stands perfectly still and stares at me. "I said I'd give you the notes. When's your next class?"

"In about forty-five minutes," I reply as I take a bite out of my bagel.

"My next one is in an hour and a half," Maggie replies and plucks the bagel from my hand. I watch as she takes a dainty bite. "So I can head home and print the notes and get them back to you before your next class."

I watch her mouth while she chews. It's a pretty mouth—and I know she knows how to use it...for more than just being sassy. I've imagined what that perfect mouth might look like wrapped around something other than a bagel. But I won't ever find out because one and done. She said it and she clearly means business.

"Okay..." I take the bagel back and tear off a big piece, chewing out my frustration. It's not that I like her, it's just that it was good sex. And so now I feel like we should have done more, and done it for longer, if it was only going to happen once. She's watching my mouth the same way I've been watching hers. Huh. That's not the sign of a girl who wants nothing to do with me, is it? So I throw out an idea. "Wouldn't it be easier if I just go with you to your place and grab the notes?"

Maggie looks at me, pauses, and then kind of lifts her shoulder and tilts her head in a one-sided shrug. "Well...yeah, I guess that could work."

She smiles.

I smile.

We make our way off campus to her apartment sipping our coffees, eating what has now turned into a communal bagel and not speaking a word. The streets around campus are peppered with students and cars zipping by. Leaves dance their way off the trees with the slightest breeze making a blanket on the sidewalk and crunching under our feet. If we were involved, I would reach for her hand and this would be a fairly romantic fall walk. But we aren't and it isn't.

When we're standing in front of the main door to her apartment building and she's pulling out her keys I say, "Are your roommates home?"

"No. You wouldn't be here if they were."

"Right." I take a step closer. The wind blows and the hem of her dress rustles against my jeans. The door swings open. "Wouldn't want them to know you're sleeping with the enemy."

"Ha. Ha," she says but her voice wobbles a little bit. Maggie steps over the threshold and starts up the long staircase to her third floor unit. "We promised that could never happen again, remember?"

"I remember." I watch her climbs the stairs, the bottom of her skirt swinging around her toned thighs. "Problem is I remember everything else before the promise too."

We reach the top of the staircase and she starts to unlock the door that leads into the apartment. She glances over her shoulder as she steps into the front hall and I flash her a devious grin. "Like I remember how hot it was when you went off like a firecracker, Firecracker."

Maggie freezes. She doesn't speak, she doesn't turn to face me as I close the door behind us and I'm not even sure she's breathing. "You did not just say that."

"I did. It's the truth and it's all I've been able to think about since it happened." I reach out and skim my fingers through her hair, lifting it off her neck. "Turn around, Maggie."

She does as she's told, which surprises me because I half expected her to tell me off for giving her orders. Her cheeks are rosy and her eyes are sparkling. "We said never again."

"We lied," I reply before I kiss her.

11

TATE

Just like the first time, half of me still expects to be slapped as soon as my lips touch hers, but once again it doesn't happen. Instead, Maggie kisses me back sliding her tongue into my mouth without hesitation, thank God. I've spent every waking minute since the barn sex trying to convince myself that I am overreacting to the encounter with her. That the high levels of frustration and annoyance that Magnolia Todd causes me mixed with the crushing levels of stress I have been carrying since the farm started going tits up caused the sexual experience to feel like it was better than anything I'd ever experienced. But it's not. It can't be. Even now, just this kiss feels like the best thing in the world.

Her hands are already undoing my fly. I'm not having sex with her up against another wall. I want a bed this time I decide, and so I drop down a little and throw her over my shoulder. She squeals and slaps my ass. "What the hell, Tater Tot!"

Luckily, I know which bedroom is hers and once I reach it I hurl her onto the bed like a bale of hay. Another squeak escapes those pretty lips and she tries to sit up but I'm crawling on top of her before she can. My hand nudges her legs apart so I can settle between them, and as she snakes her hand into my hair to pull me into a kiss, my hand glides up the inside of her bare leg. Calf, knee, thigh… I keep going. She pushes her pelvis into my hand as I cup her through her underwear.

I allow one finger to snake under the elastic and find her drenched, just like last time. She sighs and arches her back but I pull my hand away and sit back on my knees, reaching behind me to pull my shirt over my head. I feel her hands go to my fly again. I try to push her back, but she's got unreal strength for someone half my size and she stays put, managing to get my jeans and underwear down to my knees. "Maggie, I want…"

Those are the only three words I manage to say before I feel her lips against the tip of my cock and I lose the ability to speak. I think I was going to tell her that I want to take my time with her, and then I was going to push her back and kiss my way up under that little dress. But hey, this is good too.

Her hand wraps around my length and her head moves downward and suddenly her lips give way to the warm, wet heat of her mouth and tongue. If I was standing my knees would buckle, the feeling is that intense and that good. *So* good. She's doing this thing with her tongue, swirling it every which way, like my dick is an ice cream cone in a heatwave and she'll die if she lets one drop escape. Meanwhile, her plump lips make a tight suction and cause my gut to clench with pleasure every time they slide over the crown. My hands dive into that long, silky, copper hair and twist, tugging ever so slightly. Her hand clenches on my base and her tongue swirls faster and I'm about to go off like a firework on the Fourth of July. But the main event hasn't even begun, so it would be an embarrassing waste, like a firework exploding on the third of July by mistake.

Using my hands tangled in her hair, I gently but firmly hold her still and sit back on my ankles, causing a soft, wet pop sound as my dick breaks free from her mouth. Then I guide her up to eye level.

"I wasn't done," Maggie says looking up at me through her lashes with that defiant look I know all too well.

I grab the hem of her dress and pull it over her head and throw it on the floor.

"Well it's my turn," I reply before taking her mouth in a wild kiss.

When I push her back onto the bed and lie over her again I ask, "Didn't you learn to take turns growing up?"

But then I steal her answer by pushing my hand into her underwear again and taking away her ability to form words. Her mouth drops into the cutest little O shape, and her head falls back onto the pillow.

"You can make noise this time, Firecracker," I whisper against her ear before biting her lobe. "No family to catch us."

I kiss her neck and lean my body into hers, as my fingers slide in and out of her and I use the pad of my thumb to circle her clit. I stop only long enough to pull her underwear completely off and then replace my hand with my mouth.

From the first pass of my tongue, she becomes someone else. Gone is the Maggie Todd who bosses me around, fights for control, and pushes me away. This new Maggie Todd is submissive—her legs falling open as my tongue reaches her clit. And instead of pushing me away, she's got her hands in my hair, pulling me closer. She can't boss me around because she's too busy moaning, which is a clear indication she'd have nothing to say anyway because I know exactly what I'm doing. I could get very used to this Maggie.

Her hands move down my back, fingernails scraping as she arches her back and then gifts me with a pant of my name. "Oh God... Tate..."

My cock swells at the sound and then the feel of her coming against my lips.

I kiss my way across her belly and up her body, pausing to give both her perky breasts some attention. As I move on to kiss her collarbone she manages to find her words. "Condom."

I kiss her neck. "Back pocket."

She rolls over and hangs an arm down to reach for my

discarded jeans on the floor. She pulls out the condom and catches me smiling as she tears it open. "What?"

"I'm feeling victorious," I tell her. "It's such a turn on to watch the girl who lives to have the upper hand over me—and usually succeeds—let it all go because of my mouth."

"It's a really fantastic mouth when you're not using it for speaking," Maggie replies. Rolling toward me, she grabs my cock gently but firmly and I lie on my back and watch her roll the condom on. I'm holding my breath to keep from grunting at her touch.

I smile. She's back to the snark so soon after her orgasm. I guess I'll just have to give her another one. Once the condom is on, I flip her over so she's on her stomach. I lean over her and kiss her shoulder. "Huh. You weren't lying. Your ass isn't freckled."

I give it a gentle swat.

"You are a son of—" I grab her hips and pull her up to her knees before she can finish that insult.

She knows exactly what I want now and tilts her hips and arches her back—ready and eagerly waiting. I put a hand on her hip and guide myself into her. She inhales sharply, still sensitive from her orgasm, I'm sure, so I promise myself I will go slow. But I'm surrounded by slick heat, still pulsing from her release, and I grunt.

"Maggie, fuck me," I groan and my hips snap. She huffs out a sharp breath.

"This position is all about *you* fucking *me*, Tate, not the other way around," she replies and rolls her hips. "Now get to it."

I grab both hips and give her what she demands. I know I won't be able to keep this up too long. She's too tight and too wet. I'm going to come quick and hard, so I pump harder and drop forward, blanketing her back with my chest and moving one hand to her breasts and the other to her clit. She whimpers when my fingers gently pinch her nipple and then again, louder, when my thumb rubs her clit.

Her hips start keeping rhythm with my thrusts, and when I

can't fight it anymore I groan and come, softly biting her shoulder as I do.

"Tate…" She's said my name a million times and I've always wished she hadn't. But when she moans it…hell I could hear that all day. She falls forward, facedown on the bed and I fall on top of her, my face buried in her hair, my lips kissing the nape of her neck.

We stay like that for a few minutes, naked in a tangled heap, until finally she whispers. "You're heavy."

I grin and roll off. She scoots, belly down, to the edge of the bed and grabs her dress. I'm suddenly very aware—and very sad —that it's over. And now it's starting to feel awkward as the reality of what we did—again—sets in. I clear my throat, get off the bed and grab my pants and underwear. I head into her bathroom and clean up, tossing the condom in her trash can. When I come back out to find my shirt, she's got her bra and dress back on and she's yanking her undies up those perfect legs. I stop and admire the view.

"Don't do that," she says firmly. "Don't look at me like you're turned on."

"But I am." I shrug.

She smiles, clearly happy with that, even though she doesn't want to be. "You hate me, remember?"

"You hate me too," I remind her as I walk over and stop directly in front of her, reaching up and gently smoothing her hair which has that just-been-fucked tousle to it. "But for some godforsaken reason you're turned on by me too. Personality-wise we might be oil and water but sexually, we're…"

"Goat cheese and caramelized onion?" She suggests and I frown. "What? It works really well together. You want a guaranteed mouthgasm, try it."

"I'll stick with the other kind of 'gasm, thanks," I say and bend to grab my shirt off the floor. But I don't put it on right away because I'm enjoying the way her eyes keep sweeping over my chest and torso. "Anyway, we definitely know how to push each other's buttons sexually. I'll be honest, I've never had hotter sex."

"Me either," Maggie admits easily, which I wasn't expecting. She sighs. "It's because we hate each other. We're not trying to impress each other, we're both just trying to get off."

"Probably," I reply but honestly, I'm not so sure it's that simple. I really wish it was though.

"Put on your shirt, Tate," she demands.

"Why? You scared you're going to jump my bones again?" I ask with a grin. She laughs.

"You wish." She gives me a little shove with her hand in the center of my chest and I slap my own hand over it and keep it there. Now the awkwardness is being pushed out of the atmosphere in the room and lust is making its way back in.

Until her damn phone rings from inside her book bag. She pulls her hand away and scurries out into the hall to retrieve it. I finish getting dressed and wander out to find her standing there with a scowl on her face and the phone a couple inches from her ear because the person on the other end is yelling. It's her grandfather. I can hear him like he's standing in the room.

"Is this what you and that sister of yours think is good business?" he's screaming.

"It was a gamble. Sometimes in business you have to take risks, Clyde," Maggie replies, through gritted teeth. She wants to tell him to fuck off, but she can't. I wish I could.

"You're the one who wanted this fall market so bad and you're giving up a prime weekend. Because you were too stupid to win a bet," Clyde barks. "Another perfect example of why I should sell the farm. It would be better off in someone else's hands. Someone with some business sense."

"Tell him you'll get the weekend back," I whisper and she glares at me.

"You're not being fair, Clyde. It was Daisy and my idea to switch from cow milk to goat and we've improved our profit margin. And we've got other expansion plans that are built around a solid business plan and you know it," Maggie argues back. "But if you still want to sell the farm to someone instead of keeping it in the family, I'll talk to the Adlers and see if they want to buy it."

She punches end and drops the phone on top of her bag, still in the middle of the hall where she let it fall when I threw her over my shoulder. I watch her lean against the wall and run her hands through her bed head. Her eyes catch mine and I give her a soft smile. "We can't afford to buy your farm but thanks for thinking of us."

She lets out a soundless laugh. "I know. Hank and Daisy are close. He's said you guys are...tight on cashflow at the moment."

I tense and decide to change the subject. "It's cute, though, that my family is the ultimate threat."

She gives me a smile but it's flat and there's no humor in it. "I'm sure it would be the same in your house."

"Probably. I'll have to try it out sometime," I reply. She looks so down, I don't like it. "He shouldn't talk to you like that."

"He's been doing it since we were...well, born," Maggie says quietly. "We're not special. He talks to Ben, Bobby and my dad like that too. It's really hard not to hate that man."

"So hate him," I reply.

She looks at me with pain swimming in her hazel eyes. "He's the only grandfather that I've got. Mom's dad died when we were little and my dad's mom...she took off when my dad was still in diapers."

"If Clyde was like that to her, I don't blame her."

"She left her babies behind," Maggie says angrily. "That doesn't make her a saint by any means."

"You have no idea where she is? You don't want to hear her side?" I can't help but ask and walk over and stuff my hands in my pockets because I'm fighting the urge to pull her into a hug.

"Why did you get all tense when I brought up Hank?" Maggie asks, changing the subject so abruptly I blink.

"We're talking about you."

"*You're* talking about my personal business and I've decided I'd rather talk about yours," Maggie replies. "Didn't you and Hank used to be close? I remember before you went away for high school you hung out with him more than Jace."

"So you used to stalk me is what you're saying." I make a joke because I don't want to talk about the guilt I feel regarding Hank with anyone. "Firecracker, at some point if Clyde keeps disrespecting you, you should stand up for yourself. You and Daisy are working your tails off for that farm and it's clear you know what you're doing. He shouldn't get to berate you all the time."

Maggie looks confused by my kind words. Right. I'm supposed to hate her. I forgot. So I try and backtrack a little. "I mean, I'm going above and beyond for my family farm. Working in my free time instead of enjoying the perks of a full-ride and hockey stardom. If any of my family talked to me like that, repeatedly, I would walk away."

Maggie pulls herself off the wall and stares at me with a look of brutal honesty on her determined features. "Easy to do when you've got a solid shot at something else—a pro hockey career. Daisy and I have nothing but this farm. It's different."

She grabs her bag and phone off the floor and walks past me back toward her bedroom. I follow. "I do have that. But the farm has always been my end game. It's where I want to retire, and for a hockey player, even the best hockey player, that usually happens before forty."

She drops her bag on her desk chair and puts her phone down on the desk before turning to face me. "But you could sell your current farm and buy another one when you're ready to retire from hockey. And support your entire family in the meantime. You get drafted and the world is your oyster. Daisy and I only have this little chunk of land. We have to get Clyde to sell it to us or leave it to us. There's no backup plan."

"I'm not saying it's not a hard situation to be in, but he shouldn't treat you like that, Maggie," I say softly. "You're a good granddaughter and a great farmer."

"Shut up," she says softly. "Please don't start being nice."

"Also, as you know from your uncle's experience, getting drafted doesn't mean I'm instantly on easy street," I remind her because her uncle was drafted and never set a skate on NHL ice. The most he probably made a year was fifty grand which is good for a farm team player but not exactly set-for-life money.

Maggie isn't letting this NHL thing go. "Are you going to enter the draft this summer?"

I nod.

"Then you'll leave school and have real money by next year." She pauses and looks stressed about something. "But if you end up drafted by a team on the other side of the country, you may end up wanting to settle there. Why bother holding on to a farm here? And does your family even want to keep farming? Does Jace?"

"I don't think farming is Jace's first choice but it's not his last either," I say about my brother. "And for the record, even if I'm drafted, I'm not leaving school. I want a degree. It's important to me. My family wants me to drop out early, but I'm not going to... if I can help it."

She just stares at me. Her mind is spinning, I can see it in her eyes, but I don't know why what I've said has got her so concerned. I think of what she said earlier. "So Hank is hanging out with Daisy?"

"They talk when she runs into him. They've always been friendly." Maggie shrugs but then sees the concern on my face and elaborates. "He didn't gossip about anything we didn't already know, about your family and farm, I mean. The whole town knows you had issues with your new trees last year and then the barn thing."

"Yeah." I grab my shirt off the floor. "I should get going. Can you print those notes?"

My shirt goes over my head, blocking my face but I can hear her move and then I feel her hands on the sides of my torso as the shirt slips down and she's right in front of me. "I'm sorry. I didn't mean to upset you."

I can't help but flash her a wry smile and repeat her own words from a few minutes ago. "Shut up. Please don't start being nice."

She lets out a soft laugh and blushes yet again and it makes me grab her waist and kiss her. Slow and gentle like we're new lovers…which we aren't. We can't be. So I let her go and try to look like it's no big deal. "Can you print those notes?"

"I'll email them to you," Maggie replies with a smile.

I raise an eyebrow. "Was this all just a ruse to get me into your house so you could take advantage of me?"

"Honestly, no," Maggie replies with a shy smile. "But I've never had two orgasms back-to-back so I feel like you deserve a reward."

I grin and now I want to kiss her again, but I fight the urge. "So you admit, I'm the best you've ever had."

"Biggest ego…among other things," Maggie says and God she's gorgeous when she's smiling. "Now give me your email address and get the hell out of here before one of my roommates comes home."

We walk to the front door and as I grab my knapsack off the floor and shove my feet in my shoes, I give her my email. She punches some stuff on her phone and then reaches for the front door as my own phone pings. "Sent. Let me know if you have any questions."

"Yes ma'am," I say with a wink.

"Do *not* ma'am me," she warns.

"Okay, Firecracker." I want to kiss her again so I do, but only on the cheek. "You know if you ever want to double your pleasure again, I'd be game."

"This was supposed to be a one-time thing," she says flatly. "A way to take out our aggression and stress without killing each other."

"And it happened twice, so we're not good with the math part.

I think maybe if it happens a few more times it might benefit us both," I say casually. But really, I feel a lot more than casual about this. I want to have more sex with her. In fact I need it. "We both have a lot of stress to work out."

"You're not wrong," Maggie replies, surprising me but also making me incredibly happy. "I mean, if the opportunity presents itself again and the urge strikes, I won't say no. But no one can ever know. You in my bed is more than enough reason for Clyde to make good on his threats and sell the farm to someone else."

"And George would disown me. Jace might too, and the last thing I need is more shit to deal with," I add. "So yeah, I'm good with keeping this quiet. *If* it happens again."

"If…" she repeats firmly. "Now get out before someone comes home."

Maggie opens the front door and basically shoves me out. I smile the whole way down the stairs because I can feel her watching me as I go, probably checking out my ass. As I walk outside I pull up the email Maggie sent.: *Notes attached. You're welcome.* But she's included her phone number at the bottom, something I didn't have before.

Yeah…there is no "if" about it. This thing with us *will* happen again.

12

MAGGIE

I wipe my brow. I'm sweaty and stinky and just want to finish the chores on the farm so I can get home. Daisy and I have plans with Caroline and Jasmyn to go to the outdoor movie night, and I can't wait...because I know Tate will be there.

"Hey! Mags, Daze, come and see what I've been working on," Bobby calls out, and we make our way out of the goat enclosure. Ben has the goats in the milking building with Dad and Mom right now and Bobby has been working on our prototype.

We make our way down around the back of the farmhouse, behind the extension we built off the back years ago, where Clyde lives. There, behind a line of tall firs, where no one can see it from the road or the drive, is what Bobby calls Beatrice. Beatrice is a shipping container. But Bobby has been slowly and steadily working on turning her into a tiny, self-contained hotel style suite.

We both walk through the opening in the industrial plastic he has at one end and I immediately gasp. Daisy squeals. "Holy crap, it's amazing Bobby!"

I nod in agreement because words have escaped me as I look around the interior. All the walls and the ceiling, which for the past month have been nothing but metal, have been covered in drywall and the metal floor is now reclaimed wood. There are even pot lights recessed into the ceiling drywall. Bobby smiles proudly. "And that's not all."

He walks over to the wall opposite where we came in and flips a switch. The pot lights come on. Daisy squeals again and jumps up and down while I clap. "Bobby this is incredible!"

"We're not done, but we're close. And those lights are running off the solar panels I put on the roof last week," Bobby explains. "This is hands down my favorite part of working on the farm again."

"Fantastic!" Daisy exclaims and bends down and touches the wood floors.

"I still got to seal 'em," Bobby explains as Daisy touches the floorboards. "Wanted you girls to weigh in on whether I should sand off the paint first or not."

I squat next to Daisy and take a closer look. Some of the planks do have a faded red paint on them. Like the color of an old red barn. And some have a few darker marks...like burn marks. I glance back up at Bobby. "Where is this wood from?"

Bobby's grin grows devious and he looks so much like my dad. A broader, more muscular version because Bobby still has his hockey body, mostly. My dad only played hockey occasionally as a kid, was never serious about it like Bobby, and he is shorter and leaner than Bobby and Ben, but they share the same sandy hair and blue eyes that crinkle in the corners when they smile or laugh. And just like my dad, Bobby gets twitchy when he's avoiding a question.

"It's from a barn," Bobby tells me with a shrug and then he crosses and uncrosses his arms. "So sand off the paint or no?"

"I'd keep it. We can match the décor to it," Daisy says simply. "Add a red quilt or some throw pillows."

"Did you get it at the hardware store? Because I've never seen—"

"I didn't steal it...technically." Bobby says and suddenly his eyes are looking everywhere but my face.

"Bobby says he didn't steal the barn wood, he didn't steal it,"

Daisy says, annoyed. "And I agree, if someone leaves something on the side of the road…"

"Adler…" I whisper and I think of Tate and then I think of the sex…and give my head a shake and try again. His barn…with the one wall that had been burned during the cider press fire. My eyes go wide and I point at Bobby but before I can say anything he explodes.

"I didn't steal it. I was by the property line trying to wrangle Crockett and Tubbs. You know they're total escape artists and they were sneaking around by the fence, and I didn't want them to end up on the Adler property because George would shoot 'em," Bobby explains about two of our Angora goats. We have fourteen and just like all our other goats, they're named after television or book characters. Crockett and Tubbs are characters from some show Bobby loved as a kid called *Miami Vice*. "Anyway I heard Louise yelling at Vince to take the damaged barn wood to the dump and he yelled back he was busy and he told Jace to do it. So I snuck over there a couple nights ago, and low and behold the wood was still there. No one had taken it to the dump. So I just decided to get rid of it for them."

"Do they know you took it?" I can't help but ask.

"Nah. I think Vince probably thinks Jace finally took it to the dump and Jace probably thinks Vince did and George probably thinks Louise did," Bobby says. "They have a serious communication problem over there."

I feel bad, but I know Bobby is right. Tate probably wouldn't care that we had it and he's the only Adler whose opinion matters to me. I sigh. "Fine. Whatever. It does look really amazing, Bobby."

"Thank you," he smiles again. "Next up are the windows and door."

He points to the plastic opening we came in through.

"Don't steal those from the Adlers too," I quip.

He rolls his eyes but I feel a little flutter of excitement. This is really happening. But that flutter quickly sputters and drops from my belly to my sneakers. We're going to have our first, fully functional, eco-friendly cabin for a property we don't own, that the Adlers do not want to give up. That used to be something I didn't think about, but now I do. Because I've seen Tate naked. And liked it.

"Also the composting toilet gets here tomorrow, if the Amazon package tracker thingy is right," Bobby says and motions for us to follow him around the false wall he built at one end of the rectangular room.

He's already tiled the entire bathroom in these great oversized slate gray tiles. The walk-in shower is huge. And the vanity is an old dresser with a bowl sink on top and it's perfect. "Bobby you've really outdone yourself."

"Ben helped with the tiling," Bobby says and grins. "We're on budget so far and I don't see any hiccups, so this experiment is gonna be a winner, Mags. Now we just need the land for this. And the thingy you guys are working on for the bank."

"The business plan," Daisy says and pats his head like he's a toddler. "We're working on it ...but first the Adler's have to put it on the market, or the bank does."

Bobby nods and I feel squirmy inside. "Any more intel on that?"

"Well, I went to see Hank again," Daisy says. "Actually I went to get more hot wings. God they have the best sauce I have ever had, and Hank was there and we talked again. Anyway, he says he heard from Jace that they're a month behind on the mortgage and the bank sent them a warning letter already."

"What?" I say it way too loud to be normal and Daisy picks up on that immediately.

"They gotta be thinking about throwing in the towel," Daisy says.

"Can we not..." I mutter and turn to head out of the container.

"Not what?" Daisy asks. "Talk business?"

"Gossip about the misfortune of other people," I reply and

jump down out of the container home, which we have on blocks so it doesn't kill the grass.

"It's not other people, it's the Adlers," Daisy says following me out into the sunshine. Bobby is trailing behind her. "The family that took Rascal to the pound fourteen times last year because she wandered onto their property."

Daisy and her stupid cat. But she had a point. They knew who Rascal, our Maine Coon, belonged to and that cats wander. That's what they do.

Bobby nods even though he doesn't give a rat's patoot about that cat. "And let's not forget the time Vince got drunk at the town fair and tried to sucker punch me."

"Because you were hitting on his ex-wife and she'd only been an ex for like a month or something at that point," I remind him as the wind picks up and I notice Ben is herding the goats back into the pens with Clyde, who is swearing at them.

"Tanya was hitting on me," Bobby replies with a shrug and then a furrowed brow. "And why are you defending an Adler?"

I pull out my phone and look at the time. "Daisy, we gotta head back if we're going to make the outdoor movie night. I need to shower first."

"Okay," Daisy says and sprints ahead of me. "I'm driving. You're all emo or something and I don't want you driving us into a tree."

I roll my eyes at her dramatics. Bobby walks us to our car. "Who is hosting the movie night?"

Bobby asks because he used to go to Moo U and they did the movie nights when he was there too. "This time it's the hockey team," I say as I climb in.

"And they're showing *Slap Shot*? *Mighty Ducks*?"

"*Goon*," I reply.

"Nice choice." Bobby smiles. "Don't end up in Adler's popcorn line. He'll likely poison the butter topping."

Daisy laughs and I fight a frown. I'm my own worst enemy. I don't want anyone to know about me and Tate but I'm the one who can't keep a poker face. Daisy and I drive in silence the entire way back to the apartment. She stops on the porch, which is shared by all four apartments, to check the mail. We're usually very bad at that since none of us usually get any important mail of any kind, but Daisy has been relentless about checking for about a week now. She even checks it on Sundays when we aren't getting mail in case there was a late delivery Saturday evening.

Today she pulls a bunch of flyers out of the mailbox and a ubiquitous white envelope. I unlock the door and we climb the stairs to our third floor apartment and as I swing open the door at the top of the stairs Daisy speaks. "Oh my God! It's here! I got it!"

"What?" I ask.

"The ancestry site. They've sent me my preliminary results!"

"They're back already?" I ask as I walk into the front hall, and she shuts the door behind the two of us and waves the envelope in my face.

"Yes!" Daisy is so excited she's bouncing, and her high-pitched tone gets Caroline to wander out of the living room.

"What's up?" she asks, still holding her textbook and wearing her glasses.

Daisy explains she got the DNA results back. Caroline puts down her book and grabs the envelope from her and tears it open. She reads the piece of paper inside as Daisy and I stare at her. "Congratulations, you're forty-five percent Irish, twelve percent English, fifteen percent Scottish and—"

"What about living relatives? Any matches?"

Caroline hands back the paper. "You have to log in online for that info."

Daisy snatches the paper from her and heads to her room, and no doubt directly to her laptop to pull up the site. I walk in the other direction toward my own room but call over my shoulder, "I'm leaving in twenty minutes whether you guys are with me or not!"

"I'll be ready in fifteen," Caroline calls back.

She scurries off to her room as I walk into mine and start

peeling off my clothes. My only thoughts, as much as I hate to admit it, are of Tate. I think about him all the time, which is scaring me a little. He's not my boyfriend. In fact he's nothing but an accidental hookup who is open to the idea of repeating the mistake, and that's what I am to him. I have no idea how to be that person, which is probably why I am obsessing over it.

I've had two boyfriends so far in my life, which isn't bad for nineteen if you ask me. There was my high school boyfriend, Austen. We broke up three weeks after prom, and I went through the whole sobbing and eating ice cream out of the container thing like you're supposed to when you lose your first love. But by the end of the summer, when Austen went off to school in Upstate New York, I was over him completely.

And there was Dylan, who I dated very on and very off last year. I wouldn't even say we broke up. We just kind of faded out of each other's lives. I stopped calling. He stopped coming by. And then it was summer and he went back home to White Plains. He's back this year. I saw him at the library the first week of school, and we said hi but that was it. I wasn't broken up and neither was he.

And I've gone on a bunch of dates—mostly bad ones, like the cop who told me about Clyde's arrest—but nothing remotely serious. And nothing as remotely trivial as random hate sex. I wasn't sure how to do something so meaningless. Was meaningless supposed to feel so…meaningful?

Anyway, I was totally winging this but I figured ignoring him was the right thing to do, so that's what I did the one time I have seen him in the last four days, which was in class. I made sure to sit as far away from him as possible and leave before he even got out of his seat when class was over. I didn't want to be that needy girl who hangs around hoping he'll stop and talk to me.

As I get out of the shower and towel dry my hair, I hear my phone ping from where I'd plugged it in to charge on my night table. I walk over and glance at it and see it's an email alert. "Speak of the devil," I whisper as I drop down onto my bed and pick up the phone. It's Tate. He got my email address when I sent him the notes from class.

Firecracker, just wanna know if you're going to movie night?

I email him back. Just one word—*yup*—and then go about getting ready, pretending that I'm not holding my breath waiting for his response. Does he want me to go? Is he checking so he can avoid me or run into me? Why do I care so much? Ugh!

"Maggie! You ready?" Daisy calls from the hall.

"Just a sec!" I call back and as I slip into my shoes my phone pings again and I bite my lip in anticipation as I pick it up.

I'm working the concession stand left of the screen before the show. Find me.

I smile but type back, *Bossy, much?*

I tuck my phone into my back pocket and leave my room. Daisy and Caroline are waiting impatiently in the hall. "Finally!"

"Why do you look so cute?" Caroline wants to know. "It's an outdoor movie."

"I look cute?" I repeat and stare down at my outfit. It's a little chilly tonight so I put on a fuzzy gray kitten sweater and my favorite jeans, with my favorite suede booties. I did spend a little extra time on makeup and let my damp hair air dry so it waves a little...because Tate seems to like it down and wavy. Umm, I mean... I did it because I had it up all day so down is a nice change anyway.

Caroline looks down at her own ripped jeans, hoodie and sneakers and Daisy has her hair piled up in her trademark "study bun" and she's in a Disney sweatshirt with leggings. "You are looking pretty sexy for spending the night sitting on the grass in the dark with us."

"I spent all day in a pen cleaning up goat poop," I explain. "Sorry if I wanted to take it up a notch. Let's go."

I am so eager to get to the event now I basically power walk the entire way there, going so fast that Caroline complains and Daisy makes a snarky remark about how she got her workout in for the week. We pay the entrance fee and walk into the grassy quad where everything is set up. Lots of people have beaten us here and the grass is fairly full. We pick a part toward the back, and as Caroline and Daisy start to spread out the giant blanket they brought, I volunteer to go get snacks, my treat. They're so excited I'm paying they don't even question it, they just start calling out what they want.

I make my way to the stand on the left of the screen and before I even step in line, I see him. He's smiling at a group of girls as he hands them three large bags of popcorn. I try not to feel anything when I look at him but I feel *everything*. It's got to be my hormones and nothing else. I mean, I can't actually like him.

He takes a ten from one of the girls and his head dips as he makes changed out of the little metal box in front of him. One of his teammates is serving someone beside him and finishes up first. He waves me over and I hesitate. I can't say I'm waiting for Tate. I don't know what I can say.

"Maggie right?" the teammate says. "I'm Jonah. What can I get you?"

"I'll handle her needs," Tate chimes in and glances up as he hands the girls in front of him their change. "She's a difficult customer and I'm better at handling the ornery ones than you are, Daniels."

Jonah looks confused but just shrugs and waves over the guy behind me. I walk up to Tate who has a cocky grin all over his face. I cross my arms and cock an eyebrow.

"It's cute that you just labeled me a bad customer because I can't recall ever buying a thing from you before," I say like I'm thinking really hard about it. "Last year you weren't working the concession stand at the team movie night. It was that total hottie that graduated. What was his name? Mike...Danvers. Oh man he knew just the right amount of butter to put on my popcorn."

Jonah laughs, clearly eavesdropping. Tate frowns—hard. I bite the inside of my cheek to keep my smile from blowing up my face. And then I pretend to fan myself for added effect.

"I've been told that I'm more than adequate at buttering a

woman's popcorn," Tate says defensively. "Tell you what? If you're not fully satisfied with the way I butter your popcorn, you can come right back and I'll do it again. And again. I'll do it until you're completely satisfied."

Damn him. My face explodes with color. Now Jonah and the guy he was serving are both looking at us like we're insane. I dip my head, hoping my hair blocks my beet red face from their view and make sure my tone is unbothered. "Actually, you know what? Butter is bad for you, so just give me two large plain popcorns and two packs of Reese's Pieces. Thanks."

"Sometimes we need a little of the things that are bad for us. Sometimes they're fun," Tate replies casually. "And I know you're a total stick in the mud, but I'm going to give you a little butter anyway. It might loosen you up."

Oh my God I hate him, I hate that his snark, which used to make me itch with annoyance, now makes me flush with desire. What sorcery is this, Universe? I fight to remain passive and nonchalant. "Whatever, Tater Tot."

"Tater Tot?" Jonah repeats as a girl walks up to be served next.

I nod. "Yeah. I grew up on the farm beside Tate's. His child-hood nickname is Tater Tot."

"No one but you ever called me that," Tate replies as he scoops my popcorn and glances at Jonah. "She was mad because in fourth grade I started calling her Maggot instead of Maggie."

"Tater Tot is cute. I like it," the girl in line says and she grins at Tate like he's Bradley Cooper or some such nonsense.

"It's because he was about as useful and intelligent as a fried ball of grated potato," I explain to her. And when she looks at me I give a little point toward Tate's pants in a subtle, not so subtle way, and continue talking in a stage whisper. "Also...down there. Tater tot."

Jonah bursts out laughing. Tate looks like he's been shot. I toss a ten on the table and grab my stuff and leave. "Thanks for the exceptional service, Tater Tot."

That did not go as planned and with every step I walk away

from him back to my sister and my friends, I get more and more upset. I don't know why I had to insult his manhood. I mean, it's probably a good thing. It's what Maggie who hasn't seen him naked would do, so at least I didn't blow my cover. Go me?

"Why do you look like your dog died?" Caroline asks as I approach the blanket she's sitting on with Daisy.

"Tate was working the concession," I mumble and add in my head *and I think I totally screwed up any chances at a booty call tonight.*

"Ah. The arch nemesis with the killer smirk and to-die-for body," Caroline says, taking one of the popcorns from me as soon as I plop down between them on the blanket. "Yes. What a hardship. Your mortal enemy is total eye candy."

"What did he do?" Daisy wants to know, but before I can figure out a half-baked lie to tell because I can't say, "he made innuendos about the double orgasms he gave me," she turns to Caroline. "Yeah. He's superficially attractive but he isn't exactly a great person. He used to call Maggie Maggot in grade school and me Doody instead of Daisy. Which everyone bought into and it sucked."

"The horror." Caroline doesn't seem to be taking it seriously, but Daisy is right. It did actually make us leave school crying more than a few times. And the universe is clearly drilling that into my brain since it's the second time in ten minutes that awful memory has come up. "Maybe he's changed."

"Not according to Alisha Knowles. He's just gotten worse," Daisy says and my spine stiffens.

"Who the hell is Alisha Knowles?" I ask as Daisy steals a piece of popcorn and looks down into the bag and frowns. I pull one of the packs of Reese's Pieces out of my pocket and she grins. We always mix them into popcorn.

"Alisha was in my Farm to Table class last year. Nice girl but a little...unfocused. She really came to college just to party," Daisy says and rips open the candy package and dumps it into the popcorn. "She hooked up with Tate last year at the Halloween party the hockey team had at their house."

"The one where he was dressed up in that Eeyore costume and still managed to look hot?" Caroline says smiling. I'd like to say I hadn't noticed, but you couldn't not notice. I remember being annoyed he looked hot.

"Yeah. Well Alisha says that they hooked up that night, and he took her out a few times after that but then suddenly ghosted her." Daisy takes the popcorn from me and gives it a shake so the candy disperses. "Like he was supposed to meet her at a fancy restaurant. He planned it. And then he didn't show up and when she saw him the next day, he pretended he didn't know who she was. For real. Like 'Do I know you?'"

"Brutal," I whisper because it is. And it makes me very disappointed in him.

"Maggie, please say you got drinks too," Caroline says, changing the subject.

"I forgot drinks," I mutter and sigh. "You go get them."

Caroline groans. Daisy pops up. "I'll do it. But I didn't bring my wallet so lend me some cash."

I sigh and stand up. "I'll be right back. Getting drinks is easier than giving you my wallet."

"Hurry back," Daisy calls but then someone calls her name and she turns her head and waves at them, forgetting me completely.

I purposely stand in line for the stand Tate isn't at, the one on the other side of the screen. I make it all the way to the front of the line before he notices me. I pretend I don't see him looking at me while I order from another guy on the team. I order three cans of Coke, and as the hockey player digs them out of the cooler behind him, I think of Daisy's story. Would that be my fate too if Tate and I were actually dating? Is he really a guy who does that? I have no reason to not believe this Alisha girl's story. Does it even matter? I will never end up like Alisha because I can't date Tate...but do I want to keep getting naked with a guy who does that to girls?

He hands me the Cokes and I pay and turn and leave. The urge to look at Tate one last time is overwhelming so I glance over my shoulder. Turns out he's been staring at me and as our eyes connect, he jumps the counter and starts toward me.

I keep walking like I didn't notice but the fact is my gait slows so that he can catch up with me quicker. "I have a tater tot sized penis? Really Maggie?"

I shrug. "You were picking on me in front of your buddy."

"By saying you needed butter? So you go straight for the tiny penis lie?" Tate counters still walking along beside me. The place is now packed with people, so we're moving around them and stepping over them as we go. As soon as we get a couple more feet, Daisy and Caroline will be in sight—and vice versa—so I stop walking.

"It was a joke," I say simply.

"Not a joke, a lie," Tate replies. "Jokes are funny and I know you know my penis is no laughing matter."

My cheeks heat. "Neither is your ego. Besides, what are you going to do about it? Ghost me?"

"What?" Tate blinks and shakes his head in confusion. "I would never ghost you. But if you can't remember much about my penis, maybe you need me to remind you why it's no laughing matter."

"No. I mean. I don't know what I need, to be honest with you," I confess, my eyes darting up to the darkening sky in frustration.

"Where are you sitting?" His fingers wrap around my wrist for a millisecond. I look at him. The moon, which is full and bright, is glimmering in his mossy eyes and accentuating his full mouth and angular jaw, which has a little bit of stubble on it. That's new. Tate is usually clean-shaven. I immediately want the chafe of the five o'clock shadow on my lips and my neck and my breasts and my…

But he's not a good person…is he?

"Maggie. Where are your friends?" he repeats more firmly.

"About twenty-five paces to the left, near that large fir." I point, and his head turns to follow.

"Deliver them the drinks, watch fifteen minutes of the movie and then excuse yourself to go to the bathroom. Bring your phone."

"Excuse me?" I blink.

"Then meet me behind the Museum," Tate continues. "You can text Daisy from there and tell her you went home or ran into someone or went to get food or something and you'll meet her after the movie."

"Why?"

"So we can sneak back to my place and I can remind you exactly why that tater tot comment was stupid," Tate replies casually like he isn't propositioning me.

"I can't just take off like that," I reply for some stupid reason. I came here with the hopes of doing exactly that. And Daisy gets really into movies. She won't even notice or care and Caroline usually falls asleep in them, so she won't mind either. "It's too risky."

"It's worth it and you know it," Tate replies and without another word walks away.

That arrogant, cocky, annoying pain in my non-freckled ass. I stomp my way back to Daisy and Caroline. I sigh and want to kick myself because despite all my concern and confusion and the rumors and the risk, I know without a shadow of a doubt I'll be behind the museum later.

13
TATE

It takes twenty minutes—not fifteen—but she meets me by the museum just like I demanded. If someone gave me an NHL contract right now, it would probably only feel slightly better than seeing her walk toward me. Every time Maggie Todd does what I want it's a victory beyond measure because the word stubborn was invented for this girl. She doesn't look as happy as I hoped she would as she approaches, though.

I glance behind her to make sure no one else is around that would take notice of us, and then I wink at her and turn and walk toward the path that goes around the museum to the path that leads off campus. We walk in silence, an acceptable distance apart until we reach those gates. Colchester street is basically dead. No cars zipping by, no one out on the front porches of the massive, well-spaced houses. Everyone is in town or at the movie, so I let my hand graze hers and our shoulders bump softly as we continue down the street.

"I really shouldn't be doing this," she says barely above a whisper.

"Then why are you?"

"Because I'm…I don't know…bored?" She sighs.

"Ouch." I am actually a little hurt by that. She sounds exasperated and annoyed. Like she desperately wished she had something better to do.

"It's just...we both know we don't like each other, right?" Maggie declares as we turn the corner to the street where the hockey house is located. "If we keep doing this, the oxytocin might confuse the facts, and we can't get confused. I can't."

"I'm not confused by anything," I reply, and I'm happy that despite her apparent emotional conflict she's still walking down the path that leads to my front door. "What did you tell Daisy when you left?"

We climb the stairs to the porch. "I didn't have to say much. She saw Hank and some other people she knew and wandered over to sit with them for a bit. Caroline was talking to the girls beside us, so I just said I saw someone from my accounting class I wanted to talk to and would be back later. As usual, no one really goes to these things for the crappy movies."

"*Goon* is a cinematic masterpiece," I reply with a straight face and I manage to get a fleeting grin from her. I slip the key in the door, my eyes scanning the yard and street as I turn it and push the door open. No one in sight so I slip my arm around her waist and pull her inside.

The door swings closed behind us and I turn so we're toe-to-toe. She looks so...conflicted. It's like throwing cold water on my libido. If she really doesn't want to be here, I'm not going to throw myself at her. I shove my hands in the front pockets of my jeans. I'm wearing my hockey jersey. It was mandatory so everyone knew who was working the event. She reaches out and touches the shoulder of it, letting her hand trail down my arm. It feels like a goodbye, which weirds me out. I don't like it. "What is going on with you?"

"Do you know Alisha Knowles?" Maggie says and it's like skating across the ice on a breakaway and losing an edge. Unexpected and unwanted wipeout.

"Why?" I ask trying not to sound defensive.

"You know her? She's in Food Science with Daisy," Maggie says and crosses her arms.

"If she's friends with Daisy then she's told Daisy I know her," I reply and flip on the light in the hall. The old seventies chandelier flickers and floods the space with yellow light. It's harsh, but so is everything else suddenly. "Don't ask around the question you have Maggie. Just ask."

"You dated her?"

I frown but give her a sharp nod. "Yeah. And she probably slammed me to Daisy right? And Daisy couldn't wait to tell you, and probably anyone else who would listen, because that's what Todds do to Adlers."

"Whoa. Wait a minute. Do not attack my sister," Maggie says sharply and I start up the stairs. She follows, but out of anger not passion. Not what I was hoping when this night started. "And yeah this girl didn't have positive stories about you, but that's not her fault. If they're true, that's your fault."

I stop on the landing to the first floor and she comes to a halt on the last stair. "Of course you don't give me the benefit of the doubt, do you? That's fine. For the record, Maggie, this thing between us is no strings attached. That's how bed buddies work, so I don't need to explain to you my dating history, and you don't need to tell me yours."

I start walking down the hall toward the next staircase, which leads up to my room and at first I don't think she's going to follow me, but then I hear her move.

"I don't know how this works because you're the first enemy I've had sex with," Maggie blurts out as she stomps along beside me. "And clearly you don't know how dating someone works if you stand them up after months of seeing each other and then pretend you don't know who they are and humiliate them."

Humiliation. She doesn't know the half of it. I stop at the foot of the staircase and turn to face her slowly, trying to figure out how much of the flaming rancid mess that was my relationship with Alisha I should explain to Maggie. I'm infuriated that this has come up and I have to think and talk about it at all. "Are we going to have sex? Because if not, why are you here? You could be watching the movie and listening to more gossip about me."

"Yeah. I should leave," Maggie snaps and when I turn around she's already making her way down the stairs.

I find myself following her. I want to stop her, but I also don't want to stop her. Maybe this is what needs to happen. I would stop feeling so conflicted if we stopped having sex. Right? Then I realize maybe that's what she wants. For me to walk away and she has controlled this whole situation from the start, so I'll be damned if I let her control this too. So as she reaches for the door handle on the front door I speak. "What happened with Alisha wasn't my finest moment."

She freezes but doesn't turn to face me. Staring straight ahead at the closed door, she sighs with disappointment. "So you did that? You just pretended you didn't know who she was?"

Maggie's tone has dropped from indignant to incredulous, which is almost comical. This girl didn't think much of me before, and now she's baffled that she can think even less of me.

"I did. And it was infantile and had I been in a better head-space, I probably would have handled it differently," I say. "Do you want to hear my side of the story?"

She nods slowly and turns to finally face me.

"Then come upstairs."

Her face is a mask of hesitation and doubt and my defenses start to rise again, but I beat them down. I don't know why…it's just sex. If she wants to walk out the door now then I can always just have sex with someone else. I'm no Chris Hemsworth, but I've never had a problem attracting women. Why does my gut— and my heart—want me to talk through this so badly?

"Did you watch our games last season?"

"I went to a couple games," she says, confused.

"Did you know I had a concussion? Kept me off the ice for twelve days?" I ask and she slowly nods.

"Yeah, I heard about it," Maggie replies. "Why are you changing the subject?"

"I'm not," I snap and then sigh. "I had been seeing Alisha for about a month when it happened. We weren't overly serious, but we weren't just bed buddies. It was something. I thought. She made it seem like it was too, but I had a lot going on when I was recovering. The barn caught fire. I had really bad headaches, double vision, and vertigo would come and go. They kept sending me for MRIs and wouldn't let me on the ice. I had trouble sleeping, and all I wanted was to be on the damn ice again, feeling normal."

"Makes sense," Maggie says without hesitation.

"I thought so too." I pause. "But Alisha took it personally. She said I was no fun anymore and kept pouting when I wouldn't go to parties or take her out."

"She told you that?"

"No." I shake my head. I really hate talking about it. "Hank told me that was what she said when she tried to get him to fool around with her."

I watch Maggie's mouth drop open in a soundless gasp. "She tried to sleep with Hank?"

"Yeah. She ran into him at a party when I was home with one of my concussion headaches," I explain.

"So you stood her up?"

"No. I stopped talking to her after he told me. I needed time to think," I say and lean against the railing staring down at her. "I knew I was going to break up with her, but I was trying to gather in my anger and humiliation so I could do it like an adult. She made the reservation at the restaurant, and I decided I would go and talk to her afterward. But I was dreading it, and confided in a teammate. The guy you called hot earlier tonight, Mike Danvers. And then he got this sick look on his face and told me she hit on him too…and he slept with her, because she said we'd broken up already. That's when I said fuck being an adult, stood her up and just decided to act like I'd never met her."

Maggie stares up at me through her thick lashes, her expression swirling with emotions as she tries to process everything I just said. I push off the railing and stand straight, shoulders back, owning my behavior and coming to terms with it at the same time. "Not my finest moment. But I did it and I can't change it. So anyway, I'll walk you back to the movie now."

I make my way down the rest of the stairs and as I reach for the front door, her phone rings from the back pocket of her jeans. She pulls it out and, after glancing at the screen, she puts it to her ear. "Hey Daisy. Yeah, no I'm fine. I ran into some friends from my business class and we went to get food. I just wasn't into *Goon*. I'll see you at home later."

She hangs up. She takes a small step toward me and tips her head up so our eyes lock. She looks gorgeous tonight, her hair loose and wavy like I like it. The sweater, the color of a thunder cloud, makes the pink that's always tinting her cheeks more pronounced. "Now you can't take me back to the movie."

"Okay... Do you want me to walk you home?" I ask, but she shakes her head.

"I owe you an apology, Tater Tot," Maggie replies with a small, guilty smile.

"For the small penis lie?" I ask and flash her a smirk.

She lets out a breathy laugh but it dies quickly and she bites her bottom lip like she's trying to figure out what she wants to tell me but can't. Finally she says, "I don't know if hearing your side of the story makes me feel better or worse. I was having a very hard time hating you and screwing you at the same time. If you'd just ghosted that girl for no reason, I felt like I couldn't sleep with you anymore."

"Because I would be a bad person," I say.

She nods and sighs lightly. "But the problem is I'm supposed to be able to hate you and sleep with you. That's been the plan since the beginning. So if I can't do both..."

"So you should probably stop doing one or the other," I say, but inside I feel crushing disappointment.

"You're right." Maggie nods and a chunk of her copper hair falls forward, clinging to her cheek.

I reach up and brush her hair back slowly, letting my fingers skim her cheek, because I think this might be the last time I get to do that. "So, I'll walk you home?"

She blinks, takes a deep breath. "Eventually."

And then she slides her arms around my neck and kisses me, her tongue pushing past my lips with passion and eagerness that makes me want to sigh with relief. I grab her around the waist and roughly pull her against me. When she breaks the kiss she moves her lips to my ear. "Take me upstairs."

"So you're picking screwing over hating?"

"I am," she replies.

I grab her hand in mine and lead her up the stairs.

"Did you lose a bet?" Maggie says as soon as we walk into my room. "This room is the size of a postage stamp."

"Basically, yeah," I say and walk over to my desk and turn on the string of white LED lights I have coiled around the window frame. It's not exactly romantic, but it's better than the night table light which is a bulb with no shade. "This coming from a girl who lives in a pig pen."

"Not my room and you know it," she responds defensively.

"But I did notice a bunch of flower pots and boxes with nothing but mud in them out on your balcony," I say, looking for anything that might counter the hobbit hole I live in. "For a farmer you sure can't grow flowers."

"That's your fault. I had my uncle go and raid my beautiful and lush container garden when you had the dunk tank at the market, so we could give away flowers with each purchase as an incentive," she tells me and looks positively bereft for a second. I can't believe she did that and I feel guilty until she adds, "Now every time I stare out at those empty containers I curse your family name."

"Great." I roll my eyes. "Because the Adlers need more bad luck."

"You can't even stand up in here unless you're standing right in the middle of the room." Maggie turns the conversation back to my bedroom as she tries to walk around without bending her head down and fails.

"It's cozy to say the least, but it's got everything we need."

I shift my gaze to the queen size mattress on a frame I made from old wood pallets, and wiggle my eyebrows when I look at her again. She laughs and tries to cover her blush with her hands but I gently pull them away and pull her to me. I kiss the side of her neck and feel her melt against me. Then I walk her backward until she hits the mattress with her calves. She drops back onto it, and I climb on top of her without waiting for an invitation. She doesn't seem to mind. She snakes her hands into my hair and pulls my mouth to hers.

We spend the next fifteen minutes making out and taking turns removing each other's clothing until I'm in only my boxer briefs and she's in just her jeans and underwear. And even though this is our third time together—in relatively quick succession—I'm amazed that my drive hasn't slowed. There's still this overpowering, urgent need for her that I had in the barn. After we've explored with fingers and mouths and tongues until the brink of bliss—repeatedly, but neither of us letting the other reach the final buzzer—I pull back from her. It's been twenty minutes of competitive foreplay and I have the endurance for more despite the fact my cock is ready to kill me, but the guys will be showing up as soon as the movie is over, and I don't want her to get caught here. So I pull my mouth from her.

I look down at her in the dim light. She looks like a freaking angel, pale and pink in all the right places as she's laid out naked on my bed. She doesn't notice me admiring her because she's busy admiring me as I reach, naked, for the condoms in the night table drawer. She watches, holding her breath, as I carefully roll the condom on. She sits up snaking a hand around my neck and bringing her lips to my collarbone. "Can I ride you?"

"You can do whatever you want to me," I reply in a voice dripping with lust.

Thirty seconds later my perfect, flushed little firecracker is sliding up and down on my cock, back arched so her perfect breasts are pressed into my palms and her left hand is snaking down her belly to her clit. Pleasure wants my eyes to roll back in my head and my lids to close, but my brain is fighting the urge because I don't want to miss a second of Maggie touching herself while she rides me.

"You're horrible for my stamina," I say through gulping breathes. "You make me want to go off too soon."

She smiles and clenches around me—hard. I groan so loud the neighbors might file a noise complaint. I sit up, holding myself up with one hand while I grab the back of her neck with the other and pull her into a hungry kiss. By the end of it she's whimpering into my mouth and coming around my dick so hard I can't help but join her.

I fall back, taking her with me and wrap my arms around her holding her to my chest as my heart tries to figure out what a normal rhythm is again. She nuzzles against my neck and sighs contentedly. "We're getting good at this."

I smirk. "True. I don't want to stop practicing though."

She giggles.

A couple minutes later I gently slide out of her and grab my shower towel off the hook on the back of my door and head to the bathroom a floor down to clean up. When I get back to my room, she's holding the sheets around her chest with one hand as she reaches over the side of the bed with the other to grab her clothes.

"You know you don't have to leave right away."

"What if your teammates come back?"

"We've got a little more time," I say as I drop my towel onto the floor and crawl back onto the bed between Maggie and the wall and lie down. I pat the space between us. "Lie back for a second and just enjoy the moment."

She falls back onto the bed. I move closer to her and she rolls over and rests her head on my shoulder so I curl my arm around her. It feels great to hold her like this. Really great. I press a soft kiss to the top of her head, breathing in that citrusy warm smell of her hair. "This feels good."

"It does." She takes a long slow breath in and lets it out. "I'm exhausted."

"So am I. I've had a long week so far, and it's just going to get longer," I murmur. "I have hockey practice tomorrow and I have to swing by the farm after class and I have a gig at my other job tomorrow night. Third one this week, which is great money-wise but sucks in every other respect."

"Did Alisha know about your job?" Maggie asks as she traces random designs across my bare chest with the tip of her finger.

"I hadn't actually started working there yet when we were together," I explain and close my eyes, enjoying the shiver her trailing finger is creating. "I had just heard about the company and was thinking about applying. I knew though that if I did go for it, I would never tell her."

Maggie is silent for a couple minutes, her finger still moving languidly. I think she might be writing something but I can't make it out. Finally she says in a somber tone. "I'm sorry she cheated on you. Especially while you were already dealing with so much."

"I'm not sorry," I reply quickly. "I guess I was at the time, but it was a blessing in disguise. She would have done it eventually, so I'm glad it happened early on before I was more…invested in the relationship."

"Still. Cheating sucks. My high school boyfriend cheated on me," she confesses.

"Austen Henley?" I say and when she nods I laugh, but I don't mean it merrily. "Well just like Alisha, that douche did you a favor. He was not worthy of you."

"Shut up."

"Seriously. He's destined to live in his parents' basement for the rest of his life."

"He's at Syracuse. Pre-med," Maggie tells me.

"He'll end up in that basement. Mark my words," I reply confidently. "And I don't care if we're fifty and you're living six states away, I will find you and knock on your door and tell you I told you so when it happens."

"I'll be right here. Well, not in the hockey house with my sworn enemy but in Vermont. On my farm, Clyde willing," Maggie replies and pauses to look up at me with quizzical eyes before adding. "And if you get what you want, you'll be right next door. Unless you changed your mind."

"About keeping the farm? No. I mean I have moments of frustration where I want to give up." I sigh and think about the fight I had a couple days ago with my grandfather. "My grandfather got us into this mess by listening to my aunt Louise's advice on the apple trees. And no matter how little work Louise and Raquel do, he still treats them better than my dad, Jace, or me, who are all actually working our asses off to keep the farm."

"Has he always been like that? With Louise and Raquel? Because that isn't fair," Maggie says and twists around so she's got her back to me now. I curl up against her. Why am I so intent on cuddling this girl? I have no idea, but I am. There is no place I'd rather be right now, and it's giving me the strength to talk about the shittiest part of my family dynamic.

"Always. My dad acts like it isn't a big deal, but my mother was always vocal about it when they were married and she was also living on the farm," I explain. "I think it might even have been one of the things that made her want to end the marriage. She was living and working on the farm, giving blood, sweat, and tears just like my dad, and my grandfather and grandmother were taking every last extra cent and throwing it at Louise for whatever she needed. She wanted to go to college, and they paid for two years before she dropped out. My dad didn't apply to college because they told him when he was a senior in high school they needed him on the farm. When Louise got knocked up, my grandparents acted like it was the biggest blessing our family had ever received. According to my mother, when she was pregnant with me they barely acknowledged it, and when she announced she was having Jace they told her it wasn't a great time because he was due in the fall during harvest."

"You're kidding me?" Maggie says, her mouth hanging open. "That's…"

"Horrible. I know." I sigh, bury my nose in her hair and inhale the scent of her shampoo, hoping she's managed to get it all over my sheets too because I want to fall asleep to the scent tonight. I try not to think about what that urge means. "Anyway, the other day I'd had a particularly late night because I was coming back from a job and then had to get up super early for class and then my gramps called me bitching that I hadn't picked up the extra wood we needed for the barn repair, and I swear I almost quit. I'm out there in my undies getting eye-fucked by strange women while I clean their toilets and he's bitching about a Home Depot run that if Raquel or Louise were reliable, he could have had them do."

I feel her tense a little. She wants to say something. I hold her tighter. "Say it, Maggie. Whatever it is."

"Do you ever like…do stuff with them?" she asks, barely above a whisper. "Your Manly Maid clients?"

"No. Never," I say firmly.

She wiggles and turns and now her chest is pressed to mine and her eyes are glued to my face. "Do they touch you or stuff like that?"

"Some try but I remind them of the contract they signed," I say. "I'm not there for sexual favors, just cleaning. I know some guys let the lines get blurred, but I've never wanted to and I never will."

"I'm sorry I asked. It really isn't my business," Maggie says softly and then gives me a chaste kiss.

I take one of her hands that's pressed up gently against my chest and hold it in my own. She's got really delicate hands with long, thin fingers, and I remember she used to play the piano in grade school. "It's kind of your business. I mean, since we're doing this whole naked thing on the regular now."

"So this is a regular occurrence now?" she counters and I grin confidently.

"If I have anything to say about it, yeah. I mean at least until market season is over," I reply and press the fleshy part of her hand, just above her wrist, near her thumb, to my lips and give it a soft little bite. Her eyelashes flutter at that. "After that it might be harder to explain if we're still talking to each other or seen around each other. But until then, I intend to keep this up if you want to."

"I want to." Three simple words said so firmly it makes my heart beat quicker.

"So then you have every right to know what is going on with my job," I reply and take her hand and slide it down my bare skin from my chest to my stomach to my cock which is rock hard again. Her eyes flare and her cheeks pink as I press her palm against it. "For the record the whole bed buddy thing for me is exclusive. And I'd need it to be for you too."

"It is," she whispers and wraps her fingers around my length. I bite back a groan of pleasure when she squeezes me gently. "This is all I want."

I roll on top of her. "Good. Me too."

And then I occupy my mouth with hers so that we both stop talking. I feel like we're getting precariously close to saying things that we can't take back. Things about feelings we aren't allowed to have.

14

TATE

She's my first thought when I open my eyes in the morning, and that's a dangerous thing. I know it, but I can't help it. She makes me smile and not much else has been doing that lately. I rub the sleep from my eyes and throw on some clothes and stumble my way down the stairs. The house is begrudgingly alive, filled with toilets flushing and feet shuffling and alarms beeping for the fourth and fifth time, followed by moans of protest.

In the kitchen I find Cooper and Lex shoveling cereal into their mouths while standing by the sink. I push past them to grab my travel mug from the drying rack and notice the kettle is already on the stove about to whistle, so I grab a green tea bag from my stash in the cupboard marked Tate and snatch up the kettle. "Who turned this on?"

Lex and Cooper both shrug and I shake my head. "We're lucky we don't burn this place down."

I pour the boiling water into my mug with the tea bag and then refill it and stick it back on the burner. Lex has his head cocked now and he's watching me curiously. "Why you so happy?"

"Who said I was happy?" I ask and steep my tea.

"My facial muscles haven't even woken up yet but you're

smiling," Lex says and I reach up and touch my face. Then I smile even more.

"See you two at the gym," I say without explaining myself and drop the tea bag into the trash, which is almost overflowing, and head for the front door. It takes me a minute to find matching shoes in the heap that's piled next to the shoe rack, not on it. Maybe we should hire Manly Maids, I think with a smirk.

It's a cold windy morning. There're big, dark storm clouds making it look more like five in the morning than quarter to seven, but I have a job to do whether the weather likes it or not. I hop in the truck and head to the farm. I park next to the barn. There's a couple lights on in the house, but I know my brother is getting ready for school, my dad is probably out in the orchard, and Gramps and Grams are still puttering in the kitchen. They start work later and later the older they get. I don't expect to see anyone, and I don't as I make my way into the barn holding my breath.

I half expect to not find what I'm looking for, but there it is. Aunt Louise finally did something right. Well... I pause that thought as I examine the flowers. She did something half right. I'd asked her, since she works at the garden center in Colebury, to get me a deal on some flowers. I told her it was to spruce up the hockey house and then I gave her a specific list of types. Dahlias, pansies, marigolds. What I ended up with was not the ones I asked for—at least not from the pictures I Googled of them. But these were colorful and healthy looking, so I wasn't about to complain. There was a note there with the amount, and I was pleased she'd kept it in my budget too.

I load the flowers and a ladder into the truck, head on over to park like an FBI surveillance van down the street from Maggie's apartment, and wait. I'd been texting with her last night, mostly sending each other snarky comments and sexual innuendos, but I managed to subtly find out that Caroline had gone home for a few days, she and Daisy had early classes, and Jasmyn was spending the night at her boyfriend Rhys's place. Ten minutes into my stakeout, Daisy and Maggie emerge from their apartment. They're holding travel mugs and talking animatedly as they lock the door and make their way down the street. I smile as I watch her and get this sense of peace I haven't felt in a really long time.

Once they're out of sight, I take a deep breath and jump out of my truck. The risk factor in this little stunt is high. Jasmyn could come home. Daisy and Maggie could come back early. Someone in the building could not believe the cover story I have and call the police. So many risk factors, but I'm going for it anyway.

I carry the flowers to her front yard and then up the ladder, which is not easy. Neither is climbing over her balcony railing with the flowers. But I really don't like that she decimated her private garden to try and compete with my silly dunk tank trick. I don't have a ton of extra cash to throw around but with Louise's employee discount and the little cash I could spare, I manage to put something in each empty box and pot. It's not a lot, but it's something and it looks pretty, if I do say so myself. Most importantly, I don't get caught…at least not until I'm making my way down the ladder to escape and the tenant below their apartment sticks his graying head out a window and stares at me.

"Just a little emergency maintenance on the third floor. Sorry if I bothered you, sir," I say with what I hope is a credible smile.

He looks up at Maggie's balcony and back at me. "I've been complaining about my dripping kitchen faucet for three months but of course the landlord fixes the hot college girls' stuff first," he huffs and slams his window shut.

He might complain to the landlord, but I'll be long gone.

After heading home to drop off the truck and clean up, I walk back to campus and start my actual day. I don't see Maggie or hear from her the entire time so I don't know if she's discovered my little gift.

My day ends with hockey practice. The locker room is already half full and others trail in behind me at a steady pace as I undress and throw on workout gear. Today is dry land training, not ice, which means Coach Garfunkle is in charge. He makes us meditate for the first fifteen minutes. He's been doing it since the beginning of the year, and as usual, snoring starts to fill the room because some of the guys fall asleep, which then leads to uncontrollable snorts and guffaws from the other guys. Garfunkle takes it in stride, like he always does, and tells us we'll get better with practice.

Then we go in groups into the drill room to do partnered resistance training with elastics and ropes and stuff. Coach Keller pops in and out to survey us but says nothing until the end when we're back in the locker room about to hit the showers. "Nice work out there boys. I have high hopes for you in the season opener next week. I'm about to tell you who will be on that ice for puck drop in that game. And yeah it's only the first game but it sets the tone for the year. I'm telling you six days in advance of the game in case you aren't first line and want to be. Bust your ass in the coming days and change my mind. If you are on it and don't want to end up on the bench when the puck drops, then don't slack. I *will* change it."

He starts to read the names of the starting line, and mine is one of them. I want to smile and even crow in victory, but I don't want to be an asshole to my teammates who aren't on it. And Keller isn't kidding, he will drop anyone to second line or third if he's given reason to, so I sit there and just nod at my name and continue to undress.

As I wrap a towel around my waist and head to the showers, Garfunkle stops me. "I told you that crystal would help."

"What?"

"The crystal I gave you a couple weeks ago," he says smiling. "It really changed your chi. I can feel it on and off the ice. You're in a good place."

"I think I am, Coach," I say and try not to laugh. "Thanks."

He looks so damn pleased with himself I don't have the heart to tell him it's because of a hot redhead not a hunk of stone he gave me. And, as if to prove that point, I feel my chi get even brighter when I step out of the arena twenty minutes later and see

Maggie sitting on the steps, bundled in a thick, oversized cable knit sweater and leggings, sipping a coffee and reading a textbook.

"Someone should snap your picture and give it to the admissions office," I tell her as I walk over. "If I was a high school student, I'd take one look at it and immediately send in my application."

She glances up from her book and gives me the softest, most intimate smile, and I know she's been home and seen her balcony. Everything in me gets warmer despite the cool air swirling around me and my still wet hair.

"No compliments, Tater Tot. It's not who we are," she reminds me softly.

"I meant because of the latte and the nice sweater. Total Vermont vibes. What really helps sell it is the fact your hair looks more brown than red thanks to the clouds and it shields that hideous face of yours from view," I reply swiftly and her head snaps up and the look of pure shock on her face is priceless. I wink. "Better?"

"I am one second away from tossing this latte in your face," she warns and the amber in her eyes glints with mock anger.

"Don't waste good caffeine, Firecracker," I reply. "Now, what are you doing here? Just had to see my face before you ended your day?"

"Ha-ha," she says and stands up, facing me. Her eyes are so filled with awe and something else I can't place but makes me feel like a rock star. "Someone broke into my apartment today and instead of stealing stuff, they filled my empty flower boxes."

I fake shock. "Wow. That's crazy. I guess someone took pity on your horrible gardening skills, or got sick of looking at your ugly muddy barren flower boxes and decided to take matters into their own hands. Did you call 9-1-1? Is there a statewide manhunt?"

She's biting her bottom lip, trying not to smile, but she's failing. "I decided to forgo the police. I'm going to hunt this maniac down myself and deal with him my own way."

"Vigilante justice. I like it," I say grinning. "I hope this monster gets what he deserves. What, exactly, do you think he deserves?"

"Well…" She pauses and sips her latte as her eyes dart around.

I do the same, casually glancing around to make sure no one is watching us. Not a lot of people in school know about how odd it would be to see us talking and not screaming at each other, but some definitely do and I don't want to start a rumor that somehow gets back to our families.

"I think first I'll explain that it was really hard to think on my feet when Daisy and Jasmyn questioned me about where the hell the new flowers came from," she says. "And then after I berate him for that. Then…then I'll tell him that it violates all terms of our agreement. And that I hate charity. But…"

She looks down and then back up and her eyes are watery. "It was the sweetest thing I think anyone has ever done for me. That it makes me want to kiss him and…a lot of other things that I'm hoping I can show him tonight. If he dares to sneak back into my apartment or let me sneak into his."

"I'm pretty sure this vandal will most definitely let you do whatever you want to him tonight, wherever you want," I reply and have to shove my hands into my hoodie to keep from reaching out and touching her pink cheeks. "Don't cry, Magnolia. If you cry I'll have to take you in my arms no matter who might be watching. I won't be able to help myself."

She takes a ragged breath and takes one step back from me, regaining her composure. "Then I'll have to throw the latte on you."

I smile. She smiles back.

"Hey! Adler!"

She freezes and I look toward the voice It's Bennie Oldman. He's a senior and like Maggie and me, he's a local too and he worked on my farm a couple summers ago before everything started to melt down. "Maggie. Hey. I didn't know you two were…friends?"

"What? Who? No!" she barks out way too forcefully with an equally aggressive laugh at the end.

"We're just neighbors and in the same program. I was asking her for notes from a class I missed," I say which isn't a lie. It's just not the truth in this particular situation.

"I think he knows we're neighbors, Tater Tot. He worked on your farm," Maggie reminds me and Bennie laughs.

"You forget me that soon?" Bennie laughs and nudges me.

"Anyway, I have to run," Maggie says and smiles at Bennie. "Nice seeing you Bennie. And…not nice seeing you, Tate. Bye."

"Bye," Bennie says and waves as she leaves. I don't bother with an acerbic retort. I just watch her go and wish he hadn't interrupted us.

Bennie chuckles. "When I worked for you guys any Todd was a bad Todd. You know your grandfather told me it wasn't personal opinion but scientific fact because you could never trust a person with a first name as a last name."

I shake my head. "My grandmother's maiden name was Brent so that's a load of garbage. How ya been Bennie?"

"Good. Great, actually," he replies falling in step with me. He runs a giant paw through his long, shaggy hair. Bennie is extremely tall and lanky which makes his hands and feet look stupidly disproportionate. His nickname as far back as grade school has been Shaggy like the cartoon character from *Scooby-Doo*. "I was bummed when I couldn't get another summer job at your farm this past summer because you guys were a great gig, but I ended up working at the Shipley farm and it was good. Better than I thought. They're keeping me on until November part-time, so that's great."

"We really wanted you back we just couldn't afford it this season, Bennie," I say, feeling the crushing weight of guilt I felt when I had to tell him at the beginning of the summer.

"Hey man, I know. Like I said, it's all good," Bennie says easily. "I knew it wasn't just me when I saw Hank at the Biscuit."

Now that crushing guilt somehow gets even heavier. "You talked to Hank?"

"Yeah all the time. Why? Don't you?" Bennie asks and he gets incredulous as I don't answer. "Did Hank do something?"

I shake my head. "Hey, Bennie. I gotta head back to the hockey house and grab some food. Just finished practice and I'm starving. I'll catch you later."

"Yeah. For sure." Bennie nods amicably. "And if you need workers next year I'd definitely come back. So would Hank, I bet."

I text Maggie as soon as Bennie leaves my side.

Sorry about that.

A light rain begins to fall and since I don't have a jacket, only a hoodie, I pick up the pace as my phone rings and Maggie's alias appears on the screen. I didn't store her number by her real name because I didn't want anyone to see it come up. Her name is Prof Doyle, which is my Economics of Agriculture teacher. If someone looks through my phone and sees our texts they're going to think I'm having an affair with a fifty-nine-year-old professor, but I'd rather that than anyone know the truth.

"Hey."

"Hey. So was Bennie suspicious? He looked like he thought something was going on with us," Maggie says, her tone uneven from nerves.

"Nah. Bennie didn't suspect anything," I sigh.

"Then why do you sound so down?"

"He just made me feel like shit about not re-hiring him and then he brought up Hank," I tell Maggie.

"Well, he's not the one making you feel like shit there," Maggie replies swiftly. "You tense up every time his name comes up, and you get this guilty look on your face."

"That's because I do feel guilty," I tell her as the rain drops get bigger and faster. I'll likely be drenched by the time I get home. "Now can we talk about something else? Let's get back to that earlier conversation about tonight. Your place or mine?"

I hear her laugh and then she says, "How about you go have a conversation with Hank and then we can decide on the simple stuff, like where I'm going to fuck your brains out."

"First of all, I can't just walk up to him and start small talk. I've avoided him for months," I admit. "And second don't talk about fucking, you're making me hard as I walk down the street."

"Go to the Biscuit, ease that guilt weighing you down and then —and only then—you can come by my place and I'll deal with your agreement violation."

I smile at the last part, but not the first. Still, I know she's right. Not that I'll give her the satisfaction of hearing that though. "See you in a little bit."

"Text me first, so I can make sure the coast is clear," Maggie says. "And if you don't go see Hank, then don't come see me."

She hangs up before I can argue.

"Bossiest woman on the planet," I mutter and shove my phone back in my pocket. And once again, she's right. I need to face Hank and deal with any resentment he rightfully has toward me. So I find myself turning left instead of right and the next thing I know, I'm opening the door to the Biscuit and dripping all over their floor. It's too early for the dinner rush and too late for the lunch crowd, so they close weekdays between three and six. Still the one waitress inside greets me with a smile.

"Hi there. We don't open for dinner until six but I can make you a reservation for then."

"I'm actually here to see..." Hank's big frame lumbers into view. He's carrying a tray of glasses toward the bar. "Him."

Hank locks eyes with me and freezes. He doesn't look happy but he doesn't look pissed either. His face is Switzerland. "I got this, Carly."

The waitress nods and disappears somewhere in the back of the restaurant with a tray of empty salt shakers. Hank gently puts the tray of glasses down onto the bar top and then leans on the polished oak beside it. "I put on a pot of coffee if you want some.

And I got my usual afternoon snack of a couple of oat muffins in the back."

"Stop," I say with a small shake of my head. "Stop being so nice to me."

Hank blinks and then chuffs out a silent laugh. "I don't hate you for letting me go, Tate. You had to do it. I just think less of you for then cutting me off like I was just some nameless employee. But that doesn't mean I'm going to forget my manners. Then I've let you alter my morals and ethics and I lose."

"You were always too damn philosophical for a high school dropout," I say with a small smile so he knows I'm just kidding. "And also extremely on the nose."

Hank grins. "Sit down, asshole. You still take cream but no sugar because it's hockey season."

"Yeah, exactly." I sit down on one of the red leather stools. He goes about making me a coffee and slides the mug across the polished bar top when it's ready. I give him a grateful smile. "So… you like it here?"

"It's decent," Hank says as he starts to make a coffee for himself. "You know me though, I need to work outdoors, so while this pays the bills, I'm looking for something else."

"You know if we can ever hire staff again, full-time or even part-time, I am calling you," I say before taking a sip of coffee.

"Actually no, I didn't know that because you haven't told me," Hank says as he stirs a heaping amount of sugar into his coffee, and I watch with jealousy. Then he heads toward the swinging door into the kitchen. "You haven't said jack shit to me since you had George let me go."

He comes back a minute later with a bag from the bakery, which he puts on the counter and tears open with his weathered hands. Two perfect muffins lay exposed on the counter and he grabs one and motions for me to take the other. "Go ahead. I didn't have time to poison it or anything."

I huff out a small, weak laugh at that, and I guiltily take the muffin. I shouldn't because I've been an ass to him and don't deserve any charity from him, but I'm starving. I take a huge bite. "There's got to be other farm work around."

Hank finishes chewing his own bite and nods. "There is. But I've been thinking of maybe a fresh start somewhere new. There's nothing really tying me to Burlington anymore. Maybe I head out to like Georgia or North Carolina. Or Wisconsin or... I don't know."

The idea that he's been thinking about leaving makes me irrationally upset considering I've been ignoring him. "You've got friends here. And that lifelong crush on Daisy Todd will be hard to maintain from across the country."

Hank laughs and scratches his shaggy dirty-blond beard. "You hate that I have a thing for her."

"I did, yeah. But I'm an asshole, so who cares what I think?" I reply and shrug.

After a belly laugh, Hank takes another sip of coffee and cocks a thick eyebrow. "You know they offered me a job."

"Who? The Todds?"

Hank nods. "Billy, Ben and Bobby came in here about a week after I started, after you let me go, before Billy's stroke, and they said that they were going to be expanding their businesses in the next eighteen months and that they'd have work for me, full-time, if I wanted it."

Huh. Maggie hasn't mentioned anything about that. Expanding their businesses, or that they tried to hire my dear friend and former employee. What the hell else are they planning to do? They have so many goats and then the bee hives at the back of the property that I don't know what else they would have room for over there. Their land isn't as large as ours or as diverse.

"I don't know exactly what they were talking about expansion-wise, but they said my job would involve farm work and some light construction," Hank replies because he sees the look of confusion on my face. "And then Billy had one too many pints, and later that night asked me if I thought you guys would be foreclosed on this year or next."

I blink. Hank's face loses its usual passive, gregarious expression and he seems unnaturally serious. "I think that they might be looking to buy your place if you lose it."

"What?"

"Yeah, I mean Daisy comes in here a lot lately and she always makes a point of chatting me up," Hank says and a tiny smile hits his mouth, but it's wistful. "I ain't dumb enough to think she suddenly realizes what a perfect ten I am. Especially because she always swings the conversation around to your family farm too."

I shake my head. "No. I mean... I would know that."

"Why because you share a booth with them at the market every weekend?" Hank says and shakes his head when I look shocked he knows that. "It's Burlington, buddy. That's premium local gossip."

"Nah. Not just that. Because..." I glance over my shoulder. No one but Carly the waitress is here and she's still off somewhere in the back. I lower my voice anyway. "Because Maggie and I are...involved."

Hank doesn't react at first. He just keeps chewing that last bite of muffin he had popped into his mouth. But then, as his eyes level with mine, his chewing gets slower. And slower. And then he swallows whatever is left of that muffin, and it must be too big because he starts to choke.

I lean over the bar top and attempt to slap him on the back. He turns away, coughs into his hand, and when he regains his composure he turns back to me, a look of pure disbelief across his face. "You're what? Like involved...in a cult? A class project? A Wiccan ritual? Because all of that would be more believable than the other form of involvement that springs to mind."

A gust of air shoots from my lungs in a sheepish laugh and I nod. "Yeah. I know. But if what sprung to your mind was romantic involvement—*naked* involvement—then your first instinct was right."

Hank swiftly leaves the bar area and marches over to the plate glass window at the front of the restaurant. He turns to Carly as she walks out of the back with a tray of full salt shakers. "Carly, can you make sure we have enough canned goods in the back to get us through the apocalypse? It just started."

"What?" Carly says blinking.

"Ignore him, Carly. He's a better barback than he is a comedian," I call out, and Carly shrugs and heads to the other side of the room. I turn back to Hank. "So, dickhead, can you be serious about this for a minute?"

"I can but it isn't easy because it's so surreal I almost think it's got to be some kind of practical joke," Hank admits as he walks over and drops down on the stool beside me. "Jesus, Tate, the last time we talked you thought the whole Todd family was scum."

"I think a few of them still are. Especially Clyde," I reply and then stare at my coffee mug for a minute. "But things with Maggie... I don't know... Somehow I started seeing a different side of her. She's a good person."

"Is this just your fucking dick talking?" Hank counters frankly, which isn't at all like him because he's not someone who throws around words like dick or fuck, like ever. So I know this news has him rattled. "Like, do you mean the different side of her you've seen is the naked side and are you confusing good person with good in bed?"

"She's great in bed, but no I'm not confusing anything," I reply and find myself holding a breath. "I mean I don't think so. She hasn't really mentioned a new business to me though. And she definitely hasn't mentioned wanting my family to lose our farm so she can buy it. But we have talked about the farm stuff, and how hard it is for me and... Fuck."

I wrestle internally with the idea that maybe Maggie wasn't actually making small talk or getting to know me. Was she pumping me for information? My heart is furious that my brain would even entertain that thought. But even more furious that it might be true. Hank watches the war of emotions vying for control of my expression, and then he clamps a hand on my shoulder and squeezes it for just a brief second. I look up at him. "Are you here for my trusted, blunt advice?"

"I don't know," I reply honestly and run a hand through my hair before cradling my head in my hands, elbows on the bar. "All I know is that this thing with Maggie is new and crazy stupid but also exactly what I need. She makes me feel good. *Inside.* Where it counts. She's the one who convinced me to come here and face you. To tell you that I feel bad we had to let you go and it's my own humiliation that has kept me away, not anything you've done, and I'm a dick for putting that before our friendship because you're the one who lost a job and needed support. And instead I end up blurting out this secret and so now asking you for advice seems even more like a selfish dickhead thing to do."

I don't have to look up to know how he is reacting to that big chunk of emotional vomit because he squeezes my shoulder again. "Jesus, Tate. I knew you might break from all the pressure of trying to keep the farm from sinking while keeping your school and hockey going strong, but I didn't know it would be like this. Sleeping with the enemy and melting down over muffins."

I lift my head and shoot him a sarcastic smile. "Why, exactly, does she have to be the enemy again?"

Hank shrugs. "You know I've never understood that myself. I don't think there's a lot of people that know the true origin of the feud, but it's very real. I don't think anyone on either side of it will ever approve of you and Maggie. Like ever, dude. And honestly, I appreciate her sending you here, and everything you just said. But I have to wonder if she has ulterior motives when it comes to getting close to you. Like Daisy does with me."

I shake my head. "She isn't just chatting me up and batting her eyelashes, Hank. She's *sleeping* with me. She also saved my ass when someone from my part-time job recognized me at the market. She made sure I wasn't outed."

Hank nods. "Hey, look, I've never personally hated the Todd sisters. I don't think they're bad people at all, which is why I have a not-so-subtle crush on Daisy. And I'm not against you and

Maggie having some fun. But honestly? I don't think any Todd can ever be with an Adler, like long-term or even seriously entertain the thought. And Maggie is smart enough to realize that too, even if the Adler is as handsome and charismatic as you."

I roll my eyes and then Hank seems to realize something and his face grows serious in a blink. "Wait. Does she know about your job? You told her about Manly Maids?"

"No. She found out. It's a long story, but I trust her to keep it a secret," I reply and he looks doubtful. "Maggie and I aren't going to hurt each other. No matter how this ends."

How this ends. Ouch. As soon as I say it out loud, my heart feels like it's wearing a jock strap two sizes too small. I don't want things to end but they're going to—and that's not a stupid cliché, the truth really does hurt.

"Look, Tate, I'd be worried if I were you about her knowing that potentially devastating fact," Hank says frankly. He scrubs his beard with his palm again. "And I would talk to her about the farm. Tell her I'm the one who thinks they want you to fail so they can buy it. I don't care if Daisy stops talking to me."

"Yeah you do."

Hank chuckles. "Yeah I do, but if she is only talking to me to steal your farm, then I'd rather go back to admiring her from afar. And you should be the same way with Maggie. Except you'd go back to the whole loathing her from afar thing you used to do."

I nod. But deep down there is no way I can allow myself to think that she's just sleeping with me to convince me to let the farm go. She isn't that girl. She wouldn't. I just…can't believe that. Hank walks around the bar and pours himself another coffee, holding up the pot to offer me one too, but I shake my head. "I got to get home and get some protein in me. But…are we cool?"

"We were always cool, Tate," Hank says with his trademark easy smile. "Just don't be a stranger anymore, okay?"

I nod. "Yeah. Okay."

I give him a smile and head out the front door. As I make my way back to the hockey house, I have my face buried in my phone drafting an email to Maggie, but by the time I reach my front door, I discard the draft. I'm going to see her later, so I'll just talk to her face-to-face. It's the only way I'll know for sure if Hank's suspicions are right. Because Maggie isn't great at poker face and I've gotten incredibly good at reading her like a book. God I hope there's nothing to read tonight.

15

MAGGIE

I have the entire apartment to myself tonight—completely unexpectedly—which is why I texted Tate immediately and told him. That "your place or mine" dilemma solved itself when my roommates decided to go to a frat party and my sister went back to the farm to do laundry and texted me to say she was spending the night. Tate had responded with a thumbs up sign, but that was almost two hours ago, and there is no sign of him.

Is he still with Hank? Is he doing hockey stuff? Should I text him again? Is that desperate? Why do I feel desperate? Ugh.

I head into my bathroom and decide to take a long, hot shower. I turn on the water in the tiny stall and start to undress while the water warms up. If he doesn't come by tonight, a hot shower is the only way I will be relaxed enough to sleep and not stare at my phone all night.

I open the glass door and step into the shower, closing my eyes as I dip my face under the stream, careful not to get my hair wet, which I twisted into a messy knot on top of my head.

I'm squeezing my favorite body wash onto my poof when the shower door opens. I open my mouth to scream but a hand covers it so I swing, clocking my attacker in the gut. "Kopf!" I blink the water out of my eyes in time to see Tate double over and crash into the sink.

"What the hell are you doing in here?" I whisper-scream. "Are you okay?"

"You invited me," Tate gasps and groans, still doubled over. "And you have one hell of a left hook."

"But how did you get inside?" I hiss and he looks up at me with a "really?" expression.

"Your downstairs neighbor opened the main door. He thinks I'm a maintenance guy. And you have a key under your front door mat," he says. "Which is really dangerous and stupid, Maggie."

"Caroline and Jasmyn do that when they go out drinking so they don't have to worry about losing their keys and don't wake the rest of us up," I reply. "Do you know Caroline lost her dorm keys four times last year?"

"Do you know you could get murdered?"

"Are you here to murder me?" I ask coyly and shiver. "Because if your method of choice is hypothermia, you're doing a bang-up job."

"Sorry to keep you from your shower," Tate replies and his eyes sweep my naked body which I don't bother to cover because he's seen it up close and personal anyway. "Do you want me to leave?"

"No," I say without a moment of reflection. I want him here. I have been dying to be alone with him since I came home from class and found all those chrysanthemums, asters and pansies on my balcony.

"What do you want me to do?" he asks as he finally straightens up to his full height and his hand falls away from his abdomen. His eyes sweep across my naked, wet body again and it makes the butterflies in my belly go crazy and my nipples harden. His eyes seem to darken.

"Join me," I whisper and step back under the warm water, leaving the door ajar. It takes all of ten seconds and then naked

Tate is climbing into the shower stall with me. As the door closes behind him, his mouth finds mine again and the kiss is scorching. He's demanding and needy, pushing me back against the tiles and sweeping his tongue through my mouth with a dominance that makes me wet in places the water isn't hitting.

He's hard as a rock and pressing into my abdomen but when I reach for him, he steps back. His hands slide up my neck, to my face and his thumb brushes water droplets off the curves of my cheek. His eyes bore into me, serious and dark for a moment before he speaks. "Do you want to take my farm?"

The water doesn't suddenly turn cold, but the atmosphere around us does. I blink and can't quite catch my breath, for all the wrong reasons. "What are you talking about and why are you talking about it right now?"

He sighs and runs a hand over his wet hair. He can't seem to look me in the eye. "Hank told me that he thought Daisy and you have this plan to scoop up my farm if it went into foreclosure. That you've been itching for that to happen so your family can buy it and expand your business."

And now I can't seem to look him in the eye, so I close them and I hear him swear under his breath. Then I feel the blast of cool air as the shower door opens and he steps out. "Tate, wait!"

I follow him out of the shower, pausing to grab my towel and turn off the water. "I'm not doing anything to *make* you lose the farm. I just... Well, we have this idea and we want to expand and your property—"

"So you're not only blackmailing me, you're banking on me losing everything?" Tate says as he pulls his boxer briefs back on, over his soaking wet skin. I wrap my towel around myself.

"I was, but to be fair, you were thrilled we were going to lose money when you got the market booth and we didn't," I reply as he reaches for his shirt on the floor.

"That's different," Tate snaps.

"Okay, well if it matters, I feel really bad about the fact you might lose the farm now," I reply. "Even though your family is horrible to us and we owe them nothing, I don't want to see you lose it…if you really want to keep it. But I'm not sure you do."

He still looks furious. "Of course I want to keep it. I'm busting my ass and risking everything to keep the damn thing."

"Okay! Okay, it's just…" Why am I suddenly unable to speak my mind when it's never been a problem before?

He tugs his shirt over his head and then reaches for his pants. "I love that land. Unlike you, it hasn't been in our family for generations, but I grew up there. Maybe apple farming isn't my favorite thing, but there's potential to turn it into something else if I can just keep it. If I can hold on to it long enough to get some pro hockey money, I can just live on it without the pressure of making it turn a profit."

"Tate, can we talk about this?" I ask but I don't honestly know what I'm going to say.

"Are you planning on buying my farm if the bank forecloses?" he says as he buttons up his jeans.

"We…my family have mentioned it, yes," I admit.

And just like that's he's gone—out of my bathroom, out my bedroom and down the hall before I can say another word. Not that I'm going to say anything because I have no clue what to say.

I just watch him go.

I wrap my towel more tightly around myself and walk to my bay window where I stare out until he's down the street and completely out of view. I want to yell out the window and tell him to stop. I want to tell him I'm sorry. I want to explain that I feel horrible about it now that I know him—and like him, *a lot*. But I don't say a thing. I just watch him go.

Because this is for the best. This was never going to be anything. We aren't fated mates. Not destined to be together. We are enemies by birth, and that is as unchangeable as our DNA. So I throw myself down on my bed, bury my face in my pillow, and refuse to let myself cry.

16

MAGGIE

"What is your damage?" Daisy asks as I hook a left into the parking lot and she clutches the handle on the door.

"You need to stop watching eighties movies when you have insomnia," I mutter. "Your catch phrases are lame."

"Speaking of which, why were you the one wandering around last night at like four in the morning if I'm the sister with the chronic insomnia?" Daisy asks, ignoring my dig about her movie preferences.

I turn off the engine and we both get out of the car. It's a crappy day, cold and overcast, but it fits my mood. Daisy is looking at me like she's an FBI agent and I'm a bomb she has to defuse. "Can I do anything?"

I pause at the trunk of the car as I lift it and look at her. Her big brown eyes are actually soft and sympathetic. I wish I could tell her this. I wish I could pour it all out but I can't for a million different reasons, the biggest being she would freak the hell out. I don't want to see her reaction—which would be horror and then disgust—or hear her words of wisdom. Because they will most likely be "You're crazy. You can't date him. You'll destroy our family and our future."

"I'm good. I mean, I'm not, but you can't fix this. I can't fix this. It's not a big deal." I sigh because the worry and concern on her face is deepening instead of dissipating. "It's a long, crazy story I don't feel like getting into, so let's just work, okay? That will get my mind off everything."

"Okay. If you say so," Daisy says and reaches into the open trunk to grab some of the merchandise we brought.

We carry the coolers full of our cheeses to the stand. As we come around the front of the booth, my disappointment is so severe that it almost winds me. Jace, George and Raquel are there but Tate isn't. I try to casually glance around as we set up, hoping I'll spot him somewhere nearby but I don't.

"You know," Daisy says casually as we walk back to the car for another load of goods, "I registered online with the ancestry site. It allows me to build our family tree online. I've gone back super far on Mom's side. Like all the way back to her great, great, great grandmother."

"Cool," I mutter. It is cool, honestly, but I'm just not really in the mood to focus on anything. Where is Tate? Is he skipping the market altogether? Is it because he's avoiding me?

"Did you know that our great, great grandmother was named Petunia?" Daisy says and makes a face. "Petunia Harrison. And she named her daughter Amaryllis. I always thought the flower-naming thing for girls on Mom's side was cute but that's because no one named us Amaryllis or Petunia. We dodged some serious bullets."

"We did," I mutter as Dad's truck pulls into the lot. He's dropping off the stuff we couldn't fit in the car.

"Also, because I've built the family tree on their site and allowed my profile to be public and my DNA to be in their database, if anyone else matches with us DNA-wise, I'll get an email notification," Daisy says and that gets my full attention. "We'll likely find relatives we didn't know we had. There was a match on Mom's side already. This man named Evan who is supposed to be Amaryllis's son. Lives in Portsmouth, New Hampshire."

"Do not bring this up in front of Dad, Daisy," I say quietly but firmly. "Talk to Mom about it discretely when he's not around because if he knows you're on this site, he will figure out who else you're looking for. Dad is not dumb. And most definitely do not bring it up in front of Clyde."

"No. I know. I won't." Daisy nods solemnly but gives me a tiny, quick excited smile before our parents get out of their truck. "But it's exciting right?"

"In a this-could-end-in-disaster sort of way," I reply with a frown.

"Shush," Daisy says and Dad hops out of the truck and gives us a big smile.

Two and a half hours later, we're having a great sales day, but all I can think about is how Tate isn't here. Mom has already had to drop off more blue cheese because we've sold out and Dad came back with more caramels and is upselling a nice lady at the counter, convincing her she needs the bigger jar of honey while Daisy and I prep more samples. That's when the day takes a turn because I hear George say something to Jace that piques my interest.

"Where's the gift basket the city purchased?" George asks his grandson.

I glance over at them. Raquel is ringing up one customer with her best resting bitch face on full display while Jace hands another one a sample of their caramel apples. George is digging around at the back of the booth, I assume for this basket he mentioned.

"I left it in the cooler because I didn't want the apple butter to get too runny," Jace explains.

I can't help but stare as he walks over and opens a cooler and pulls out a nicely decorated wicker basket filled with Adler Farms products. George admires it. "Did you decorate this, Raquel honey? It looks wonderful."

Raquel turns away from the customer without so much as a "thanks and come again" and beams at her grandfather. "Thanks Gramps. I worked on it last night. I would have done much better if Jace had bothered to give me more notice."

"I think it's lovely, doll." George kisses the top of his grand-daughter's head and then turns to Jace with a frown. "You really shouldn't spring stuff on your cousin like that. She's talented, but it isn't fair."

Jace rolls his eyes. "Next time I'll find the ribbon and glue gun and do it myself."

"That's not the answer. Stop being a smart ass," George snaps.

"Hey folks!" Ethel Morris walks up and smiles from under the brim of the biggest straw hat I have ever seen. "Happy Market Day!"

"Hi, Ethel," I say smiling back. Everyone else greets her just as warmly. "Are you here to grab some goat cheese? Honey?"

Ethel smiles warmly. "Oh sweetie, I'm not doing my personal shopping just yet. Business before pleasure. My city always comes first. I'm here for the gift baskets."

"What gift baskets?" Daisy asks before I get the chance.

"Not your concern, girls," Jace says firmly and turns to Ethel with a smile as he hands her the basket George was yammering on about. "Here you are, Ethel. It's under budget too at forty-five dollars and forty-nine cents. But we'll round down and call it forty-five. Because we love our city as much as you do."

Ethel beams at that, although it's hard to really see her face with that silly hat. Seriously, the thing is like a flying saucer on her head. She takes the basket and puts it down on the table in front of her as she rummages around in the fanny pack around her waist. She pulls out a fistful of money and counts forty-five dollars into Jace's outstretch hand.

"Ethel, do you mind if I ask what is this for?" Dad asks.

"The town hall sent an email to the fall market participants. You didn't get it?" Ethel looks confused and digs in her fanny pack again and pulls out a rumpled piece of paper. She smooths it out and clears her throat like she's about to give a speech.

I watch my dad's face contort in frustration as Ethel begins to speak. "Dear fall market entrepreneurs, the town council would like to purchase gift baskets from each of you at a cost of fifty dollars or less per basket, per booth. These baskets should feature the best of your products and will be raffled off by the city during our new annual Harvest Festival. It's our way to give back to you, our local businesses while also promoting all you have to offer. Please be sure to include marketing material about your business and its location as we hope it will attract you new business. Sincerely, your town council."

Ethel looks up smiling.

"We didn't get that email," I say with anger igniting inside me as I see Jace's smug smile. "We don't have a basket for you."

"Oh… I…" Ethel looks at the paper again and after a minute she looks up, relieved. "Oh it's okay. You're not on the list, so we couldn't pay you for it anyway. No worries."

She shoves the paper back in her fanny pack and picks up the basket.

"No. I mean we should have been on the list. We're part of the market. We are half of this booth."

Ethel looks stricken. "But you and Tate agreed not to share the booth last time we talked, remember? You never told us you changed your minds."

"They didn't. The police officer told them they had to share," George Adler barks at poor little Ethel who looks more confused than ever.

Daisy and I exchanged panicked glances. Shit. Daisy steps up. "We can throw together a basket today and run it right over to you at city hall before evening."

"But there's only allowed to be one basket per booth." Ethel waves the wrinkled per in the air again. "We don't have the funds for more than that, and the Adlers have already made this basket."

I glare at Jace. He just shrugs at me. "Sorry. It's our booth. I guess when the sheriff or whoever forced us to share, they didn't bother to include this. Not our fault."

"You're a piece of—"

"I wonder why Officer Humphries never told me he made you

share after all? Maybe if he tells the mayor about the arrangement we can squeeze in a basket from you in the budget," Ethel says, still looking very confused, and I realize that if I don't drop it, our little arrangement will be exposed.

"No worries, Ethel," I say loudly and then smile as brightly as I can muster. "It's a lovely idea. We'll get in on it next time. Have a great day."

Ethel smiles and wanders off with the Adlers' basket.

"You feel awfully good about yourself, don't you?" Dad snarls at Jace who looks so full of himself I kind of want my dad to slug him.

"Look, Mr. Todd, no one wants you and your stinky cheese here to begin with," Raquel pipes in.

"Shut up, Raquel," Daisy snaps.

"I know you weren't raised by anyone with class, but that's not how you talk to people young lady," George Adler growls.

"You want to talk about class, George, really?" Dad actually looks like he might hit someone now and I panic and step in between him and George. "The guy who goes out for a beer and comes home two days later when he's got a newborn at home."

"Your drunk daddy tell you that?" George hisses. "Must have been one of his drunken hallucinations. My wife is still here. Where is his?"

"Okay everyone just STOP!" Daisy hollers so loudly that people walking by stop and stare.

"Great, one of the redheads is making a scene," Raquel mutters.

"Dad, go home. We've got this," I say and wrap my hands around his bicep, which feels tense and hard. I look down and see his fists in balls. I squeeze harder and give him a little tug. "Seriously, Daddy, please. Don't do this."

He glances down at me and he softens, both his stance and his expression. He gives me a small smile. "You're right, Magnolia. He isn't worth the time it would take to knock him out. No Adler is worth our time."

After this discovery, I think he might be right. And it makes my heart ache.

The rest of the day drags on painfully and when it's finally five o'clock, I don't know whether to laugh or cry. Daisy and I have to pack up on our own because we sent Dad home, so it takes longer than I want. Raquel disappeared before the market ended, and George takes off with one load of stuff leaving Jace on his own. He's folding up their banner when I walk back to get ours.

"So where is Tate?" I ask. "Why wasn't he here today?"

Jace looks up. His eyes are not green like Tate's, but they're the same shape and hold the same intensity when he glares. "Why should I tell you?"

I shove our own banner in the box with our honey. "I go to school with him, so I will find him whether you like it or not."

"He had a hockey thing. You know they have their first game next weekend," Jace says. "And for the record, even if he was here, nothing would have changed."

"So he knew about the gift basket?" I ask.

Please say no. Please say no. Please say no.

Jace nods. "He knew. He told me what to put in it."

I walk away without another word, but Jace isn't finished talking unfortunately. "He doesn't want you here any more than the rest of us do."

I hate that I think he's probably right, but I know for a fleeting minute that not so long ago, that wasn't the case.

I drive back to the farm with Daisy and busy myself with putting away all our market stuff and products that didn't sell. My eyes keep wandering over to the shipping container. I hate looking at it now. Daisy watches me with concern but doesn't bug me. Mom appears on the back porch. "You girls come in and grab dinner before you leave. I know you're not eating enough, and I made roast chicken with the gravy you both love."

"Thanks, Mom," Daisy says and kisses her cheek. All I can do is muster a smile and a nod.

But as we make our way across the backyard toward the

house, I realize I'm not going to be able to eat a thing or get through idle chit chat with my family. And if any of them bring up the Adlers and what happened today at the market with the gift basket, I will probably cry out of frustration and sadness that Tate would not only do that to me but is so done with me he didn't even show up to tell me himself. And then I'll have a lot of explaining to do, so when we get to the porch I walk toward my car instead of walking through the screen door my mom is holding open.

"Maggie, where are you going?" Mom asks, concern crinkling her forehead.

"I forgot about an assignment due tomorrow. I need to go home and get started," I say with a frown to sell it. "I'm sorry. This week has been a blur and I just spaced."

"That's not like you," Mom continues to look worried. "You sure you don't have just half an hour? You need food."

"Can you drive Daisy home with a doggie bag for me?" I ask with a hopeful smile.

"Will do," Mom says.

Luckily, Daisy was too hungry to even stop and eavesdrop on our conversation because she would totally pepper me with a billion questions: What assignment? Which class? Didn't you just say a couple days ago that the semester workload was light so far?

I hop in the car and make my way down the drive. I pause and then turn the other way on the main road—the way that leads to campus and the hockey house and not my apartment.

It's a little after seven thirty when I park across from Tate's. The lights are on in what seems to be every damn room in the giant, old house. Great. It means his teammates are likely home. There is no way to be stealthy here. If I go in there, everyone will know. I take a deep breath, try to talk myself out of it, and fail.

I march up the steps and bang a closed fist on the front door.

"Come in!" someone yells.

I open the door and step inside. It smells good. Like,

simmering tomatoes and fresh basil. I take a few, small tentative steps. The living room is right off the front door and two guys—Lex and Cooper if my memory is working—are sitting there on the battered couch playing a video game on the TV. Hockey, of course.

"No! No fucking way!" One of them howls as the other one leaps up off the couch in victory.

"Loser!" Cooper yells and points to the guy sitting down who tosses his controller on the scuffed wood coffee table with disgust. "You are cleaning the toilets next week!"

"When did you get good at this?" Lex grumbles. "If only you were as good on the actual ice."

Kicking back in two beat up recliners, watching it all unfold, are the identical twins—Patrick and Paxton. I don't think they live here, but it makes sense they'd be hanging out here.

"Hey all," I say and they all turn and look at me.

"Hi," Patrick is the first to greet me with a big smile. "I bet you're not here for me, unfortunately."

"No. I'm here for—"

"Tate," Lex says and he smiles too. It's less confident and more awkward, in a cute way.

"Tate!" Patrick yells. "You might want to run."

"What are you going on about, Graham?" I hear Tate's voice from the back of the house. He wanders out of what I assume is the kitchen, barefoot and in a pair of faded jeans and a Moo U T-shirt, holding a dish towel. He looks relaxed and gorgeous and it makes my heart twist painfully.

He looks up and sees me there and freezes. Patrick and Lex are now glued to the scene in front of them, their eyes bouncing back and forth between Tate and me like the audience at the U.S. Open watching a finals match.

"We need to talk," I say flatly.

"I don't want to talk," Tate replies, in a monotone. "That's why I didn't go to the market today."

"You should have been there to see my face when I found out

you screwed us out of the gift basket money and publicity," I snap and cross my arms. "I was furious. And hurt. You would have loved it."

Tate just stares like he didn't hear what I said or doesn't understand it. "Are you drunk?"

"Do I look drunk?" I bark.

"Well, you're a little flushed," Patrick pipes up. "People get flushed when they drink."

"Patrick, can you go stir the sauce for me and make sure the pasta doesn't overflow?" Tate says and tosses the dish towel at him. It hits the back of his head. "Dinner's almost ready."

"Make Coop do it. I don't even live here." Patrick reminds Tate.

"Lex should do it. He's the house chore whore now," Cooper suggests, grinning.

"Can someone just stir the fucking sauce?" Tate snaps.

Lex nods and picks up the dish towel from Patrick and walks toward the kitchen without a word. Patrick just sits there, still staring at Tate and me like we're his own personal television drama. Tate flips him the bird and then looks at me and points at the stairs. "Let's go finish this in private."

"Oh come on! It was just getting good!" Cooper complains.

I follow Tate to the stairs and we climb them in silence all the way up to his room on the third floor. As we enter his room I try not to think about the last time I was here and how well that argument turned out. If only I could be that lucky this time around.

"What the hell were you talking about down there?" Tate asks as he leans his butt on the edge of his desk.

I want to pace but the room is too small, so I just fold my arms across my chest and stand near the door. Why does everything hurt so much? This was just supposed to be a physical thing without strings, so whether it finished with a bang or a whimper it shouldn't make my chest ache. "Ethel sent you an email saying city hall would pay for gift baskets from each farmer's market vendor that they would then give away at an event later this month."

He stares at me for a long moment, like he's frozen. Then he says, "What?"

I know instantly his confusion is real, not fake. I feel it in my bones. "Jace said you got the email. He made it seem like you purposely didn't tell us."

"And you believed him." Tate tilts his head to the side in disbelief.

"You left my house last night so angry and you didn't show up today," I reply.

"And you think I'm *that* guy?" Tate questions and then lifts himself off the desk and sighs. "Of course you do. I'm an Adler and you think we're all just genuinely assholes."

He walks across his room and grabs his phone from the nightstand where it's plugged into a charger. As he starts punching something on the screen someone calls up the stairs. "Adler! Dinner is ready!"

"Start without me!" Tate yells back. "But leave me some or I will beat you with my hockey stick."

He hits speaker on his phone and holds it out in front of him. It rings twice and then I hear someone answer. "Hey, Tate."

"Jace, did you fuck over the Todds?" Tate says bluntly.

"What the hell are you talking about?"

"Something about a gift basket every booth member was supposed to supply and you got an email about it," Tate refreshes his memory. "And you didn't tell the Todds, or me."

"I didn't screw anyone," Jace says and Tate opens his mouth to speak but Jace keeps going. "Well, I did, but I had every right to. It's our booth, Tate. Not theirs. You never said they had the right to anything other than one side of the booth. And I did tell you about the basket and you told me to handle it, you were swamped. So I did handle it by not telling the stupid Todds and not bothering you with that little bit of info."

"You're splitting hairs Jace, and it's bullshit. You should have told them," Tate replies. "We're going to give them half of the money we were paid for that basket or we're going to go tell Ethel it's a joint basket and pull out some of our products and let them add theirs. Those are your choices."

"Fuck that," Jace snaps. "You know what? You didn't even bother to show up today so I made a decision and I'm sticking to it. Gramps knew about it and thought it was a good idea, and it's technically his farm, so deal with it. I'm done playing nice with these jerks and it's annoying everyone, by the way, that you've turned so soft."

"I'm not soft. I'm sensible," Tate replies angrily. "This feud has gotten out of control and since neither of us want to give up our land and businesses and move away, we need to learn to work together. So grow up, Jace. I'm not done with this. We're going to make it right."

"Whatever. Good luck with that." The line goes dead as Jace hangs up on his brother.

Tate swears under his breath and tosses his phone on his bed and then he looks up at me. "I'm sorry. My brother is a bigger dick than I realized."

"To be fair, Daisy might have done the same thing," I reply softly.

"I'll make this right somehow," Tate promises.

Then we stare at each other awkwardly for what feels like an eternity but is probably a minute. I take a deep breath, but it feels like my lungs are pinched. "I'm sorry about the other night."

"Sorry I found out you're trying to steal my farm?"

"I'm not trying to steal it. I just… I have plans for it if you guys can't keep it," I reply, and I feel like shit when he looks at me because he looks so hurt. "I feel bad about it now. I have for a while. I don't want you to lose your farm now. But I still need more land to advance my plans for our business."

Tate keeps staring at me, but the hurt in his green eyes seems to be dissipating at least a little bit. "What are your plans?"

I bite my lip. He frowns. "Okay. You should go. We had team

meetings today and I managed to squeeze in a workout too and then I cooked that huge meal down there to keep my mind off you, so I'm going to go eat it now."

He walks across the room and out the door and I follow because I don't know what else to do. When we reach the ground floor I realize if I walk out that door, this thing with us is done. I grab his hand as he's about to walk into the kitchen, where I can hear a bunch of guys talking and dishes clanging as they eat. He turns to face me.

"After you eat, can I take you somewhere?"

"Why?"

"Because I want to show you what my plans are," I say and I feel scared and nervous, like I might be making the biggest mistake of my life. But what if I'm not? What if this is exactly what we all need? A leap of faith. An olive branch.

His eyes scrutinize my face and then he smiles cautiously and takes my hand and pulls me into the kitchen. "Hey boys, try and chew with your mouths closed. We have a female guest joining us."

Four guys stare up at me in various stages of devouring the spaghetti dinner in front of them. They all look baffled that I'm there—and about to eat with them—but they all smile, wave, grunt or give me other forms of a welcome. Tate offers me the empty chair and grabs another one from the hall.

The meal is delicious, and I'm pretty sure it's not just because I'm starving. His sauce is meaty and garlicky and the pasta is perfectly al dente. I devour every spec that Tate had heaped onto my plate, which amuses the guys. Lex watches me in awe as I reach for a second piece of garlic bread. The twins both smile.

"Gotta love a girl with an appetite," Patrick says with a smirk.

"I'm a farm girl," I say with a guilty smile. "We know how to eat."

"So...like you two don't hate each other anymore?" Lex asks timidly.

I feel Tate's hand land on my knee under the table and he squeezes. "We're working on a peace treaty."

I nod. "It's a work in progress."

No one brings it up again, and I happily munch on another piece of garlic bread while they talk about the upcoming hockey season. When dinner is finished and there isn't a scrap of food left on the table, Tate stands up. "Enjoy doing the dishes, Lex. I'll see you guys later."

His teammates all wave or call out goodbyes. And when we get outside and start down the porch, I dig my keys out of my pocket. "It's best if I drive."

"Okay," Tate says easily and climbs in my passenger side.

Ten minutes later I park at the bottom of my family's driveway. It's after nine now—on a Sunday—so I'm confident Ben and Bobby have gone home and one of them probably dropped Daisy off at our apartment too. There's a light on in the upstairs left window, which means Dad and Mom have retired to their room. Mom is probably reading or knitting and Dad is watching some sports channel, probably trying to catch highlights of the Patriots game. Clyde lives in the self-contained apartment at the back end of the house that my dad and uncles built for him the year I was born. I don't know if he's awake so we're going to have to be stealthy, which is why I'm parking at the end of the drive, so no one sees my car.

I turn to Tate. "We're going to have to hop the fence and walk up, through the field."

Tate smirks. "Can't get caught with the enemy."

"Exactly." I nod and get out of the car. Tate follows.

I lead him to the fence and hop over. He follows and we make our way through the dark field in silence. "Where are your little monsters?"

I smile. "The goats sleep in the barn."

As we come up the back side of the field, we pass the series of oblong, white bee hives and Tate starts to walk faster and makes a wide birth around them. I smirk. "They won't bug you."

"I've been stung more times than I can count in my life, so I don't believe you," Tate replies. It's dark out but even with just the quarter moon as our light, I can see his eyes just bugged out of his pretty little head and I laugh.

"I had no idea a big bad hockey player was so terrified of a little bee."

"They sting!" Tate hisses back.

"I've never been stung," I say and shrug. "But I also wear gloves and the whole gear. Daisy doesn't though."

"Your sister is officially a badass," Tate replies. "And quite possibly has a death wish."

I laugh again but make sure to stifle it as the house is now within throwing distance. And as we round the corner of it, the container house comes into view. Tate's walk slows and he squints, as if it will help him figure out what he's looking at. "If that also houses bees, I'm running back to the car screaming, so say goodbye to your stealthy mission here."

"Nope. Trust me," I say and reach for his hand in the dark. He links his fingers through mine without hesitation and lets me lead him toward the structure despite his apprehension.

We get to the sliding doors Bobby and Ben installed at the one end of the container, and I pray they didn't lock it. I pull on the slider, and thankfully, it opens. I let go of Tate's hand to take my phone out of my pocket as I step inside and turn on the flashlight app. It does a decent job of illuminating the small space. Tate's quiet, but he also turns on his flashlight and walks around the place slowly. "You guys built a house. Out of a shipping container?"

"It's a micro-cabin," I explain. "Basically a self-contained hotel room. There's a bathroom back there."

Tate follows my finger to go check out the bathroom behind the half wall. The composting toilet has been installed and the sink has too. Ben has tiled two of the four walls so far. It looks really good. "It's also eco-friendly. There's actually electricity from solar panels but I don't want to turn on the lights in case someone sees. It's a prototype to see how easy it would be to create. We want to build six or seven of them and open a resort. One with an existing house we could turn into a bed and breakfast with a restaurant on the first floor that serves only farm-to-table dishes. And a barn that we can turn into an events hall where weddings and conferences and yoga retreats can happen. And a lake to pepper eight or ten of these units around."

He's not stupid and he understands what I'm saying immediately. "My property. That's where you were hoping to put these."

"Yeah."

I don't know what he's thinking as he wanders around the place for another couple of minutes. He doesn't storm off, so I take that as a good sign. I follow behind him like an eager puppy as he paces the space. Finally he turns and looks at me. "It's a brilliant idea."

"Thanks."

"I can see why our farmland would be perfect," he replies. "So why are you telling me about this?"

"Because I'm an idiot," I reply and sigh. "I like you and I want you to like me too."

He steps right up to me, his hands cupping both sides of my face before he gently leans his forehead down to mine. "I do like you. More than I ever thought possible."

My arms move upward and I press my palms against his back just below his shoulders. He feels warm despite the fact it's a cold fall night and air is blowing into the room from the open slider. He kisses me. It's slow and sweet, until it isn't. Eventually his tongue finds mine and we're making out like horny teenagers.

"You forgive me?" I ask as his mouth moves to my neck and his hands slide down from my face, cupping my breasts through my sweater.

"I understand you," he replies. "I would have thought of my farm for this too if I were you."

"It's freezing in here," I walk over to the door. "Let's go back to the car."

"Or just let me warm you up," Tate says and opens the zip up Moo U hoodie he threw on before we left the house.

I close the sliding door so the air stops bustling in, and I walk up and slide my arms around his broad, warm torso as he wraps the hoodie and his arms around me.

"These are amazing and a really great idea," Tate says after a second of just holding each other in silence.

"It would be perfect for a resort farm," I say and find myself holding my breath.

"My family doesn't have the talents to make it work," Tate says and I feel his lips on the top of my head. "I mean, Jace could probably learn to build the units, but we don't have the culinary skills to run the catering-slash-food side of things. And Raquel and Louise would love to play hosts but wouldn't lift a finger to actually change over rooms and all that actual work that would be involved. My grandparents just want to retire. The only reason they haven't is they don't have the money."

"If only our families didn't hate each other's guts," I say, tipping my head back to look at him. A sliver of moonlight is cutting through one of the narrow oblong windows my uncle cut on the side of the container. It's making him look angelic. "If we partnered, we could do this. George and my dad could tend the goats and apples, My mom could keep up with the bees and goats, keeping the actual farm aspects running and handling the farmer's markets. Raquel and Louise could run the front of the bed and breakfast, you and I could put our marketing degrees together and handle the marketing and advertising, Daisy, my mom and your grandma could handle the catering, and Jace and my uncles could do the handyman upkeep."

His lips land on mine in a fleeting chaste kiss. "That would be perfect, but as we both know, there is no such thing as perfect. And our families' feud is irreparable."

He kisses me again, but it's urgent this time, not fleeting. And I respond with passion and need because I need him—and makeup sex—because we don't have much more time to break up and make up. In five short weeks, the fall market season will end and so will this—us. Because our families won't allow anything else.

As if reading my mind, his hands find their way under my sweater.

"It's too cold, isn't it?' he whispers as he moves his lips from my mouth to the column of my neck.

"You'll make me warm," I say with certainty as my hands reach for his belt.

There're no more words as we kiss and undress each other. I push his hoodie off his shoulders and he yanks his arms out of it and lays it on the floor. I come up behind him before he can turn back around and kiss a trail between his shoulder blades as my hands snake around his abdomen, and as one slides his zipper down, the other pushes past the waistband of his boxer briefs.

I wrap my hand around his cock and he groans. "I swear I've never been as hard as I am with you. The second I see you, you do this to my dick. No matter how much sass you throw my way, I want you."

He lets me stroke him, long and hard, for two slow pumps before turning around to face me and kiss me, our tongues tangling the second our lips meet. In seconds, the rest of our clothes are all gone, in one big pile on the floor and he lays me on top of them, and then stretches out on top of me. I can't feel the cold air around us. I can only feel his warm skin, hard muscles and harder cock pushing against my thigh as he nips at my left nipple, causing my back to arch. His eyes shift up to my face. "You look so fucking beautiful like this in the moonlight."

I feel a flush and he smiles in satisfaction as one of his hands slips between my legs and two fingers graze me. "Tate, I need this. No teasing. Get the condom."

I feel his whole body turn to stone for an undeniable second and I know exactly why. He forgot condoms. I whisper out a string of expletives. Tate starts to lift off of me but I reach up and wrap my hands around his neck, stopping him. "You have condoms in here? In the house?"

"No," I say and bite my lip.

"Maybe your dad has some?"

"Vasectomy," I explain. "My parents got pregnant with me by accident and Daisy only two months after my birth, before my mom even thought it was possible. They only wanted two, so they made sure there was no chance of more."

"Clyde?"

"The last time Clyde had a girlfriend was the year before I was born apparently, so anything he might have would be expired and my uncles don't live here to leave contraception lying around." I sigh and kiss him chastely, pulling him closer so he's touching every part of me again. I push my pelvis up and it bumps the tip of him. He fights a groan and loses.

"We need to stop talking about your relatives because the mood is imploding," Tate replies and rolls off of me.

"What I do have is an IUD," I say and suddenly he's rolled back on top of me.

"What?" Tate blinks down at me.

"I'm protected. You think I'm going to just rely on condoms? No way," I say. "But I've never told a guy I use other protection because I've never wanted a guy enough—or trusted him enough—but I do with you."

"Really?" Tate seems stunned. "I know I'm clean. I get a full physical every six months and they include STD tests. And I've never had sex, ever, without a condom."

"Well, we don't have to now. We can do other stuff," I say even though I really, really want him. All of him.

"I trust you too, Maggie," Tate says softly and then I feel his fingers at my folds again and I arch my back. "And I want you so much right now."

"Then no teasing," I say but I'm also pushing down on his hand, begging his thumb to find my clit, which is does and I moan.

"Maybe just a little teasing," Tate whispers against my collarbone. But after his thumb rolls against my clit one more time he shifts positions, and body parts, and runs the tip of his cock over my opening.

I grip his shoulders and bury my face in his neck as he starts to slide inside.

This is everything. He is everything. We are everything.

Those simple concise thoughts are the only thoughts my brain can form as Tate starts to move inside me. He isn't fast or rough, but he's breathing against my neck like he's run two marathons. "This… Jesus. It's so good like this."

He's not wrong. This feels so good and not just physically but emotionally. I feel like I'm giving him something and he's giving me something, and it's creating butterflies in my belly that are their own unique breed, like nothing I've ever felt before.

His thrusts are already as ragged as his breath, and I am writhing and panting and desperate for my own release, which comes on the heels of his judging by the noises we both make. My body goes limp a minute later and Tate's does the same.

He turns to bury his head in my hair, his lips by my ear. "Well that was…"

Everything. It was everything. Oh my God I'm in trouble.

"That was…indescribable." Tate finally finishes his sentence.

"Yeah."

He lifts his head to hold my gaze. His thumb slides gently across my cheekbone. "Maggie…I think I don't want this to end when the market does."

Now we're both in trouble.

"I love that you just said that, but I hate it too," I confess and suddenly feel like crying. "Because it feels good to know I'm not alone in my feelings, but it means we're both doomed instead of just me. Because our families will kill us."

He opens his mouth to argue with me, but a sound outside has us both shut up. Something—it sounds like something metal— crashes. And then Clyde's voice drifts through the air. "Stupid, dumb watering can. Who left it in the middle of the porch? God damn it."

"Shit!" I mouth the word, not even daring to whisper it.

Tate rolls off me and I crawl off our bed of clothes and we both scurry into them as quickly and quietly as possible.

"Will he come in here?" Tate whispers and I shush him even though he whispered it so quietly even I almost didn't hear him.

"Normally I would say no," I reply softly. "But if he's drunk, all bets are off. I can't predict drunk Clyde."

Once I get my sneakers back on, I scurry over to the long, high oblong window that faces the house and peek out. I see a shadow move on the porch. Clyde is dropping his drunk ass down in the porch swing that is beside the door to his small apartment. He kicks at the offending water can but misses.

"How are we going to get out of here?" Tate asks.

I take his hand. I'm rolling the dice on Clyde's level of sobriety being close to nil when I say. "We're going to walk out."

Tate looks horrified but lets me walk him to the door. I quietly slide it open and hop down into the grass. Tate hops down next to me and turns and slides the glass door shut. I grab his hand again and we turn away from the house and start walking toward the field. We make it three steps.

"Who's there?" Clyde slurs loudly.

"Just me Clyde," I call back trying to do it as quietly as possible so my parents aren't disturbed. This might work if my mom and dad don't show up. If they hear Clyde or me they'll wander out here and then the shit will hit the fan. "Heading home. Good night."

"Who is with you?" Clyde calls and he tries to get up off the porch swing but fails. He swears again.

"Gotta get home, Clyde."

"That your sister? You two working on that silly tin box instead of doing schoolwork?" Clyde growls.

I take a deep breath. "Yep. That's why I'm leaving now, Clyde. Got schoolwork. Bye!"

"You two girls are useless," Clyde snarls more to himself than me so I don't even bother with answering. "I can't believe you two are my only heirs. Building tin boxes and expecting people to live in them. What a joke."

I keep walking down into the empty field, past the bees, and over the fence. I feel Tate's hands on my waist as I climb it, making sure I make it over. When he hops over and we get to the car, he turns me around and presses me to my door instead of letting me get in. "My grandfather is right about him. Clyde Todd is a total asshole."

I nod. I've long ago lost that inherent instinct to defend my grandfather just because he's blood. "I won't argue that."

He tucks my hair behind my left ear and leans his body into mine. "You know you're far from useless right? Your idea is actually smart and progressive, just like moving the farm to goats and bees instead of cow dairy."

"Thank you. I know," I say proudly. I've never doubted my business sense. Even before college, I had great business instincts. "But I have to put up with Clyde because if he really wants to, he can sell the farm to a stranger. He's the only one on the deed. He wouldn't put my dad on it, and my uncles didn't want to be on it. Now that dad has had a stroke, Clyde's more hell bent than ever on selling it. He doesn't want to wait for Daisy and me to graduate to take it over."

"Then I will sell you my land," Tate promises and I smile because I think he actually would try. But the Adler farm isn't his either. Not alone. Although I think George has made Louise and his dad Vince official co-owners.

"Let's go." I get in my side and he gets in the passenger side, and we drive for a few minutes in silence.

Finally Tate says. "Did Clyde actually think I was Daisy?"

I grin. "He has horrible night vision and the beer goggles also don't help."

He laughs loudly. "Oh my god I wish we could tell her because Daisy's head would explode."

I pull to a stop in front of the hockey house and he reaches to undo his seat belt. "Come in."

I shake my head even though I don't want to say no. "I can't. Daisy knows by now I didn't go straight home this afternoon like I said I would. If I don't show up before midnight, she will have her spidey-sense activated and she won't stop harassing me until I tell her where I've been. She'll know it was a boy."

"You mean her weird doppelgänger intuition. Because you're creepy twins?" Tate has the smirkiest smirk that ever smirked on his face right now. I remember when it used to make me want to punch him but now…it makes me want to kiss him. So I do.

"I hate you."

"No you don't," Tate replies and cups my face. "And we're not breaking up."

"We're not together, remember?" I reply. "We're just scratching an itch. Not a big deal."

"Oh we're a big deal," Tate argues and kisses me again. "The biggest deal. The kind of deal that either destroys families or merges farms."

"Tate, what the hell are you talking about?" I ask and pull back because the more he kisses me, the more I think anything is possible, and that's dangerous.

"Do you want to be my girlfriend?"

I stare into his forest green eyes and open my mouth to answer. To say no, of course not. This isn't a possibility, and I don't entertain fantasy. I'm a no-nonsense, farm-raised, salt-of-the-earth Vermonter with a business brain. A logical one. I can't waste time on impossibilities. "Yes. More than anything."

"Good because I want you too. As my girlfriend, as my person." Tate kisses me again and for one brief, perfect moment I let my heart do a victory dance. "So we're going to do it. We're going to try and make this work."

"How?" My brain asks, essentially kicking my heart into submission. "No one—and I mean no one—will be okay with this."

"Jace will be," he says but it doesn't sound all that confident. "I mean, not at first, but if I explain it to him. Tell him how sure I am about you, he'll come around. It might take some time but he will. And as much as your sister both annoys and slightly terrifies me, she will too. Don't you think?"

"Maybe. But there will be so much judgment and yelling first," I reply honestly.

"It's worth it," Tate replies.

"Yeah. It is." I nod and he leans in to kiss me again but I pull back. "But Daisy and Jace are just the tip of the Todd-Adler iceberg. My dad and your dad used to get into brawls in high school. And your dad despises Bobby for allegedly hitting on your mom, and George and Clyde. George and Clyde—"

"Are the reason we're together, so we should thank them," Tate reminds me jokingly but then he grows serious. "Look, it's definitely not going to be easy, but maybe this is exactly what will finally stop all the drama. And if they can actually learn to tolerate us together, and then tolerate each other. Maybe merging the farms can happen."

"Tate…"

He kisses me, hard, and then reaches for the car door. "Just think about it."

"Okay." I nod.

He closes the car door but instead of walking up to his house he turns back and motions for me to lower the window. I hit the button and it slides down so he can lean in. "Look, it sounds crazy, I know. But crazy things happen. Hell, if someone had told me just a few months ago that the first person I would make love to would be Maggie Todd, I would have told them they need a shrink. But that's exactly what just happened tonight. So why not this too?"

Did he really just say that?

Tate winks and says, "Night, Firecracker," and I stare after him, speechless, as he walks off with my heart.

17

TATE

Five days later the sun is barely up when she crawls out of my bed. She has to go back to her apartment before Daisy wakes up and finds her missing. We've fallen into a system of sneaking out of our homes at night and sneaking into each other's beds and leaving before anyone can catch us. There's also a few clandestine meet-ups in hidden corners of the campus in between classes or before and after my hockey practices. I'm almost one hundred percent certain some of the guys like Lex and Jonah have figured out we're together, even though no one has seen her come and go from the house, but no one is talking about it and that's what counts.

My dick gets hard watching her get dressed in the early morning light, so when she leans back down to kiss me goodbye I try to pull her back into bed. But she has more willpower and common sense than me and doesn't let me. "If I stay another minute, Daisy will catch me doing my walk of shame and that's not how I want to tell her."

I groan, even though I know she's right. "Okay. But you're still planning on telling her today, right?"

Maggie nods and pulls her hair up into a ponytail. She snuck over here at one in the morning in workout wear and running shoes so that if anyone caught her sneaking out—or in—she could say she had insomnia and went for a run. "I was going to tell her on our way over to the hockey game. That way she doesn't have a lot of time to yell at me or run home and tell the family, and she'll be forced to watch you play and hopefully you can woo her with your talents."

"Who doesn't want their sister with the best defensemen in the tri-state area?"

"Daisy hates big egos, so you might wanna rein that in." She gives me another quick kiss but makes it to the door before I can grab her again. "Have a good day and a kick ass game. I'll see you at the Biscuit afterward."

"I'm going to kiss you. In front of everyone," I warn.

She smiles. It's big and bright and drop-dead gorgeous. "I hate PDA but for you, I will make an exception."

She disappears, closing the door behind her and I get out of my warm comfortable bed, like a lovesick fool just so I can watch her jog down the street. My God, I'm in love. With Maggie Todd. The world is officially upside down, and I like it better this way.

I try to catch some more Zs but I can't. I'm tired but I'm restless. Not just because Maggie is supposed to tell Daisy today, but because I also want to tell Jace. So I decide I might as well get that done and throw on some clothes and get in my truck.

As I barrel up the long drive to the farm, Dad is on the porch, sitting in one of the Adirondack chairs, probably on his first coffee break of the morning. I park behind his truck and hop out. "What's going on, son?"

He sounds concerned. I smile. "Couldn't sleep. Thought I'd see if I could steal Jace for breakfast before he has to go to school."

Dad pulls off his tattered Patriots baseball cap and scratches his thick, dark hair. "I'm sure it won't take much convincing. But make sure he actually goes to school, okay?"

"Of course. Why? Has he been skipping?" I ask as I climb the stairs to the porch.

Dad nods. "Your Ma got a call from the vice principal two

days ago. Because apparently it was his fourth sick day in the last two weeks."

"Shit." I shake my head. "He has nine months left and then he's free. What the hell is he doing?"

"Maybe ask him over pancakes," Dad replies. "Because your Ma is pissed not just at him but at me for not noticing he was doing it. At this point, she wants him to move into her place in town and you know we need him here. But I need him to graduate, so…I'm thinking about it."

As if on cue, the screen door swings open and Jace walks out. The sleepy expression on his face shifts to confusion when he sees me and then annoyed when he sees Dad. "I'm going. I'm going. I'll take a selfie with the school bus driver if you want proof. You don't have to have Tate drive me."

"I was actually here to take you to breakfast," I tell him. "But if you want that selfie with sixty-year-old Eddie the bus driver and his vibrant array of seventies concert shirts, feel free to say no."

"I'm in."

"Straight home after school, Jace," Dad calls out as we make our way to the truck. "Not only do we have apples to pick, you're grounded."

"I know. I know." Jace rolls his eyes aggressively as he slams my truck door.

I hop in and get us on our way. Jace talks about the farm and football the whole way to the diner, and I let him because I don't want to rile him up before we get there—and I drop my bomb. He tells me about the progress they're making with the barn and how we, luckily, have less crappy unsellable apples than last year. "And Dad was able to make another payment on the mortgage, so the bank is easing off for now."

"Really? How? Why didn't he tell me?" I ask.

"Raquel actually contributed some of her paycheck," Jace says scratching at his pathetic excuse for beard stubble. He's trying to go for the scruffy hipster look, but he's only eighteen and his beard is duck fluff at best. "And Dad took a drywall job last weekend."

"What?" I steal a stunned glance at Jace. My dad used to want to be a builder and have his own contracting business. He even took night school courses when I was young and was in the drywallers' union. But my grandparents needed more and more help at the farm and so he gave it up. Or so I thought.

Jace nods. "Yeah. It was hell at the farm because we had to work twice as hard all weekend and Raquel, of course, didn't show up to work Saturday. We had more visitors than ever but Gramps wouldn't even let me call her and yell at her because she donated half her paycheck to the mortgage, so she earned her day off, he said."

"You donate every hour of your damn life. So does Dad," I say, annoyed, as I pull into a parking spot. "Why does he always cut her and Aunt Louise so much slack?"

"He never expected Raquel to give up her senior activities, but Grandpa flat out told me to not ask for money for silly parties just because I was graduating," Jace says and jumps out of the truck as I turn it off. He leaves his school knapsack on the front seat.

"If you want to go on the trips, I'll find a way for you to go, Jace," I say and he shrugs.

"I kind of wanted to go on the ski trip in January, but it's no big deal," Jace says. In the back of my head I make a mental note to save money for his trip. "Are you excited for the game tonight? We're all going. The whole family."

"I am. A little jittery but that will pass. First game of the season is always a little nerve-wracking," I explain as I open the door to the restaurant and Jace walks in.

We find a booth and slide in. After the waitress pours us both coffee and takes our orders, I stare at him while he stirs in an alarming amount of sugar to his coffee. "Jace. You have to graduate."

He sighs but doesn't lift his eyes from his mug. "I will. Relax."

"Can you do it without making it as hard as possible? So Mom and Dad don't fight more and lose years off their lives with worry?" I say and sip my own coffee.

He finally looks up and frowns. "Yeah. Fine. I just...who even cares if I graduate? I could get a GED, you know. It's not like I'm going to college."

"Why not?"

"Because I'm definitely not getting a full scholarship like you, even though my grades aren't hideous. We don't have the money, even for state school," Jace reminds me what I definitely already know.

"You will qualify for aide, and I'll hopefully be making enough money to pay off your loans in a couple of years," I remind him. "And even if the pro thing doesn't pay off, I'll have the farm back on its feet and will help you pay them off. We paid for Raquel's ridiculously overpriced online cosmetology classes. We can pay for you."

"I don't even know what I would take." He sighs.

"I thought you wanted to go into the veterinary program?"

"I did, but it's not practical," Jace says and pauses to sip his coffee. "We don't have animals on the farm, and that's where I'm going to end up. Just like you."

"What if we didn't need you for manual labor?" I ask. "What if we had animals that you could tend to? Or even better, enough other people to run the farm so you could start your own veterinary practice?"

Jace blinks his eyes which are similar to mine but lighter. "Please don't say we're changing over from apples to cows or something? Because even just changing tree types is part of the reason we're circling the drain financially. I doubt making even bigger changes will help."

"The Todds moved from cows to bees and goats with little to no hiccups," I say calmly, but of course he looks at me like I just invoked the name of the devil.

"The Todds are our business icons now? Shit, we really are in trouble," Jace snarks. He reaches for the sugar dispenser and I stop him.

"If I have to watch you add more sugar to that tiny mug of coffee I'm going to get diabetes," I say and then move back to the subject. "The Todds are doing well with their new plan. So well, they have expansion ideas. For more things that have more return and less risk than the standard farming we've all been trying to do."

He raises an eyebrow. "And how do you know that?"

"Because unlike the rest of you, I've actually held a conversation with one of them," I say and silently add *and, you know, seen one of them naked.*

"Which one?" Jace wants to know, his left eyebrow still arched. "Daisy Cute-But-Psycho Todd or Maggie Hot-But-Evil Todd? Or Clyde Drunk-And-Nuts Todd. Or—"

"Maggie," I interrupt because he will literally list every person on their family tree with some sort of ridiculous nickname if I don't. "And she's not actually evil. She's smart and kind and…"

Jace's eyes grow two sizes and I know he knows what's coming. "You didn't."

"I did. I am. And it's good, Jace. Really good."

He makes a face. "Oh God I don't want to know about your sexual exploits."

"No I'm not talking about the sex part," I argue and smile. "That's actually better than good. Way better. But I'm talking about the relationship part. I like her. A lot. In fact, I kind of think I could love her."

"How?" Jace asks in a disbelieving hiss. "I just…after everything with that family? How on bloody earth do you even go there?"

"Trust me, I didn't plan it, but it happened." I shrug. "And I don't want it to unhappen, which is why I'm telling you. And eventually everyone else. But I need your support first."

Jace is blinking—repeatedly. He picks up his mug, puts it

down without taking a sip and then picks it up again. Then puts it down. "Tate... I don't know if I can."

"Why not?" I challenge. "Think about it. Really. There've been a ton of scuffles with the Todds over the years, but do we even know why at this point? Can't we just make a concerted effort to let the stupid feud go? Working with them at the market hasn't been horrible."

"It hasn't been great," Jace counters.

"Because we've been actively trying to push each other's buttons," I say and pause as the waitress walks over and drops our orders in front of us.

I got avocado toast with a side of smoked chicken apple sausage. Jace got a bacon double cheddar omelet with a side of smothered hash browns and pancakes. It all looks delicious but after thanking the waitress, we both ignore our plates.

"Tate, even if *I* accept you dating a Todd, Dad won't. Grandpa definitely won't," Jace says.

"They will lose me if they don't," I reply and to be honest, I didn't know I would say that until I did. But it feels good. "Not just because it's Maggie either. I mean, who knows. Right now she feels like end game, but life is full of curveballs. This isn't about her, specifically. If they don't accept that I'm with her, and actively try and mess things up, then they care more about the stupid feud than they do about my feelings, and I'll walk away. From them and the farm and everything."

Jace looks at me in stunned silence. I let him. He needs time to absorb this, and I've said all I have to say. I sip my coffee and reach for my fork. Finally Jace speaks. "Maybe that's what needs to happen. Not you disowning the family, but letting the farm go. What are we even fighting for here? Gramps is tired and wants to retire. Dad misses drywalling. God if he'd just stuck with that and stayed out of the family farm, maybe Mom wouldn't have left him. She hated how Gramps and Gran never treated Dad well, like they treated Louise, and it was the real hole in their marriage. So maybe we need to just sell it."

"Or, you know, merge it," I say and he freezes, with a forkful of food in midair. "Maggie has an idea, and I like it. We'd be happier and more profitable and so would the Todds."

"Unless we all kill each other," Jace says and shakes his head, finally diving into his meal.

Halfway through our breakfasts I say. "Can you keep this to yourself? I want to be the one to tell everyone else. Eventually."

"I'm more than happy to not be the bearer of bad news," Jace replies quickly.

"But you'll have my back when I do tell them. And all hell breaks loose?" I ask and try not to sound as nervous as I am. I honestly don't know if he will support me.

"I don't agree with this, but I'll have your back," Jace confirms and gives me a small smile. "You can't very well pay for my college if I disown you."

I laugh. "Thanks for the support."

His smile fades and his light green eyes grow serious. "You really like her?"

I nod.

"And more importantly, you really trust her?"

"One hundred percent."

He nods but he doesn't smile. "I don't. Sorry. This feels…like you're gonna get burned."

"Give it time," I reply. "She's not going anywhere, so all I ask is that you have an open mind. Please."

"I can do that, I guess," Jace says and shrugs. He's still skeptical and I can't blame him. Maggie and I have a long, rocky road to pave but at least Jace is willing to let us try.

"Love you bro," I say as I get up to pay.

"Gross." Jace smiles and makes a face. "She's already making you soft."

I laugh. "Soft is something Maggie doesn't make me."

"GROSS!"

18

MAGGIE

Everything has already gone awry. I wanted to talk to Daisy on the way to the game, but she didn't come home. She stayed at school after her last class and I had to walk over with Caroline and Jasmyn, who both noticed my mood was off. Caroline said I was a big ball of anxiety, and she wasn't wrong.

Now it's moments before puck drop, we're surfing down the row into our seats, and Daisy is still nowhere to be found. Jasmyn and Caroline sit but I stand and glare at the entrance. Where is she, damnit?

"She'll be here, relax." Caroline reaches up and tugs on my arm to try and get me to sit down.

"She didn't tell either of you why she wasn't coming home before the game?" I ask. "Where she went?"

They both shake their heads. "She said it was important and all would be revealed later."

I stare at Jasmyn after she announces that and she just shrugs. "What the hell does that even mean?"

Neither answer because neither knows. I sit because I don't know what else to do. I told Tate I would tell her before the game, so that after the game at the Biscuit we could actually hang out together without causing a scene. He texted me earlier and said he had told Jace, who promised to keep it quiet and that he was okay with it. "Okay" was the best we knew we could expect, so I was relieved. I was hoping the same from Daisy, if I could just damn well tell her.

Finally, as the players skate around the ice in warm-up, my attention is drawn to something other than my missing sister. Tate. Just watching him glide over the ice with his teammates makes my heart flutter. He looks so hot in his uniform. I know that sounds ridiculous because you can barely see him with the helmet and face cage and everything but man, my ovaries don't seem to care.

And then he looks up and scans the crowd and he finds me— stares right at me—and I swear we're eye-fucking in front of everyone.

"You know, Maggie, if I didn't know any better I would swear that smile on your face is for your mortal enemy," Caroline says with a side-eye glance.

I reach up and touch my lips and yup, I'm smiling. I hadn't even realized. I glance over at Caroline and both she and Jasmyn are staring at me with curious looks. "Yeah well, you're wrong," I say calmly. "He's not my mortal enemy anymore. He's…"

"Oh my God!" Daisy's voice cuts through the din of chatter around us. "I so didn't mean to be that late. And yes, Mags, I got your nine hundred text messages. I know I was supposed to meet you at the house and you want to talk. Sorry, sorry, sorry! But I'm here now so, yak away." She drops down dramatically beside me.

"Where the hell were you?"

She's staring at the ice. "I had to do a thing. You'll see. Eventually. It's a surprise. A glorious surprise."

"I don't like surprises," I reply, feeling a dark sense of dread start to swirl in my belly, sucking up my Tate butterflies like they're the cow in *Twister*. "Spill it now."

"Nope," Daisy replies firmly and shakes her head. I have to lean back to avoid being clipped by the end of her high ponytail which starts swaying back and forth. "Now why don't you tell me what you wanted to say to me before the game gets started and this place gets even noisier?"

I open my mouth and the announcer blares over the sound system welcoming everyone and blabbering on about the upcoming season, the team, and a whole bunch of other stuff that I'm sure everyone wants to hear but me. Argh.

Then it's National Anthem time. Then Daisy announces she's thirsty and has to pee and will be right back. Then the game starts. Caroline switches seats with Jasmyn so she's right beside me and when I ask her why she grins and says, "I have a feeling you're the real show tonight and I want a front row seat."

"Shut up," I say and turn my attention back to the ice. Tate is in a corner of the rink fighting for the puck with one of the Boston University players—and he wins. The crowd roars and so do I. Caroline laughs. "You may want to tone it down a bit when Daisy gets back or you won't have to tell her you're shagging him, she'll figure it out on her own."

My head snaps toward her so quickly I almost give myself whiplash. She's just smiling serenely, like some wise old prophet who knew all along. "I'm not just shagging him, I'm dating him. And I'm falling in love with him. Fast. Faster than his slapshot."

Her response is to squeal and clap her hands and then wrap me in a bear hug. I laugh. "I have a feeling Daisy's reaction won't be this enjoyable."

"Not at first, but you know her, she'll come around," Caroline replies and tucks her blonde hair back behind her ear. "She'll see you're happy and he's a good guy and she'll chill out. But, the rest of your family…that's a harder sell."

"I know," I reply and sigh. "But let's just start with Daisy."

Five minutes and one goal—thankfully by us—later and Daisy is back with four hot dogs and a giant drink. She hands out the hot dogs, getting all the toppings of preference right for each of us. I look at Caroline, my eyes screaming "well I can't tell her now, we're eating!" So the entire first period goes by without me saying anything about the fact that I'm dating Tate.

During intermission, Daisy is gone again. She comes back smiling—and it's not just any smile. It's her I'm-up-to-something smile. She first debuted it when she was five and she gave Tess, our old lab, a manicure using our mom's reddest shade of nail polish. The manicure was administered in our parents' bedroom, and most of that nail polish ended up on their white throw rug.

"What have you done?" I ask mimicking my mother from back in the day.

Daisy's smile deepens. "You'll see soon enough."

"Daisy, you're making me nervous and nauseous," I say, the hot dog I ate sitting like a brick in my belly.

Daisy ignores that and cheers with the rest of the arena when we score. I see Tate skating toward his bench, arms in the air. "Did Tate score that?"

The announcer answers me over the speaker. "First goal of the season for defensemen Tate Adler."

I start to clap—loudly. Daisy's eyes grow wide and Caroline laughs. I ignore them both and keep clapping, adding a wolf whistle for good measure. Now Daisy's mouth is hanging open. "What on God's green earth are you doing?"

"Cheering for our hockey team," I reply coolly.

"You're a little aggressive about it considering it's the devil's spawn that scored," Daisy says bitingly and I take a deep breath, hold it and turn to face her.

"Maybe it's time we stop the hate," I say firmly.

"Nope. He's earned it," Daisy replies just as firmly.

"He really hasn't earned *my* hate," I say. "In fact, he's earned my respect and my…like. He's earned my like."

"He's earned your like?" Daisy repeats and shakes her head, her nose scrunching up in revelation. "What does that even mean? You *like* him?"

"I do. A lot."

"So he's your friend? Are you insane? You think he's your friend?" Her voice is climbing in octaves with every sentence and it's freaking me out.

"I think he's my boyfriend," I clarify.

"You think what?" Daisy gasps. She puts a hand to my forehead. "Are you sick? Did you hit your head? Are you out of your freaking mind?"

"Actually, I know he's my boyfriend," I reply. "I mean at first, it was just sex. Angry sex. Hate sex, even...although I don't know if we ever really hated each other. But if we did, we don't now. We really like each other and we want to be together."

"Be together? Like, as in, a relationship?" Daisy is in shock, which I expected. But there's something more...there's panic. I don't understand why, but she is panicking. "But what about the gift basket opportunity he stole from us?"

"Jace did that, not Tate," I say. "Jace never told him about it."

"What? No. No, Jace said that—"

"Jace lied," I say. "Apparently he hates us as much as, well, every other one of the Adlers. But Tate gave him hell for that gift basket thing and talked to him and Jace is okay with us giving this a shot."

"Magnolia, this can't be happening," Daisy says, which is another sign she's panicking. She never, ever calls me by my full name. She grabs my hands and then lets them go, and runs her hands into her hair completely destroying her ponytail.

Her panic is making me panic, so I start to babble. "I really, really hope that you'll be okay with this after you get used to it. Because honestly, Daisy, if you just give Tate a chance, you'll like him. And you'll like him for me."

"No. No," Daisy insists shaking her head emphatically. "We hate him. We were blackmailing him. He knew the rules and he broke them and now we screw him. Because he has done nothing but try and screw us and Hank said..."

"Hank? Hank said what?"

"That Tate is stealing our business," Daisy blurts out. "Hank said he knows about the container home project and he was going to do it himself. Instead of with us."

"He knows because I told him. He's not stealing anything," I say. Tate mentioned he was going to hang out with Hank again the other day, and that Hank knew about us so he must have mentioned the business idea. And as I have the most sickening realization of my life, the buzzer for the end of the second period cuts through the arena. "Daisy. What did you do?"

"Our sponsors for tonight's game include The Biscuit in the Basket." Daisy jumps out of her seat and looks at the Jumbotron above the ice where a picture of the Biscuit's logo is being displayed on top of a close-up of one of their tables filled with food.

The announcer keeps talking, announcing Tito's Pizzeria as another sponsor and a picture of a fresh-out-of-the-oven pizza flashes up on the screen. Daisy tries to push past me and escape down the aisle but I grab her and won't let her go. She stares at the screen above like she's watching a train wreck and then I realize she is…because the announcer starts to speak again. "And our newest sponsors, Manly Maids."

And there—splashed across the Jumbotron for the entire arena to see—is the picture I snapped of Tate Adler in his underwear holding a feather duster.

Everyone recognizes him. You can hear it in the rumble of gasps, giggles, claps and whistles that erupts. They think it's a joke. I drop my grip on Daisy's arm as my eyes find Tate on the bench. He's staring up at the Jumbotron while his teammates either seem confused or are laughing like the fans. But his coach definitely is not laughing. I want to die.

"Maggie, I didn't—"

"Don't talk to me," I say in a low, growl of a voice. "Just don't."

I push my way down the aisle. I have to find Tate after the game, because I know he won't be finding me.

19

TATE

"She's out there."

I look up at Lex's remorseful face, like it's somehow his fault Maggie Todd stabbed me in the back—and the heart. I give him a curt nod of thanks. "I'll go out the back exit."

"Do you want me to wait for you?"

I shake my head. "No. Thanks."

He nods and reluctantly turns and leaves me alone in the locker room. I finish drying off from my shower and get dressed, trying not to think about what's about to happen. Coach asked me not to leave after the game. He didn't look angry, he looked gravely concerned, which was actually worse. I'm tying up my shoes when I hear someone clear their throat and look up and see Coach Garfunkle standing in the doorway. "Coach is ready to see you."

"Thanks," I say and stand up. I feel like I'm a pig going to slaughter. I can't believe this is happening—and that Maggie would do this.

Coach Garfunkle claps my shoulder as I pass and then hands me a crystal. "Put this in your pocket."

I look at the hunk of bright green stone he's pressed into my palm and then back up at him skeptically. "I don't believe in this stuff, Coach."

"You don't have to," Coach replies and then gives me a small smile. "Think of it this way, you need all the help you can get and this can't hurt."

I slip the rock into my pocket, but the dread in my gut doesn't lighten. If anything, it gets heavier with every step I take toward Coach Keller's office. And as I see the dean walk out of that office and head down the hall in the opposite direction, the dread is so crushing I almost can't bring myself to walk into the office. But I do somehow.

Coach Keller looks up from his desk, his face grim, and as I walk toward the chair across from his desk he shakes his head. "No need to sit. You're not staying. You need to go home."

"I'm being kicked out of school?" I say.

Oh my God.

The gravity on Keller's face lightens slightly. "What? No. Not yet. There's been no final decision on what to do with you, but you're suspended from the team until the decision is made, so no practice tomorrow and possibly no away game for you later this week."

Fuck. The dread comes back like a bowling ball rolling through my innards.

Keller sighs loudly. "What the hell were you thinking, Adler?"

"I was thinking my family was behind on mortgage payments and I needed to help," I say honestly. "And that job was maximum pay and minimum hours, so it didn't interfere with my classes or rink time."

"Well that's not true now is it? Seems like it's interfering with everything." Keller frowns. "I'll be at the meeting you have with the dean tomorrow, and I'll fight to keep the blowback from this minimal."

"Thank you, sir.

"And I want you to show up there with proof you've quit that damn job, like a copy of your letter of resignation," Keller demands as he sits back behind his desk.

"I don't know if it's the type of job that requires a letter," I say quietly. "Most guys just stop showing up."

"It may not require a letter, just like it doesn't require pants, but you're giving them a letter so we have the proof we need," Coach barks and shakes his head.

"Yes, sir." I nod. He flips open his laptop so I assume I'm dismissed and start for the door, but he calls my name gruffly before I can leave.

"I'm sorry about your family's hardship Tate," Keller says, the hard lines of his face barely visible because his expression is softer than I've probably ever seen it.

"We're managing to hold on," I say even though my shiny new plan for the farm's future was stabbed through its heart, just like I was when that photo hit the Jumbotron.

"You know, if you can just stay focused, as soon as you enter that draft your financial troubles will be over," he tells me firmly. "I believe that, Adler. You've got what it takes."

"Thanks, Coach." His words should be helping me feel better, bringing me some kind of relief, even minimal, but they feel like they're falling through me instead of filling me up.

I make my way out of the locker room the long way, making sure not to use the main entrance where Lex said Maggie was waiting. Instead I head out the back exit that no one ever uses. Someone else is waiting for me there. It's Patrick. Or Paxton? Telling them apart in the moonlight is even harder than the sunlight—until he speaks. "It's time to drown those sorrows in tequila and a good pair of boobs."

I should decline but Patrick wraps an arm around my shoulder and drags me away, and I decide to let him. Chances are Maggie will show up at the hockey house sooner rather than later, so the longer I stay away from there, the better. And although boobs is the last thing I need, a shot of tequila or six might numb the ache in my chest.

Two hours later, I fall off my chair.

Patrick and the rest of the team cheer like I just scored another goal. Assholes.

"Okay, I am officially cutting you off." Hank's voice floats into my ears from somewhere behind me, and then I feel his hands under my arms as he pulls me to my feet. "And I'm getting you something to eat."

"I'm not hungry," I tell him.

"I don't care," he replies and points at me. "You're eating."

"The staff here is so bossy," I mutter and Jace chuckles.

On the way to the Biscuit I realized I had seventeen text messages. Ten from Maggie and seven from family members. Mostly Jace, but even Grams texted me. And someone—likely my dad or mom since they were both at the game—left a couple voicemails too. I only responded to Jace, telling him I was going to the Biscuit and then I turned off my phone so I couldn't look at Maggie's messages at all.

Was it infantile? Maybe. But I didn't care. I was like a wounded animal, and I just needed to crawl off and lick my wounds. Jace showed up about an hour ago after he settled my family down and promised them he'd get answers. They were all at the game and according to Jace their reactions vary from irate to confused and everything in between. He's been trying to get me to go back to the farm to explain myself but I won't leave, so Jace is drinking pop and waiting until I'm drunk enough that he can force me into his car. That time has probably arrived, but I still don't want to go face my problems.

The guys, thankfully, have done a great job of distracting me. We talked about the pictures, and I explained everything to them when I first got here. Everyone seemed to be relieved when they found out I wasn't instantly expelled and that Coach would go to the meeting with me. I tried to absorb their confidence and their positivity, but all I really absorbed was tequila.

Hank drops a giant basket of fries in front of me and a pint glass filled with ice water. "Eat and drink nothing but this. Got it?"

I try to salute him but judging by his face it's not the best impression. He rolls his eyes and walks off but not before pointing at the other guys. "No more booze for him guys. I mean it."

Everyone nods. Jace steals a fry as he jumps off his seat. "I'm heading to the can and then I'm gonna take you home. To the farm. Dad made me promise, so eat up."

I groan. The last thing I want to do is head to the farm, but I know I don't have a choice. My family needs an explanation for what they saw tonight. I shovel two fries into my mouth and chew.

"Tate."

Shit.

"Sorry Maggie, but he's not in a good place to talk to you," I hear someone say—it might be Paxton.

"Tate. Please," Maggie says but I refuse to look at her. It's going to hurt to look at her. That ache in my chest will start to overtake the blissful numbness of the tequila if I look at her. "I had no idea. I swear."

"Please go away. I can't right now," I say and my voice sounds so dark.

Jace is going to wander back from the bathroom any minute and if he sees her here he will go off like a cannon. It won't be pretty. I push the fries away. She's still standing there. I have no choice. I get off my chair, almost tipping over again, but Patrick reaches out to steady me. I turn and look at her.

She's been crying—a lot, judging by her blotchy red face and puffy eyes. My heart wants to break for her but it can't because it's already in pieces. "Maggie you need to go. I can't right now. You don't want me to, trust me. If we talk right now..."

I don't finish that sentence because I don't know what will happen, but I know none of it will be good. I'm angry. I'm hurt.

I'm confused and scared and frustrated. I'm a lot of horrible things, and I'm too drunk not to take it out on her.

"I just need a second. Just one. Please."

"No. Fuck just..." I glance over toward the bathroom doors. I see four, thanks to my drunken double vision, instead of the usual two which is not at all helpful. "Fuck."

I march toward her, take her arm and head toward the doors. I don't think I'm doing a very good job because I clip two tables on my way and trip as I reach the door, almost falling onto the sidewalk beyond. Maggie helps me stay upright and pushes me back against the brick wall beside the door.

Why does she have to be so pretty, even all puffy-faced? Why do I want to hold her even though she may have ruined my life? "You're not fair."

"Daisy did it," Maggie says.

"How could you let her?"

"I didn't know until it was too late."

"You two tell each other everything. Your words." The disbelief dripping from my voice is something she can't miss.

"Well she didn't tell me this," Maggie replies and the anguish in her pretty eyes is more than apparent. "You think I would do this to you? Now?"

I don't answer that. "She did it because you told her about us?"

"She did it before I could tell her."

I tip my head back and feel the rough bricks behind me. "Why didn't she know? You were supposed to tell her before the game."

"I know. I tried. It got all screwed up. I'm so sorry."

"That isn't going to help me if I lose my scholarship and have to drop out," I reply angrily.

"It was a mistake."

"This whole fucking thing has been nothing but mistakes, Maggie," I blurt out, and she looks like I slapped her.

The door to the Biscuit swings open and Jace is standing there, his eyes narrowed with disdain. "What the hell is *she* doing here?"

"I came to explain," Maggie says.

"Come on. Let's go," Jace says to me as he waves me over. Then he turns back to Maggie. "There is no explanation in the world that can make me forgive you for what happened tonight. And I'm going to work like hell to make sure he doesn't forgive you either."

"Jace…"

He glares at me. "Shut up and let's go."

We walk down the sidewalk to Gran's little ancient hatchback. He unlocks the passenger door and tries to shove me inside. I don't want to let him but it seems like my muscles have been replaced by Play-Doh. Jace turns back to Maggie, who must still be standing nearby, as my ass hits the old seat. "I asked him point blank if he trusted you this morning when he told me about the two of you because I wanted to know how he could. Because I didn't. And it turns out I was right. You might not have done this, but you're still the reason it happened."

I turn to get out of the car and tell Jace to leave her alone but he slams the door shut in my face and by the time I get it open again, the sidewalk is empty.

20

TATE

When I turn the corner to start down the long hall to the dean's office, my heart stops. There's a girl sitting on one of the benches that lines the administration building hall. And for the split second I think it's Maggie my heart floods with warmth for the first time since that stupid picture hit the Jumbotron forty-eight hours ago. But then she looks up from her phone and turns to face me and I realize it's Daisy, and my heart turns cold, back into the dead organ it's become.

She stands up as I continue down the hall, intent on walking right by her. "I'm here to help."

I stutter step at her words but refuse to stop walking. "You can't help. Go away."

"I'll tell him I did it. I'll even lie and say I photoshopped it. You never worked there. I was just trying to screw you over," Daisy says stumbling along behind me.

Finally I stop and turn to face her. She looks even more like Maggie when she's anguished. I never really wanted to know that. "Daisy, if you do that then you'll be in trouble. They'll see it as bullying which is strictly prohibited and you'll lose *your* scholarship."

"But I deserve to," Daisy says.

"No you don't." I can't believe I am saying it. It's true, but I still don't want to let her off the hook for anything she's done. Especially the part where her actions made it clear an Adler dating a Todd is destined for failure no matter what. "And I already admitted to having the job, so don't bother. I'll take full responsibility and I'll handle the consequences."

I turn and keep walking but just like a typical Todd, she is not done. "Okay then can you please stop punishing Maggie for this?"

And now I've stopped walking again. My fingers in the pocket of my coat grip the crystal Coach Garfunkle gave me because I actually decided to bring it. It might not help save my scholarship, but maybe it can keep me from murdering Daisy Todd. She scurries up to stand in front of me.

"I'm not punishing her. I'm...I don't know what to say. My family will never ever get on board with us dating now. They know you did this. They know Maggie shot the picture and blackmailed her way into the booth. They know it all, and now this is doomed, Daisy. I don't know how to make this work."

"If you get back together I'll be on your side," Daisy says. "She's a mess."

"I am too," I admit and sigh. "Daisy, I have to deal with this other mess right now, okay?"

She opens her mouth like she wants to say more and I'm sure she does but, luckily, she gets that it's not the time. She nods. "Good luck, Tate, and I'm very sorry. I am."

"Thanks for the apology," I say and continue down the hall to the dean's office.

I hold my breath and square my shoulders as I knock. The door is opened by Coach Keller. He nods and I see a flicker of approval in his stern expression because I wore my best suit. I walk in and prepare for the worst.

An hour later, I shake both their hands and walk out of there still a student with a scholarship and still a member of the hockey team. I'm also now employed part-time on the campus grounds crew, so I'll be tending the lawns and helping shovel and de-ice the grounds when winter comes. The pay isn't bad. As coach Keller acerbically pointed out when the dean told me the news, "It's not Manly Maid money, but you can wear more than just your underwear."

"In fact fully clothed is a requirement," the dean had added.

I had a one-game suspension but I could still attend practice and after that, all clear. I was back on the team and back on track. It couldn't have gone better. And the first person I want to tell is Maggie.

I step out of the administration building and start down the steps pulling my phone out of my pocket and reread her one and only message since this all blew up.

I'm so sorry. I didn't do it but I'd do anything to fix it. To fix us. I'm sorry.

I leave campus and jump in my truck because I promised my family I would head straight to them with the news of my fate. The whole drive there I think about telling Maggie. I craft forty different text messages in my head but none of them sound right. She should know I didn't lose my scholarship or spot on the team. But there's so much more to say, and I don't know how to say it.

I pull up and park next to the barn and pull my phone out again and start to respond to her last message.

Dean took pity on me. Still have my scholarship. We should probably talk...in person.

I stare at the screen waiting for a response but then I hear a voice I'm not expecting at the farm—my mom's. "Tate! You're back. What happened?" She turns and calls into the house through the screen door. "Tate's back!"

I look up and see her on the porch, wrapped in a cardigan and holding a coffee mug. It takes me back. She used to wave goodbye to us like that as we made our way down the drive to catch the school bus. Only her face wasn't creased with worry back then like it is now.

"What are you doing here?" I ask. She hasn't been to the farm, that I know of, since the divorce unless it was to drop us off after weekend visits, but she never got out of the car.

"Your dad said I should come here and wait for the news," she explains as the door behind her opens and my entire family floods out of the house. Even Raquel and Louise are there.

"What happened?" Dad demands, his tone clipped and tense.

"I've still got my scholarship."

Everyone blurts out various words of relief.

"And I'm still on the team, but I am suspended one game, so I won't be playing this weekend," I say.

"Shit," Dad hisses.

"Oh Tate, I'm sorry," Mom says sympathetically.

"You deserve it for screwing a Todd," Raquel says judgmentally.

"Shut up," I snap.

"Don't tell her to shut up," Louise barks at me. "She's not the one embarrassing her family and screwing up her one big shot in life. A shot that could save this damn farm."

Before I can respond, Grandpa does. "Your aunt Louise is right, Tate. The suspension will show up on your record with the team and it might affect your draft rank. Some teams are going to see you as a problem now, and it's all thanks to that little bitch."

"Do not call her a bitch," I yell. "I warned you the other night. You do not insult Maggie in front of me, ever. I wasn't kidding."

Grandpa looks completely offended. "You go near that girl again and I swear you won't have to disown me. I will disown you."

"So will I." My grandmother speaks up for the first time since this whole thing started. Even when I ended up back here drunker than a skunk with Jace the night it happened, she didn't say a word. The next day when I told them the whole story, from taking the job to getting caught doing the job by Maggie to the blackmail to the way my feelings for her changed, Faith Adler didn't say a word. Not one.

"Grams..." I say softly. I didn't think she would necessarily be an enthusiastic defender of my choices, but I thought I could count on her to be neutral at least.

But now her eyes are teary and she shakes her head. "You leave well enough alone when it comes to that family, Tate. They…they have no place in our lives. That decision was made long before you came along, and it needs to be respected."

She turns abruptly and storms off into the house. Grandpa chases after her. Jace looks as bewildered and taken aback as I am right now. My mother on the other hand just looks fed up. She furrows her blonde eyebrows and lets out a sigh. "What the hell is it with this family and the Todds? I never understood it. Maybe if you all just gave it a rest you'd be happier."

"Tanya, with all due respect, you don't have to deal with it anymore, so don't get involved," Dad tells her.

"Hating someone is like drinking poison and expecting the other person to die," Mom tells him and points. "That's all of you right now. And yeah, I got out, but my sons are still part of this shit show and I want Tate to be happy, even If it means dating a Todd."

She marches down the porch steps and kisses me on the cheek before she gets into her car and drives off. Dad just stares at me for a moment longer from the porch and then shakes his head. "I'm very happy you dodged this bullet, Tate, but I'm still disappointed you gave the Todd family the ammunition to fire the shot. And if you do it again, it won't be forgivable."

He goes inside. Louise and Raquel follow, so now it's just Jace and me. He gives me a small smile. "Well, that went well."

We both let out a dry chuckle. He jumps off the porch, walks over and hugs me. I accept it without one of my usual quips or jokes. When he lets go, his face is more serious than I think I've ever seen it. "Tate, they aren't kidding around. I have never seen Grams so distraught or angry."

"I know. Me too," I admit. "But I just don't get it."

"To be honest, at this point neither do I but I do know one thing…" Jace pauses and his expression grows sympathetic, "…

you aren't going to be able to change their minds. So are you really walking away from the family and the farm? You can't, Tate. Please. Don't."

I hug him again. "Maybe if I just gave them some time…"

"Yeah, maybe," Jace says but everything about his tone and expression says he doesn't think all the time in the world will make a lick of difference.

I get back in my truck and drive back to the hockey house. I'm exhausted emotionally and physically. My body has been carrying so much tension since this started, and I've barely slept but still… When I see Maggie sitting on the front steps, I feel better: lighter, stronger, happier.

As I get out of the truck, she stands up and I walk right up to her but stop short, about a foot away. She is a sight for my sore eyes and even more so for my sore heart. She's wrapped up in a puffy white winter coat and if she's wearing makeup I can't see it. She looks tired and sad but so damn beautiful. I shove my hands in the pockets of my dress coat to keep from reaching out and touching her because I don't think that will make anything easier.

"You look gorgeous in a suit," she says in an appreciative whisper, like it's taboo for her to admit that. "I didn't mean to just blindside you here, but I was out for a walk when you texted me the news and said we needed to talk, so I just thought I'd swing by. So we can have that talk."

"I was just at the farm, telling my family," I explain. The wind whips around us, cold and harsh which seems fitting.

"They must be relieved," she replies.

"Yeah, their meal ticket is still intact," I quip harshly and her face twists with pain.

"They love you, Tate, for more than just your earning potential. Even I can see that," Maggie says.

"But not enough to let me date you," blurt out. Maybe it's too blunt. Maybe it's too soon to just throw that reality out there, but I do. And she doesn't even seem surprised by it.

"I told my family everything," she says. "Clyde went straight down to the realtor in town and listed the farm."

"Oh my God, what?" I stare at her waiting for her to say she's making a really unfunny joke but her eyes fill with tears and she just nods her head. I finally pull my hands out of my pockets and grab hers with them. "Maggie, that's insane. Just because you dated me?"

Dated. I used the past tense and we both catch it and our eyes meet.

She blinks and looks away. "Yes and because I also told them I wanted to merge the farms and create a partnership and that I told you about the container units."

She takes a ragged breath and exhales in a gust that turns the air white. "I didn't have to. I didn't have to tell them anything. They never had to know about any of it, but I just... I am sick of the fighting and the lies and all of it. So I told them everything, and Clyde went off like nothing I have ever seen."

"Was he drunk?"

"No, actually I think if he was it would have been less terrifying," Maggie replies. "He hates your family on a level I have never experienced before."

"What are you going to do now if he really sells the farm?"

"I don't know what anyone in my family will do," Maggie replies quietly. "Everyone is basically losing their shit, and I just ran back to my apartment and hid. Even Daisy disappeared today. She said she was going on a drive to clear her head and would be back by midnight."

"I saw her this morning. She wanted to help with my meeting with the dean," I say, my fingers still laced with hers. "Everyone in my family is being as irrational as Clyde."

Maggie nods. She lifts her head again and speaks the words I don't want to say. "I think we need to take a breather here."

"I don't want to, but I think you're right," I reply and every word, as it tumbles from my mouth feels like it's taking a piece of my heart with it. "Just for now. Let everything settle down a little. I can concentrate on hockey."

"I can get the winter marketing plan for the farm in order and concentrate on school," Maggie replies. "Even if he is selling, it will take some time and I'll be damned if I'm going to tank all my hard work with the farm in the meantime."

We stare at each other. God, I can't believe that there was a time when avoiding her was as easy and normal as breathing, and now the idea of going back to that makes me feel like I'm suffocating. She pulls her hands from mine. "I'm going to go."

I just stand there like a chump and watch her start down the street. That lasts all of forty seconds before I break into a sprint and catch her, spinning her around and crushing my lips against hers. And she kisses me back...until she doesn't. Pulling away and inhaling sharply.

"That won't be the last time I kiss you, Maggie," I find myself promising. "It's just the last time for now."

"Don't make promises you can't keep, Tater Tot," she says back and then keeps walking away. And this time, I let her.

21

MAGGIE

I'm sitting on the balcony, staring at the flowers Tate secretly planted. I've been coming out here a lot despite the cold weather at all hours of the day and night to stare at them and imagine him planting them. Reliving the feeling I felt when I saw them and realized what he had done for me. How he must have felt about me to do it. The first serious frost will happen any day now and they'll wither and die, and that will be the last thing about us to be taken away against my will. I hear someone walk into my room and then Daisy whisper-yells my name. I don't bother to get up. I left the door to the balcony open so it only takes her a second to find me.

"It's freaking freezing out here, you lunatic," Daisy chastises me and wraps her arms around herself. "Get inside!"

"I'm wrapped in three wool blankets and a quilt. I'm fine," I say flatly. "What are you doing up and dressed at barely seven in the morning on a Sunday?"

"I'm fixing things," Daisy says and walks over and yanks me out of my chair. She pulls me back into my room and closes the door behind us, leaning against it. "Shower. Get dressed. We're going on a road trip."

"I don't want to go on a road trip," I reply, and instead of following her orders I flop onto my bed.

"Magnolia," she sighs. "I found our grandmother."

The words seem to take a minute to float across the room and settle in my brain. As soon as they do I sit up, which is a little hard in my blanket cocoon. "What?"

Daisy pulls herself off the door and walks over to stand in front of me. "The genealogy site matched us. It happened the day after the whole Jumbotron nightmare so I didn't tell you. You had so much going on and to be honest, I wasn't sure if it was legit."

"But you think it's legit now?"

Daisy nods and uses both hands to tuck her hair behind her ears then laces her fingers behind her neck and stares at me with excited brown eyes. "I know it's legit now because I met her."

"Oh my God, what?"

This was not how I was expecting my Sunday to go. This will be the sixth day since Tate and I put things on indefinite hold. I was going to spend it like I've been spending all my days, zombie-walking through my daily chores and tasks: homework, farm work, attending class, blah, blah, blah—and then curling up in a mournful ball and thinking of nothing but him.

"Remember that day I told you I was going for a drive to clear my head?" Daisy says. And I remember it because it was only three days ago and it was also the day Tate found out he didn't lose his scholarship. "I drove down to Gray, Maine, where she—our grandmother Elizabeth, who goes by Betsy—lives. And we met and we talked and now I need you to meet her and talk to her."

"Right now? We're driving to Maine?" I am so confused. "Daisy why did you keep this from me?"

She frowns. "I'm telling you now. And no, we're not driving to Maine. She is in Colebury for the weekend and we're meeting her there. That is, if you want to meet her. She really wants to meet you."

"I do. I think." I'm conflicted, to be honest. But Daisy met her and she is eager for me to do the same, so I will. I nod. "I'll go shower."

I start peeling off my blanket cocoon.

Twenty minutes later, I meet Daisy in the kitchen where she hands me a travel mug of coffee and my coat. I realize, as we walk down the stairs from our apartment and out the front door of the building that she's holding two mugs, not just one. "You're double fisting caffeine this morning?"

I climb into the passenger seat and she gets behind the wheel, putting her travel mug in one holder and reaching back to put the other one in the holder in the back seat. "We're picking someone up."

That's when I start to panic. "You are not surprising Dad or Uncle Bobby or Ben with this are you? Because that's just going to fracture our already splintered family tree even more."

She shakes her head and turns the car off our street and toward campus, which is not the way to Colebury. "I've told Dad and he told Bobby and Ben."

My jaw drops so hard I think I might have dislocated it. "When the hell did you do this?"

"Last night," she replies. "I didn't want to tell them without you, but Mags, you've been an emotional puddle. Completely justifiable and partly my fault, so I just went ahead and decided to try and sort this all out myself."

Daisy looks so serious and adult right now with a stern brow and tight jaw, that I almost forget I'm the older sister here. And then, as if there weren't enough surprises in the last half hour to last a lifetime, she pulls to a stop in front of the hockey house.

"What the hell are you doing?" I ask in horror as I watch Tate emerge from the house and make his way to the car. My eyes fly to Daisy in sheer disbelief and panic.

"I know this is hard to believe, but he needs to be there too,"

Daisy replies. He slides into the backseat wordlessly. "There's a coffee there for you. Cream, no sugar the way Hank told me you like it."

"Thanks," he tells Daisy.

My eyes collide with his in the rearview mirror.

"Hi. I miss you," he says simply.

"I miss you too." I smile softly but it hurts. A lot.

"You two are going to be the death of me," Daisy says as she starts to drive. "And I mean that quite literally because by the end of today, you might want to kill me."

"I still have no idea why I'm here," Tate says. "Can someone fill me in? I'm already on very shaky ground with my family. If they find out I went joy riding with you two…"

"All I know is Daisy found our grandmother and I'm going to meet her," I say.

As Daisy turns onto the on-ramp for the highway, she starts to tell Tate what she told me—about the ancestry site, the DNA swab, the match with a woman in Maine and her meeting with that woman.

"She has red hair," Daisy explains with a content smile. "Well, mostly gray now but not totally. And she looks a lot like Maggie. And she didn't abandon my dad and his brothers. She was forced out of their lives by… Clyde and circumstances. But she swears she tried to keep in touch with letters and Christmas gifts. I haven't confronted Clyde about it. I'm leaving that up to Dad and our uncles just like I'm leaving it up to them to contact her if they want. But I'm not leaving it up to you, Mags, because there's other stuff I think will change things for you."

Daisy's eyes shoot up to the rearview mirror to look at Tate. "Things that will change life for you, too."

Tate leans forward so his head is between Daisy and me. I get a whiff of his scent. It's honestly nothing special—a blend of deodorant, shampoo and laundry detergent but mixed with the heat of his skin and pheromones, it sends my stomach into back-flips and my heart aches harder than before. "I still don't understand but as long as I'm back for the harvest festival tonight, I'm good. The farm has a booth and so does the team, so I'm double-booked."

"Of course. I'm not kidnaping you overnight or anything," Daisy assures him. "Trust me."

"With you, Daisy, that's not easy," Tate says and I know it hurts Daisy, but he has every right to feel that way.

We drive the rest of the way to Colebury in silence. Somewhere along the forty minute drive, my hand slips back and I feel his fingertips tangle with mine. We shouldn't be giving in to temptations but we do, and I don't care how pointless and stupid it is—it feels good.

Daisy pulls into the parking lot of a place called the Busy Bean a little after nine in the morning and we all get out of the car. "They didn't feel comfortable coming into Burlington just yet so we agreed on here," Daisy explains as we walk toward the front door.

"They?" Tate questions and Daisy pauses with her hand on the door, glances inside and turns back to me and Tate.

"Just please keep an open mind. Both of you."

She opens the door and holds it for me and Tate to step inside. The place is cozy and smells like espresso beans and buttery baked goods. My eyes scan the room. There're a few people in line by the counter with a display case of decadent-looking muffins and cookies and a smiling blonde lady serving everyone. To the right side of the room there're tables and chairs clustered about, and I see a patio at the other end for warmer days. My eyes bounce around to all the occupied tables and stop dead on one in particular. Before Daisy even says a word I know the woman with the shoulder length strawberry-gray hair and camel-colored sweater with her hands clenched together on the tabletop next to an untouched muffin is my grandmother.

She's sitting next to a raven-haired woman who is talking but her gaze floats up to us. Daisy waves and she stands. Betsy's amber eyes jump from me to Daisy and back to me and she smiles, tears brimming in her eyes. I can see her internal struggle to contain them and I'm having the same one. Tate's arm gently wraps around my shoulders.

The woman she was talking to stands too. She's got near black hair, peppered with gray and dark green eyes. The color of…the color of Tate's.

"Hi again," Daisy says easily to our grandmother and they hug. Then she hugs the woman with the green eyes. Daisy takes a deep breath. "Maggie and Tate, this is Betsy Levy, formerly Elizabeth Todd."

"Hi," she says simply. "Oh my you are beautiful, Magnolia."

"She is," Tate pipes in and reaches out to shake her hand which she accepts. I can't seem to move at all so I just watch, wordless.

"And this," Daisy says motioning toward the other woman. "Is her life partner. Marty Dunn. Formerly Martha Adler."

Boom.

Seconds tick by with nothing but the bustle of the coffee shop and the chatter of other customers buzzing around us as we all stand still and silent. Then Tate speaks, his voice high yet rough. "What?"

"I'm Martha Adler," the woman repeats. "Well, I was when I was married to George Adler. Your father…he's my son."

I finally move, reaching out and grabbing Tate's hand in mine, hoping my touch steadies him the way his does me. Because it's all I can do while this bomb goes off in front of us.

22

TATE

Daisy motions for us to sit across from the couple, and Maggie and I do. Then she reaches for a chair from a nearby empty table for herself but she doesn't sit. She announces she's going to go get us some food and drinks and urges Betsy and Marty to tell us what they told her earlier this week.

They do.

Betsy's side of the story is easy to accept. She married Clyde, her high school boyfriend, because it was expected of her. They were young—nineteen—both local kids with not much else expected of them except to get married, have babies, and in Clyde's case take over the family farm. And that's what they did. But was it love? According to Betsy no, not for either of them. The only really shocking part is that Clyde wasn't a heavy drinker back then. Shortly after Maggie and Daisy's dad was born, my grandfather bought the farm next door and moved in with his wife and infant son—my own father. That part is the history I know. But the young wife was supposed to be Faith Brent Adler. That's what I was always told.

"George and I were even less of a love story than Betsy and Clyde," Marty explains to us all as Daisy comes back with three fruity smelling teas and a variety of muffins. "George was the hotshot playboy in my hometown. He was out for any conquest he could get. I was trying to convince myself I didn't like girls. So we slept together, and I got knocked up."

"With...with my dad?" I croak out. I can't believe this. How is this true? How did I never know? How does my dad not know?

Marty nods and continues. "We married. We were both miserable from the beginning. He cheated like it was his job. I tried to leave him, but he promised he would change. We both just needed a fresh start. A simpler life. So he convinced me to buy a farm with the little money we had and move to Vermont."

According to both Betsy and Marty, George and Clyde became fast friends. Best friends. And their wives did too, helping each other out with the kids and confiding in each other about the dismal state of both their marriages. And then...they fell in love.

"I know the history books like to portray the seventies as a decade of free love and liberal awakening, but that wasn't exactly true everywhere," Betsy says, gently placing a hand over Marty's as if she's trying to comfort her. "And Clyde and George, when they caught us, made sure it wasn't the case for us."

"Our great, great gramps was a judge," Daisy interjects as she reaches for a poppy seed and lemon muffin. Neither Maggie nor I have touched any food or drink and neither have Betsy or Marty. "Clyde's mom's father, and he made it clear Clyde and George would retain custody. Full custody."

"George was still cheating and he had knocked up a waitress in town named Faith," Marty adds and she might as well have just punched me in the gut. "Your grandma, as you know her. So he convinced me, pressured me, to sign away my rights and let Faith adopt Vinnie."

Vinnie. Nobody calls him that. In fact if they try in front of George he corrects them. Now I know why.

"He swore that Faith would love him and treat him like her own. There was no way they were going to give custody to two adulterous lesbians, not back then. So I gave them Vinnie, legally," Marty says, her voice breaking and a tear slipping down her cheek. I don't know if I forgive this woman. I don't know anything except that I'm not going to make her pain worse right now by telling her that they lied. They didn't treat my dad the same as they did their daughter Louise. And now I know why. And he will too. I intend to tell him.

"This is a lot to unpack," I say and Maggie's hand reaches for mine under the table. I squeeze it and my shoulders relax a little. "I had no idea that you exist."

Marty nods. "I know. I'm sorry. I am willing to stay gone if that's what you think is right. But Betsy... She always wanted to reconnect with her boys, so when Daisy found her... Well, her truth is impossible to tell without mine and I wasn't going to deny her this. She's the love of my life."

"That part I get," I admit and squeeze Maggie's hand again. She looks over at me and blushes.

"These two are like madly in love and stuff," Daisy announces, pointing at us and smiling. "But George and Clyde and everyone else refuse to let them be together."

"You're not exactly innocent there, Daze," I can't help but remind her.

"That's why I'm doing this," Daisy says, looking me in the eye with a pained expression. "This feud, the hate that has infected all of us thanks to George and Clyde's lies, stops here. If you let it."

"So you are dating?" Marty asks me and Maggie.

"We were. But our families are making it impossible," Maggie says. "Clyde is threatening to sell the farm out from under us, and Daisy and I have hinged our whole future on it."

"Wow." Betsy shakes her head sadly. "History really does repeat itself."

"Don't let them do it," Marty says firmly. "Please don't. I regret a lot of things in my life, but I don't regret not letting anyone keep me from Betsy."

We talk for about another half hour. They ask Maggie and me

all about our lives and we tell them and they tell us about their life together in Maine. Marty explains she had purposely kept herself from Googling anything Adler-related for decades but after they met Daisy, she did a Google search and was blown away by my hockey achievements. "You know, my dad was a hockey player. He was good but didn't make the NHL. He would be so thrilled that he has a grandson about to be drafted."

Wow. Hockey is literally in my blood. I love that.

"I'm entering the draft," I have to correct because I don't want to jinx anything. "Whether I'm actually drafted isn't a guarantee."

"Whether you do or don't, you've accomplished a lot and you should be very proud," Marty says and then her smile fades and her eyes grow somber. "Listen, Tate, if you decide not to tell your father and your brother about me I understand. And if you decide you don't want to see me again, that's okay too."

"I want them to know. They have a right to know and to be honest, I don't want to carry this secret around with me," I tell her. Her face clouds with worry. "If you're worried that they will have a problem with you being gay, I can say without an ounce of doubt Jace and my dad won't care about that in the slightest. You never trying to reach out to us...that's a whole other thing that is going to take some time and forgiveness. But they can't forgive you if they don't even know about you."

Marty smiles tentatively. "Well, Daisy has our contact information. Feel free to reach out, or give it to them, or whatever you feel is best. Thank you for meeting me. It...it was a dream come true."

I reach out and hug my grandmother for the first time.

We wait until Betsy and Marty drive away before getting into Daisy and Maggie's car. Daisy slides behind the wheel again but I grab Maggie's hand and pull her into the backseat with me before she can climb into the passenger seat. I reach across her and lock her seatbelt in and give in to the urge to kiss her at the same time. She lets me and kisses me back.

"If I see anything that's rated R back there, I am pulling over and separating you two," Daisy warns. I break the kiss reluctantly and find her eyes narrowed as she stares at us in the rearview.

"Relax Doody," I joke and wink at her. "The last thing I want is to give you a show."

Daisy huffs in disapproval at her unwanted childhood nickname and pulls out of the parking lot. Maggie snuggles into me and I watch the Vermont scenery on the side of the highway—jutting rock and trees with colorful leaves—blur by. This is all so much, and maybe I'm in shock, but I'm not freaking out. I'm worried for my dad, but I'm hopeful too because the truth will be exposed and whatever happens next, at least it will be based in honesty. And I am going to be honest with my family too—about what I want and who I want.

"Can you drop me at my farm, Daisy?"

"If you never call me Doody again, yeah I can," she says and I feel Maggie's body shake against me as she giggles.

"Deal," I say. Ten minutes later, Daisy starts to slow and pull to the side of the road beside my driveway. "No. Drive right on up."

"Umm…" Daisy glances back at me with wary eyes. "Doesn't George own a shotgun?"

But she turns up the driveway anyway and stops just in front of the house. I turn to Maggie. "See you at the Harvest Festival tonight?"

"Ah…" Maggie blinks up at me, confused.

"Just come. Please."

"Okay," she relents.

"And bring some of your products," I tell her. "Honey, caramels, goat cheese, but not the stinky kind. The mouthgasm stuff you once told me about."

She laughs and I steal a much quicker kiss than I'd like and get out of the car. As I close the door, I hear Gramps's booming voice as he barges toward me from the barn. "What the hell are they doing here?"

Daisy is already driving away when I turn to him and

respond. "They're dropping me home so I can talk to you. About Martha Dunn."

George's face turns a shade of gray that matches the fading paint on our farmhouse. I walk up to him slowly. "Gramps, it's time for the truth."

23

MAGGIE

I walk into the Harvest Festival being held in Battery Park with trepidation. Not because this is the first year the city has held this festival and I don't know what to expect but because I don't know what to expect from Tate or the Adler family or even my own family at this point. We swung by our own farm after we dropped off Tate at his, and no one was there except my mom. She said my dad and my uncles had a big blowout with Clyde over the news Daisy had shared and they'd all disappeared.

I reposition the bag that's on my shoulder filled with our products, like Tate asked, and wander through the park. Daisy stays close to my side. Most of the town seems to be here enjoying the event, browsing the artisan booths, ordering from the food trucks, hanging out in the little beer garden, or riding some of the rides and playing some of the games. With the fairy lights in the trees it's like a mini-carnival, really. I glance over at the tiny stage where a band is tuning up. Next to the stage is a small beer garden and that's when I see my uncles and my dad sitting at one of the picnic benches there. I grab Daisy's hand. "Look. Five o'clock."

She turns her head and squeezes my hand. "They look...sad? Maybe angry? I can't tell."

"Let's go find out." I tug her with me as I cross the grass.

Uncle Bobby sees us first and gives us a small wave and a smile. "Hey girls."

My dad looks up, shocked. "Did Mom send you out looking for us?"

"She worried we killed the old man?" Ben asks as he lifts a half-empty pint to his lips.

"No we're here...just for us and happened to see you," I say, not willing to throw Tate's name out there right now. It feels like it would be throwing gasoline on a fire.

"Did you? Kill Grandpa?" Daisy asks timidly and I'm shocked she called him grandpa. We haven't done that since we were about seven.

Dad smiles up at her. "No honey. He's still alive. Still gonna sell the farm out from under us. Still an asshole who has no remorse about tearing up years of letters and cards and making his kids think their mother abandoned them."

Ouch.

"Are you guys mad at me?" Daisy wants to know. "For finding her?"

The three of them shake their heads in unison.

"Nah, Daze," Bobby says. "I'm not sure I want to meet her yet...but I'm not mad at you for finding her."

"You did the right thing telling us the truth, Daisy Mae," Dad says and smiles at her softly before turning to look at me. "You meet her too?"

I nod. "I think I like her. And her wife."

"They aren't legally married," Daisy interjects. "Marty and Betsy. In fact Betsy is still legally married to Clyde."

"What?" Bobby gasps and Ben and my dad look equally stunned.

Daisy nods. "I'll stop talking now. I feel like there's been enough plot twists."

Daisy's words mean nothing because when it comes to plot twists, apparently the universe isn't done.

"Hey. You came." Tate's voice hits my ears and I spin to find him standing just a little behind me in a pair of jeans and his hockey jersey. He's smiling at me. It's big and warm and makes me smile back without even thinking about it.

"I got the stuff you asked for," I say and hold out the bag.

He takes it, glances inside it and nods.

"What's going on?" My dad asks and he stands up without his cane. He wobbles and Tate instantly reaches out to grab his elbow to steady him. Dad pulls his arm away and leans on the picnic table for support. "I'm fine. Why are you here, Tate?"

Dad doesn't sound overly aggressive, but I don't like where this might be heading. Please, may he not make some big stink about me talking to an Adler. This has got to end.

Tate steps closer to me and by doing so is now closer to my dad. Ugh. He looks my dad straight in the eye. "Mr. Todd, sir, what's happening is I asked your lovely daughters to bring some of your farm's products here so I could add them into the basket the city is raffling off. The one that was supposed to be from the farmer's market vendors. I didn't think it was fair my brother cut you guys out of that, so I'm making it a co-branded basket."

"Oh." Dad seems confused by Tate's words. And to be honest his tone is kind of throwing me off too. It's mild mannered and polite. No Adler has ever used that tone with a Todd. Not in my lifetime.

"Well as long as that's all you want from his lovely daughters," Uncle Ben quips tersely and gives Tate a bit of a glare.

"Jesus, Uncle Ben, don't you think it's time we cut all this crap?" I say angrily. "Just be civil. Please."

"For the record, Mr. Todd, that isn't all I want from your lovely niece," Tate says to Uncle Ben. His tone is less mild and more frank than it was a minute ago but still polite. "What I want is to be her boyfriend again. Publicly this time. For all the world to see. If she'll have me."

"Oh my God," Daisy gasps excitedly.

Tate looks at me. My dad opens his mouth to say something

but I snap up a hand and hold my palm up in his direction, silencing him before he can say a word. Tate winks at me. "You good with that, Firecracker?"

"I'm good with that, Tater Tot," I reply and my chest feels tight because my heart is swelling so hard and so fast I can barely breath. "So good with that."

And then Tate kisses me, hard and firm, but PG-13 because there are too many eyes watching us for anything else. When he ends the kiss and wraps his arm around me, I turn back to my dad and uncles. "Tate's the best thing that has ever happened to me. He makes me happy. And he makes me crazy, in the best and sometimes worst possible way. He just makes me…more. And I've never been happier, so just like your mom—my grandmother —I am not giving that up. But I'm also not giving you guys up, so you have no choice but to learn to live with it."

"Now if you'll all excuse us, we have to go fix that basket and give my family the same speech," Tate says. "Have a good night."

Daisy is clapping wildly as Tate guides me away, toward the other side of the park. When we're out of sight and earshot of my family I stop him. He looks down at me with his smirkiest smirk. The one I love and hate with equal passion. "I was good, wasn't I? That was some award winning, high quality romantic content right there."

"Yeah, you knocked it out of the park, Romeo," I tell him and I sound sarcastic but my smile says I actually mean it. "Except the kiss was lacking."

"What?" he gasps.

"Yeah, a little lackluster. Boring, really," I say and fake a yawn.

He grabs me by my waist and tugs me right up against him and then he kisses me again. His lips claiming mine with force. His tongue stroking mine with abandon as I fist his jersey in my hands and try not to moan. "Better?"

I have to catch my breath before I can answer him. "It'll do."

He laughs at my fake nonchalance and pulls me into a hug. I cling to him tightly, because I can—right here in public with half the town wandering by, I can claim Tate Adler as mine. And even more amazing is the fact that I want to, more than anything else in the world. Whoever said your world can change on a dime really wasn't kidding.

"We really do gotta get the stuff into the basket before the auction starts," Tate tells me and ends the hug, only to take my hand in his as we keep walking.

"Is your family here? Do they know about Marty?" I ask him and glance up to see his reaction because it'll likely tell me more than his verbal response will.

Tate's smile fades and his jaw tightens as he nods. "Yeah. I told George I know and he lost his shit on me, but then he called my dad in from the orchard and sat him down and told him everything. There was a lot of yelling."

"I'm sorry," I say not because I feel responsible but because I sympathize.

"They're still at the farm, talking it out. I think it's gonna be okay in the end. One day. Just not today."

I give his hand a squeeze. Jace, Raquel and Louise come into view a few feet away, and Tate smiles down at me and winks. "Ready to profess your undying love for me again, this time in front of my family?"

"Who said anything about love?" I quip.

"You didn't have to say it." He shrugs. "You're head over heels for me. I know it."

Our eyes meet and I really want to come up with some zippy burn about his ego or something but for the first time in my life, I've got nothing. He dips his head down a little so he can whisper by my ear. "Don't worry, Firecracker, if this was a competition it'd be a draw because I'm skates over helmet for you too."

I scrunch up my nose. "Did you just make that up?"

"Yeah. Another winner huh?"

"No. God no," I say with a laugh.

"Okay, how about I just stick with the basic fact that I'm falling in love with you then?"

Oh my God.

"Really, Tate?" Raquel's voice cuts through this perfect moment like a lawn mower ripping through a quiet Sunday morning. "After all this shit blowing up with our family today you're going to add this silly fling with her on top of it all?"

"Raquel, your cousin just told me he is falling in love with me and unfortunately for you, that makes me way more than a fling," I announce. "So feel free to bitch about it, but do it somewhere else. We're having a moment over here."

I take the bag of goat cheese and honey from Tate and hand it to Jace. "Can you go add these things to the gift basket? I've got to kiss your brother again."

"Gross," Jace mutters but he wanders off toward the gift basket table by the stage.

I wrap my arms around his neck as his circle my waist. "Wow. Your speech was almost as good as mine."

"Almost?" I blink. "Are you kidding me right now?"

"Just shut up and kiss me, Firecracker," Tate says.

"So bossy," I whisper back and shake my head in mock judgement. But then I do exactly what he demands and I kiss him, long and slow, because the fight—at least for this Adler and this Todd —is finally over.

24

TATE

I roll down the window and take a long, deep breath. The sweet, humid Vermont summer air fills my lungs. I close my eyes and exhale then lean the other way and inhale my other favorite scent —Maggie Todd. She giggles and squirms when I nuzzle her neck, her silky copper hair sliding against my cheek and jaw. "Stop it! I'll drive us into the ditch."

I let out a disgruntled huff. "Whose dumb idea was it to do this again?"

"Mine. And shut up," she says smiling. "Work doesn't stop just because you've been drafted, Tater Tot."

The draft was held in Toronto three days ago, which was lucky because it's close enough that we could afford a bunch of plane tickets so my mom and dad and Jace and Maggie could all be there with me. I knew from all the sports agents calling me nonstop over the last couple of months and Coach Keller's opinion at the end of the season that I might go in the top fifty. But first round, thirteenth overall? Shit, that crushed even my wildest dreams.

She pats my knee. "Farm work will keep you humble."

"Yeah. Yeah." I grab her hand and hold on to it, then I tilt my head out the window and take another deep breath. "Brooklyn isn't going to smell this good."

"Nope, but it's only a five hour and forty-seven minute drive or a one hour and fourteen minute flight," Maggie says, and although her face is placid and calm, I know from the accuracy of that statement that she has done a lot of thinking about this too in the last three days.

If and when I ever do make it on the ice for Brooklyn, she will likely stay here. At least to start. We've got our families talking again and we've even started helping each other out with farm work, when needed – lending equipment or a hand for stuff as required. A merge of the farms is definitely on the table. Right now both our dads, her uncles and even Louise and Raquel are onboard. It's just Clyde who vehemently opposes it and my gramps and gran... step-gran that is, who are leery. But by the time we graduate I think it will be a done deal. And that kind of scares the shit out of me but she can't run a farm from Brooklyn, and Maggie this idea is her baby so how can I ask her to leave it? Luckily, I don't have to worry about that immediately since I've decided to stay in school and keep playing for Moo U, at least for the next year. Our farm is still struggling a little, but not as much as it was, and we've managed to fix the barn and the cider press and have started selling our cider again.

I take her hand I'm holding and slide it up my thigh. "I wanted to spend the day in bed with you getting over jet lag."

I've been unofficially living in her rental apartment all summer with her and her roommates. They don't mind the extra body because I do almost all the cleaning, but not in my underwear anymore, thankfully. Maggie laughs as she turns onto the road that leads to our farms. "There's no time difference between here and Toronto, so no jet lag. And yes, both farms need our help today and you know it. But if you play your cards right, later I'll sneak you into the barn and take care of this."

Her hand moves to the front of my jeans and she palms my

cock through the denim and it starts to spring to life—and then stops immediately as she drives up my farm's driveway and I see the big banner strung up on the front porch.

Congratulations Tate!

"You ambushed me!" I gasp as I see the field that leads to the orchard filled with people and picnic tables with balloons tied to them. Everything is in the Brooklyn team colors. She parks the car and her amber eyes glint deviously. "Ambush is better than blackmail isn't it?"

She hops out of the car and I follow. As soon as my feet hit the dirt, the crowd erupts. Everyone is here; Hank, Maggie's entire family, my family, the coaches from the team, some of the players who live within driving distance or stayed in town for the summer, and—my step stutters—our grandmothers.

They're standing next to Daisy and Jace, as far from my grandfather and grandmother as possible, but they're here and no one is brawling. That's progress.

Maggie grabs my hand and pulls me forward. "Everyone wanted to celebrate with you. And everyone promised to play nice. Except Clyde, so he's at home."

God I wish that old man would get with the program. Thankfully, he won't be selling the farm because Betsy is still entitled to half of it, and she announced in their initial divorce proceedings that finally started a few months ago that she wanted Daisy and Maggie to have her half. Clyde doesn't have the money to buy her half, but Betsy has the money to buy his half, so he has finally shut the hell up with that threat.

I hug everyone and take their congratulatory hugs back and then George fires up the grill and Jace turns on some music, and we have an honest to God party. It's been a rough few months in the Adler and Todd homes as everyone adjusts to the truth. But my dad has started a relationship with Marty as have Jace and I, and Betsy is on civil terms with her sons too and great terms with Daisy and Maggie.

As much as I am thrilled to be drafted and hopefully play in the NHL for at least a few years, I'm going to miss this place and these people. Maggie leans in as we sit at a picnic table across from Daisy and Jace who are arguing about his musical choices. "Don't look so wistful. You haven't gone anywhere yet."

"I know," I say and kiss her cheek.

"You two are so cute," Marty says with a smile as she sits next to me with a plate of different salads. Since I know she's not a vegetarian, I think she's too nervous to approach the grill because George is manning it. "I'm so proud of you, Tate. For the draft and for everything else."

I smile.

"Martha!" Gramps's gruff voice cuts through the din of voices around us and I bristle for a second. "Got some ribs ready. If you still like 'em."

Marty looks like you could knock her over with a feather, which I get because I feel that way too. Marty stands. "I do. Thanks."

She walks over to the grill. And I smile.

"That's the face I need on your pretty mug tomorrow at the farmer's market," Maggie says. "Luckily, we have booths beside each other so you can stand in between them both and draw customers. Everyone will want to meet Burlington's number one draft pick."

"Thirteenth," I correct her.

"You're the number one pick *from* Burlington, Vermont," Maggie says with a wink. "And number one in my heart."

"Wow. That was so cheesy it makes me miss those days when all you threw my way was shade," I quip and she laughs and lets me cup the back of her neck and pull her in for a kiss.

"You two never stop." Jace mutters and makes a gagging sound as he gets up and leaves the table.

Maggie breaks the kiss and she stands up. "I'm done with insulting you, but I'm willing to revisit some other old habits."

She starts to walk away.

"Where are you going?"

She looks over her shoulder. "The barn."

"Magnolia Todd, don't ever change," I whisper as I sneak away to follow her.

ACKNOWLEDGMENTS

Thank you to Sarina Bowen for allowing me to play in your world as well as for graciously and generously sharing your wisdom on writing, marketing and publishing. Just like your books, you are magic. Thank you to my family, especially my husband Jack, who have been there when I needed them, even when that sometimes means not 'being there' so I can work. Thank you to my agent Kimberly Brower. Thanks Kimberly Cannon and Katie Kenyhercz for their editing prowess and to Jane, Jenn, Emma, Natasha and the rest of the team behind Heart Eyes Press for all the help and heavy lifting you did for this book, and this series extension in general. Thank you to the fellow True North world authors, especially my Moo U teammates. You've all been so much fun to work with. Thank you to Catherine for sharing your beautiful little balcony in Paris, which is where Maggie and Tate were created. Thanks to my beta readers Sarah J, Melanie T, Lex M and Jenn D for your feedback and support. Thank you to the bloggers for all you did to support and promote this book, and all you do - for all authors - every day. And to the readers, new and old, who gave this book their time; I appreciate it so much and I hope Tate and Maggie blindsided you, in the best possible way.

Made in the USA
Columbia, SC
13 May 2021

37887222R00143